Also by Ken Filing

Awash in Mystery
Unfinished Flight
Epic in the Forgotten War
Blazing Vengeance
Heartbeat in the Amazon

Mistress

OF THE AMAZON

KEN FILING

Order this book online at www.trafford.com
or email orders@trafford.com

Most Trafford titles are also available at major online book retailers.

Print information available on the last page.

ISBN: 978-1-4907-6166-4 (sc)
ISBN: 978-1-4907-6168-8 (hc)
ISBN: 978-1-4907-6167-1 (e)

Library of Congress Control Number: 2015910162

Trafford rev.   06/27/2015

 www.trafford.com

North America & international
toll-free: 1 888 232 4444 (USA & Canada)
fax: 812 355 4082

Without Teddy's input, suggestions, and corrections, none of my books would be complete works. This book is lovingly dedicated to her.

Preface

Mistress of the Amazon is a work of fiction. All of the characters alive or dead are fictitious and not intended to resemble anyone, past or present. The cure for dengue also is but a myth. The author has based his story on historic fables and myths that tell of warrior women living in past centuries. When the conquistadors of Spain came to the New World and encountered these Amazon women, they in turn named the gigantic river after this legendary tribe of sexually liberated women. They called it the *Amazon River*. Whether or not the interpretation of these historical fables and myths has been altered by those who choose to pass them on from generation to generation is not documented. A recent dig in the south of Russia has uncovered the grave of a warrior woman complete with armor and weapons. She was tall and showed evidence of a violent death. DNA was taken and compared with a modern-day tall blonde child living with the Mongols. It matched. It is only one of several studies and documentation that show that there were tribes of tall blonde warrior women who fought fierce battles, captured men for sex once a year, killed them, and only kept the female children. This story tells of one such woman.

Chapter One

Without moonlight, the star-filled tropical sky was blotted out by an unusually low overcast. It seemed to hang in long tendrils, making the night black as pitch.

The village of females was quiet except for the soft crying and an occasional sob from the women who served the Amazon warriors. These loyal women were near total exhaustion from carrying the dead and wounded back from an intense battle.

The surviving golden skinned warrior women had carried the lifeless, inert body of their leader back from the battle against the Yano-Matis warriors. It was one of the few times in the history of this unique tribe of dauntless Amazon women that they had tasted defeat in such an agonizing way.

Many of the women warriors had been killed or were suffering from fatal wounds. Only a few escaped with minor cuts and bruises. Even they were defeated in spirit, especially when they saw their inspirational leader, Cassania, fall to her knees and wage a relentless battle from this kneeling position. Even from this vulnerable situation she was intimidating, swinging her machete at any enemy who dared charge this brave blonde warrior, jabbing her dagger at any foolish enough to get within her reach and past the arcing machete.

The Yano-Matis warriors had never, in their many battles, encountered such strength and fury.

Alas, she was outnumbered and finally overwhelmed by the battle-experienced hoard of skilled warriors. The many wounds soon took their toll on this magnificent fighting machine. She slumped to the ground.

The other golden skinned Amazon women had waged a relentless battle, and the forest was strewn with the bodies of Yano-Matis, some slain and many wounded.

But the women were outnumbered and were beaten by a superior force. The enemy had a brilliant and experienced leader as well.

And yet, that Yano-Matis leader was respectful of the fighting acumen of golden skinned women, and when he saw the blonde leader fall to her knees, waging that relentless battle, and finally succumb to overwhelming odds, he signaled his warriors to cease and fall back.

He saw the few remaining women warriors, bloody and beaten, stand staring at the body of their inspired leader. She was now lying inert on the ground, with wounds that no warrior could have survived, even with half as many major wounds.

The chief called a halt to the battle he knew he had won, but with deep respect for these outnumbered Amazon women who gave no quarter. They fought until only a few remained standing. Those that still stood slowly dropped their weapons and gathered around Cassania. All were grim. They stood abreast, three on each side, gazing down in disbelief at their champion who lay sprawled out in a beaten heap. They stooped and gently lifted the body of their inspirational leader, raised her high overhead, then slowly walked away from the field of battle. It was strewn with bodies of warriors from both tribes.

One of the women took command and instructed those left standing to collect their wounded and help them back to the village. She ordered one wounded young warrior to return to the village to alert the servant women to come help to collect the dead and other mortally wounded.

It was a slow, solemn ceremony, and the trek back to the village was led by the six women bearing the body of the blonde, golden skinned leader. They held her high and walked slowly, their own bodies bloody and beaten. These were the last remnants of the fabled Amazon women whose stories of battle and survival dated back to the fifteenth century when the first Portuguese invaders came to their land.

The Portuguese soldiers told tales of these huge blonde fighting women in the Amazon basin and thereafter, the stories of battle with these huge women who gave no quarter. They were called Amazons.

Some stories told of men fighting along with the women. The men were always on the forefront and were the first to be killed. If their men turned and ran or attempted to retreat, the huge women killed them before they could escape or turn tail.

Many different legends were told of why and how the fighting men became a part of their civilization.

Numerous unbelievable tales were told of the amazing feats of this tribe of women, some no doubt exaggerated, but nonetheless the tales kept growing and each told of the heroic battles waged by this aggressive civilization of tall women.

No one has lived long enough to experience the complete story of why or how this tribe of golden skinned women came to be, or even how long they have existed. There are many tales and stories told by the tribes that the warrior women were in the Amazon basin long before the Portuguese and Spanish. It was those foreigners that invaded this huge land of rivers and jungle. They were enticed by the rich natural resources and battled all indigenous tribes, as well as the women warriors.

How and when did the women come to this part of this world? Legend has it that the first savage women fighters were a group in the ancient region of Sarmatia, living in the steppes of the southern part of Russia 2,500 years ago. They were tall and blonde and fierce archers who cut off their right breast in order to shoot an arrow with more accuracy. They were a tribe of women, and only if they killed a man in battle were they allowed to mate. They then did away with the man or used him in battle at the forefront to take the brunt of enemy fire. None of the men would survive.

Legend has it that these brave and ferocious women migrated to Mongolia, where recent DNA tests have determined that descendants are living today, proving that the ancient tribe of women is not a myth.

Could the migration of some of these women have continued east to the present-day North America? Then south, looking for a new uninhabited area, to finally settle in the foothills of the Amazon basin? Yes, it's possible . . . very possible.

We only know of what legends the early tribes and Europeans have passed on down in the last many hundreds of years.

Now, would this tragic battle be the end of these last vestiges of this unique civilization?

***

Nardania, the second-in-command, now gave orders as the beaten procession entered the village through the cleft in the rocks so cleverly hidden from the outside world.

"Take our leader into her hut, lay her on her mat, and summon the shaman to perform the last rites as is our custom. After she has finished, she can tend to the wounded. And lastly, after we have laid out the dead, she can also carry out the custom of last rites on them."

The able-bodied women did as they were told, and when all but Nardania left the hut, she knelt beside the woman that she so admired and had known from childhood.

She spoke quietly and respectfully to the bloody hulk lying before her, "I will clean and tend to you myself, my noble leader. We have faced and overcome many obstacles over these many years and no one will touch your body but me."

She gathered water and oils and prepared to clean and arrange the body of this magnificent creature. As she started on the beautiful face, she hesitated and stopped cleaning.

"Are my eyes playing tricks? Did I see an eyelid flutter?"

She carefully moved the blonde hair away and stared further at the face of the beloved leader.

"No. It must have been a nerve contraction."

She was wiping the mud and the blood from her face when a shallow, labored breath of air escaped from the slightly parted lips. She was aghast.

Nardania put her ear on the leader's breast and listened for some sign of life from the strong heart of this woman who had never lost a battle. It was very faint, but yes, there was a beat, though very slight and very slow, coming from her chest.

She quickly rose and scampered out, screaming for the shaman, "Come quickly," she called at the top of her voice. "Our leader lives. She needs your help. Bring herbs and anyone you need to help. Our leader's heart is still beating but she needs your help. Hurry . . . hurry."

Nardania ran back into the hut, followed quickly by the shaman and her assistants.

They quickly took charge and immediately started applying salves and ointments to the wounds. They worked for hours, stitching and attending to the worst wounds first.

The shaman attempted to pour a vial of liquid into Cassania's mouth. Most of it dribbled down her chin, but some ran into her throat—very little, but enough. She gagged and a low groan escaped from her lips.

Soon they had done all they could and the beloved leader lay very still on her mat, covered with a light woven shawl.

As they gazed at the inert body lying before them, there was a very slight movement of the shawl. Short breaths came from the lips of their patient now on a regular but shallow basis.

They set up a watch over her so that she would never be alone and in need of something.

That night, a ceremony calling on the spirits, was performed by all the shamans around a fire in the main courtyard. It was an age-old ceremony intended for all the dead and dying but also with great emphasis on the recovery of their leader.

The population of the village had vastly changed. It now consisted of many more servant women of normal stature and of varied ethnic backgrounds. The tall blonde warriors, always in the minority, were even fewer now. The battle was extremely costly.

This change greatly affects the future of the tribe of blonde warrior women, a lineage that spans hundreds of years and spanned several continents.

Chapter Two

The days passed slowly. Nardania kept a vigil by her leader's side, even sleeping on the ground next to Cassania's mat. When she had to leave for a short time to tend to village business, she assigned two women to stand guard and come running if any change occurred.

This constant vigil and the duty to take charge of the village were becoming threats to her health. She also had wounds that must heal from that dreadful battle against the warriors of Yano-Matis. She had fought relentlessly. Yes, they indeed were formidable foes.

She was resting in the shade after finishing the noon meal served to her by one of the servant women when several of her warriors approached and stood waiting for permission to speak.

She looked up and in a low tone asked, "Yes, what is it?"

One of the warriors stepped forward and said, "Forgive us, Nardania. We wonder about the condition of our glorious leader. We only get rumors and second-hand information."

Nardania stood and answered, "Forgive me for not keeping everyone informed. She is our leader and all are concerned. Please pass on the information that she is still unconscious, but seems to be getting some strength back. Her wounds were devastating and the shamans are doing miracles with the herbs and roots that they gather in the jungle. We are able to hold her head up and allow some broth to trickle down her throat. She will occasionally stir and moan but does not respond to outside stimulus."

"Will she survive?" asked another.

"Of course she will," Nardania firmly and loudly stated as she abruptly turned to head back to the hut.

As she entered, she quietly asked, "Is there any change?"

The tallest warrior turned and said, "You've only been gone a short time. There is no change. Why don't you go to your hut and rest yourself? You look terrible and we can watch over our leader as well as you."

"It is my duty as second-in-command to watch over her."

"And what good are you in your weakened condition if our leader needs help? We can summon you and the shaman if need be."

Nardania's shoulders sagged. "You are right, of course. I will stop to see the shaman for some healing herbs and then go to my hut to heal my body so I can be of help when our leader comes to." She respectfully stroked Cassania's blonde head, then turned and left the hut, mumbling, "Call me if there is any change."

***

Weeks passed. Nardania had set up a scheduled watch of two women at all times to be with their beloved leader while she lay unconscious. She was well cared for, with daily sponge baths and bedding changes. Care was given to her wounds, which were healing nicely, with aloe and other healing herbs administered by the shaman.

The Amazon women were far advanced in medical procedures compared to some of the tribes in the rain forest. Nardania's wounds had almost completely healed and she was finally able to bring the village together. She was faced with the loss of over half of the total population, mostly the warriors and hunters. Much work and many assignments were needed to heal the sick and bury the dead. She took charge, trying to help the village recover from a devastating loss.

It was a sunny, pleasant afternoon when a servant woman came running to Nardania's hut with the news that Cassania had opened her eyes and was very restless.

"Nardania, she keeps calling for you and is thrashing about like she is still in battle. Her eyes, though open, are glazed and not seeing."

Nardania jumped to her feet and cried, "Run to get the shaman and bring her to our leader's hut. I will meet you there."

As Nardania burst into the hut, she saw two of her warriors holding Cassania down in her mat. Cassania was fighting and seemed to draw on a strong force from within. Some of her wounds were seeping from the extreme activity. The warriors were doing all they could to contain her.

Nardania held Cassania's head and spoke into her ear with gentleness, "Please, great leader, lie back so we can treat you. The battle is over. You are at home with your friends."

Cassania seemed to lighten her struggles for a moment but resumed with even more strength, then suddenly she collapsed, spent and weak from the extreme effort.

She was panting in short breaths when the shaman entered with her bags of herbs and roots.

"Please, Shaman, save our leader," begged Nardania.

"Move aside and I will do my best," she answered.

The shaman withdrew a vial and poured a combination of liquids into it. She said, "I'll need two of you to elevate her head and shoulders but keep her steady. Nardania, I'll need you to hold her mouth open and then keep her from spitting up the liquid that I will pour down her throat. Quickly, do as I say."

The shaman poured the bitter liquid down the throat of the struggling Cassania. She forced it down as Cassania tried to reject it but was too weak to battle the four strong women. It trickled down her throat.

She coughed, trying to reject the liquid. But after a slight delay she slowly succumbed to the drug and now lay quietly on her mat.

"What will happen now?" Nardania asked the shaman.

"She will rest peacefully for a few days and then we must do this again. We must keep her in a state where she is not aware of her surroundings until her body heals to the point where she can restore her senses so that she no longer needs to battle. We may need to keep her this way for a complete cycle of the moon, maybe even longer if her wounds don't heal well. I will keep one of my assistants with her at all times. I may require help to administer the drug every few days. Nardania, I will depend on you for this help."

"I will be at your beck and call when needed," answered Nardania.

***

The next two months passed slowly as the more seriously wounded warriors died and funerals were common. The other wounded were treated but some would never fight again. The Amazon army was decimated, with only a few able-bodied warriors left.

Since the servant women had more freedom without the Amazon's watching over them, they grew more independent. Some of these women were captured during raids on tribal villages along with some men of choice to perpetuate the growth of the tribe. The women were kept to serve. The men were disposed of after their usefulness was over.

A few men had been confined recently, and when the women found more freedom, a few rebellious ones turned the men loose and they all escaped together. Other women were born in the village, and though young, they did not meet the standards of the Amazon warriors and were made servants. They too were unhappy with their plight, so again these women escaped into the jungle.

Through the ages, the Amazons were very particular of the men they captured to copulate with. They must be big, tall, light skinned, and healthy. It was more and more difficult since now armies, such as the Portuguese and Spaniards, were no longer raiding the basin as in the ancient times.

With all things considered, the population of this once-thriving village was dwindling to a fraction of what was once a force to be reckoned with.

It was under these conditions that the great leader Cassania awakened from her drug-induced dormant condition. The shaman had decided that her wounds were healed enough and that hopefully her mental anguish was stable enough for her to come back to the real world.

Nardania was alongside her mat when she awakened.

"Hello, my leader. Do you know me?"

Cassania opened her eyes and turned her head slowly to look at Nardania. She stared at her for a moment and said, "Yes, my able assistant. Why are you here in my hut?"

Nardania smiled and said, "I'm here to assist you and help with your wounds from the battle."

Cassania looked confused for a moment. "Is the battle over? Did we win? Why are back in the village? We should get back to the battle field to help our wounded. It is not good to leave them overnight. Go back before nightfall and collect them."

"No, my leader, we did not win. We lost many and you have been close to death for two turns of the moon. Our shaman put you in a deep sleep to keep you from injuring yourself further."

"I don't understand. It was only a few hours ago that we waged a fierce battle. I remember the Yano-Matis tribesmen charging me one after the other. I remember going down to my knees to continue fighting, and then I fell forward from a blow from behind. I lay still for an instant, trying to rise up but must have lost consciousness. I awoke with my face lying in blood-soaked mud, but I couldn't move or even see but I could hear from what seemed far away. The great chief of the Yano-Matis called to his warriors to cease and fall back. I was thankful because I thought he had given up the fight and we won. Then everything went black. The next instant I awoke here in my hut with you beside my mat."

"All that you remember is true, great one. But no, we did not win. The Yano-Matis chief called back his men in respect for the fierce battle we had fought and to give what few of us that were left time to collect the body of our leader and the rest of our wounded. He was not only a fierce warrior but a man with respect for his enemy."

"I am very confused. Can I rest now and collect my thoughts?"

"Of course. I will stay outside your door to answer any need that you may have."

Nardania and the rest of the attendants all left.

Cassania closed her eyes and tried to reconstruct what she envisioned happened in the past few days but was in fact the past few months.

Something bothered her. She tried to remember, to reconstruct those moments before the battle, those lingering moments. Yes, now it was coming back. But could that have been a dream?

Chapter Three

The thought process became clearer to Cassania as she became more alert. But her thoughts were still muddled. She had lost several months of time while under the healing drugs of her shaman, though it seemed like only moments.

The time of battle had slowly returned and she knew now that they were on the verge of losing when she was cut down by a superior force. She had resigned herself to that. She also knew that many of her fellow women warriors had not made it through the battle, and she was deeply saddened by this. But her second-in-command, Nardania, could give her more details when she was able absorb them.

Meanwhile, what bothered her most was the time before the battle. During the time, they captured a tall white woman missionary and then lured her husband, a doctor, to try to rescue her. She knew he would try his best. The two of them were held as prisoners here in the village in the longhouse but separately at first. Things were going so well on the plan to strengthen their line of warriors, which in the past had somewhat deteriorated. They needed new blood, and these two captives were perfect to give them a new start to add to their tribe of warrior women. It would take some time, but they were still strong and this couple would make them stronger.

She closed her eyes, deep in thought. *Yes, yes, if only we would have had more time. It was a last-ditch effort on my part. How foolish that I thought I might be able to progress things hurriedly. Now I must regain my strength, and with the help of Nardania, rebuild our tribe to the glory it was when the ancients were here.*

"Nardania," she called, "come help me get on my feet."

Rushing in, Nardania cautioned, "No, my leader, you are not ready. Give yourself some time to gather your strength."

"Nonsense, you told me it has been two months since the battle and we have only half of our people. It's time to start rebuilding."

She stood with Nardania's help but felt dizzy and she staggered. But this strong woman regained herself and slowly walked to the door leading out to the village commons.

When she entered the common area, the women who saw her cheered and soon others came running to see what the excitement was and then they cheered. Their beloved leader was back on her feet.

She greeted them with a slight wave of her hand, quieting them, and weakly but with resolve in her voice said, "We shall again become the scourge of the Amazon basin. This is the start of a new era."

It seemed to inject new energy into the crowd. They again raised their voices in support of their risen leader.

And yes, desertion of the depressed servant women ceased. As Cassania regained her strength it seemed to carry over to the whole village even further. Both the warriors and the servants worked together doing their job as before and only a few months passed before they were on a scheduled program rebuilding the Amazon tribe.

***

It was on a peaceful day of rest when Cassania summoned Nardania to come to her hut.

"Yes, my leader, what can I do for you."

"Sit with me, my faithful companion, I must tell you some facts that I've kept to myself because I had no idea of the outcome."

"This sounds serious," muttered Nardania.

"Yes, it is most serious and I'm very nervous about revealing this to anyone, mostly because of the time and circumstances of this incident and especially the irreversible outcome of it."

"Please, Cassania, we have known each other since childhood. We grew up almost as sisters. We trained together to become warriors and even pledged to give our lives to protect each other. There is nothing that you can tell me that would alter my feelings and devotion to you. Please understand that."

"I do understand and I beg you to hear me out."

"Of course."

"Our plan was to capture the tall white woman and hopefully integrate her into our village as a means of strengthening our line with strong children. Whether that was possible was yet to be seen, but the important part was to lure her husband to try to rescue her. That would give us ample opportunity to capture him, without harming him, it was especially important that he come to us intact and strong."

She thoughtfully continued, "He was the perfect specimen for impregnating our young warrior women. He would give us a continued line of strong women that we could train as we were trained."

"Yes, my leader, and it went according to our plan and would have worked if the Yano-Matis had not interfered," said Nardania.

"I know," Cassania now hesitated.

The room became quiet.

Nardania waited, knowing what came next was the revelation of the reason she was sent for. She sensed Cassania's deep thought.

Cassania finally continued, "I had sensed that we were up against a force we possibly could not overcome. We had come this far with the woman and now had the perfect man in our midst. He was still unconscious with the sleep-inducing drug used when captured, but would soon awake and alert his mate of his presence. I convinced the shaman to let me give him the drug that would keep him in a peaceful state of rest and tranquility, also to let me give him the drug that would arouse his desires to copulate even while he slept. I preferred that he not be aware of my plan so as to prohibit resistance from him."

Again she hesitated and nervously took a deep breath.

Nardania, who had been impatient, suddenly sat up straight, sensing what came next and anxiously said, "Yes, yes. Go on. Tell me."

"I had been keeping track of my cycle and I knew that night was the perfect time for ovulation. I dismissed the guards and was alone with the imprisoned man. Since he was semiconscious, I carefully fed him the drug to put him a state of euphoria. He became perfectly relaxed in minutes. I then gave him the drug to arouse his desires, not knowing how quickly or how well it would work. I did not want him to awake to arouse his mate or others." She hesitated. "It took just a short while, and it was obvious that it was working. He was a healthy man . . . very healthy."

Nardania shifted uneasily on her stool. Beads of sweat appeared on her upper lip as she throatily whispered, "Yes, yes! Go on."

"I had prepared myself for the act and had the minimum of clothing on, so I proceeded. As he lay there on his back, I acted as the aggressor and straddled him. It went very well and was over much more quickly than I thought it would be. I slowly and quietly stood. The shaman's drug had been very effective on him. He stirred as I left but was still asleep. When he awoke I'm sure that if he remembered anything, it would have only been as in a dream, the type of dream that happens to a healthy man from time to time."

"I'm sure there is more to the story but I have heard enough to understand," said a relaxed but breathless Nardania.

"He would have made our village better by the offspring he could have provided," said Cassania.

"I'm sure of that, and probably some happy young maidens too," Nardania chuckled.

"Now I must tell you my dilemma," Cassania said.

"I'm afraid that I know your dilemma," answered Nardania.

"My monthly cycle has not come and I thought perhaps it was because of the trauma of my wounds and the induced coma. No, that is not the case. I am pregnant, Nardania."

"Yes, I thought so. Have you seen the shaman?"

"Not yet. You are the first to know. I will go tomorrow."

Chapter Four

The two veteran warriors knew that this was an important event in the future of the village. The leader was pregnant and if the offspring were a female she could be the future of their clan. To rebuild the Amazon civilization to what it once was will take several generations, but this could be the start. The shaman was told and proper incantations took place to assure that it would be a female—at least, that is the shaman's belief.

The important thing is the health of Cassania. She is still very weak from the wounds inflicted in the brutal battle with the Yano-Matis tribe. Nardania took it upon herself to be the caregiver to her dearest friend and vowed to carry this pregnancy to full term. She was a constant companion and would not allow any mishap to befall her care.

Months passed and Cassania was now well into the pregnancy. It was estimated that she would give birth on the next full moon. The whole village buzzed with the expectant arrival of what all hoped would be the next leader.

"Have you given any thought what name will be given to this child of destiny?" asked Nardania.

"Yes," answered Cassania, "she is a gift from the god of the fire mountain. The mountain has been more active lately and is anticipating the birth of this child."

"I have seen smoke coming from the crater at the top of our mountain, so I believe what you say to be so," said Nardania with a slight quiver to her voice.

"Do you remember many years ago when we captured the men on the river? With them was a man they called their priest. He was a holy man and he spoke a language not like any we had heard before while he was captive. He would say his incantations each day with bread and wine. I was very young and curious. I tried to speak to him. He was kind and taught me words in his language. He called it Latin. A word that I remember was *calida*. It meant fiery or blazing. That is what I shall call my daughter, *Calida*. She will be the fiery one, the one that will be a blazing warrior, the one who will lead those to come after we are gone. She is the future."

***

It was a warm and humid night, an unusual night for the Amazon village purposely located at this ideal spot. It was higher in elevation than the surrounding rain forest. Off in the distance, in the surrounding mountains, the volcano that guarded the village rumbled. It was as if it was announcing an event. And indeed such an event was about to happen.

In Cassania's hut, the shaman was chanting incantations while Nardania was mopping the brow of the leader of the Amazon women. She was in the beginning stages of giving birth. A moan came from her dry mouth.

"I need water," she croaked.

Nardania dampened her lips and said, "It will be soon, my leader."

"Yes, the pains are coming more frequent now. You should get the midwife."

"She is here, my lady. I will move and give her some room."

It was not a moment too soon. The baby came fast and was born quickly with no complications. Cassania was born to be a mother and this was her first and would be her only child.

It was a girl as expected. She was long in girth with gangly, straight legs and arms. Very much like her mother, she would be tall. Her skin tone was not as golden as her mother's, it was lighter. It was a slight olive tone, a beautiful combination to blend with golden hair, not as blonde as her mother's but a slight shade darker. It was a striking combination even for a newborn baby. She indeed was destined to be *Mistress of the Amazon.*

***

The years passed and Calida matured into a young maiden. She was trained by her mother and by Nardania in the ways of an Amazon warrior. She was intelligent and learned quickly.

When she asked questions about her heritage, Cassania was evasive. Calida was taught, as all young Amazon maidens, the tribal custom of the superiority of an Amazon woman over all others, male or female.

"Mother, I have heard stories about the bitter battle with the Yano-Matis tribe. Was it as terrible as they say?"

"Yes, my child, it was devastating. It was during that time that I met your father."

"Oh. What happened to him?" she asked with hesitation.

"He went back to the Yano-Matis village, where he is a missionary and a doctor. He is a good man."

"Can you tell me more, Mother?"

"No, child, I've probably told you too much already."

***

As a small child, Calida showed this nurturing side inherited from her father, and many times when finding damaged small animals or wounded birds she took time to nurse them back to health. Sometimes it frustrated Cassania when Calida asked questions of the shaman on the many herbs and roots that she used for cures.

When Cassania had given Calida permission to accompany the shaman to the rain forest to gather herbs for her cures, she voiced her concern to Nardania, who answered, "You must remember, my leader, that her father was a doctor and practiced medicine in the Amazon basin without outside help. She only comes by this naturally."

"Yes, you're correct, but she is also a natural-born leader too. I'm very proud of her. She will be a fine Amazon warrior someday."

***

It was very unusual for a shaman to pass on secret cures to those not destined to become a shaman. But she realized perhaps, someday, shamans may die out and even become extinct due to the loss of herbs in their habitat. All this is due to the shrinking rain forest and the healers like her not able to harvest the natural cures. She knew that Calida was a special young maiden and that passing on some of this knowledge may be of benefit to the tribe.

"Pay attention, Calida, and I will show you the most common herbs and how they are used. Later I will give you some very secret cures known only to a chosen few."

"Yes, please show me. I want to learn all I can about helping others."

"First of all, you may hear of many fallacies that we as shamans do not refute and we let the imposters make fools of themselves with their incantations and hallucinogens. They are sometimes called medicine men. A real shaman knows the correct cures and I will teach you."

"I want to learn," answered Calida.

"Watch and listen."

They trekked to the rain forest, where the heat and humidity was greater than at the higher elevation at the village. The tree canopy was dense with many tall kapok trees. Some grew as high as 200 feet with trunks 10 feet in diameter. They stopped and the shaman parted a thick growth to pick a plant, making sure to leave some of the same plants and not take it all. She wanted to save some to reproduce.

She said, "This plant is called the foxglove. We have known of it for many centuries and now the white man knows of it. It has an important use to treat a heart condition more common to the white people than to our people. They have named it *digitalis* and it has saved many lives."

They moved on.

"Today I want to gather some herbs to heal wounds. I used most of my stock healing wounds after the battle several years ago. I didn't replace it then but may need some for the future now."

"What do you use?"

"There are several but I like the sap called *sangre de drago* or dragon's blood. It is the color of blood and is a good healer. I also use the bark from the *icoja*. If mixed properly it becomes an alcoholic maceration and disinfects as it heals."

They trekked on.

"Ah-ha. We are in luck. This herb is hard to find. It is called *sangre de grado*. The sap is very effective against diarrhea. This dreaded condition has caused death from dehydration and can happen quickly if not properly treated. Also, I was told by the ancients that it also contains an agent called cicatrizant, which has been known to fight tumors."

They went deeper into the rain forest. Soon the heat was oppressive.

"Here, this is the camu tree. Its fruit is called camu berries, and when eaten, will cause a sense of wellbeing. If one is in distress it can calm the fears that overwhelm a person when demons possess his body. This can happen in times of the death of a loved one."

At each stop the shaman collected what she needed and not more.

They entered a grove of smaller trees.

"Here is the annatto, sometimes called the lipstick tree. Not only is it a good insect repellant but is known to lower the blood pressure. On ahead I see the cacao trees. It was used for centuries by the Aztec Indians and Mayans, both civilizations now extinct. They knew it was good for tiredness and also to reduce fever and some anxiety. The white man uses the bean to make chocolate.

"And one more, it is a fruit called graviola, used to reduce swelling but more important as a sedative and treatment for convulsions. Some have said that its leaves are a cancer fighter or even a preventer. I have no proof of this but white men are studying its properties.

"That is enough for today, my child. We must start back. Can you remember what I have shown you?"

"Oh yes, and I want to learn more. Can I help you in the village?"

"That may not be possible, child. You are destined for other things. Our leader has planned your future."

They started the long journey home and arrived well after the sun had set.

The next day, Calida was tending to a bird with a broken wing. It was one of many injured animals that she had mended and she was deep in her task.

She was startled when her mother called, "Calida, come into the hut."

"Yes, Mother," answered the gangly eleven-year-old girl, "as soon as I make my little friend more comfortable."

"I said come in *now*," Cassania said with great emphasis.

Calida jumped to her feet, very well aware of when she must move quickly and ran to the hut.

"Here I am, Mother. Is something wrong?"

"Please sit, child." Cassania composed herself for a moment and then softly said, "No, my daughter, I just felt it was time we talked about your future. You will soon reach the age where you will have your time of the moon each month. This means you are becoming a woman and no longer a child."

"Yes, Mother, Nardania has mentioned this time to me while training in the skills of becoming a warrior. I have been using the long bow and Nardania said I'm almost as good as she is. She took me hunting and I bagged two of those obnoxious, pig-looking creatures. She said that I'm not yet ready but I think I am, Mother."

"Yes, dear child, very soon—"

Before she could finish, a tremor shook the hut and wall trappings fell to the floor. Small bits of the overhead material floated to the ground. Both Cassania and Calida jumped to their feet and stood unsteadily while the earthen floor trembled.

Calida was frightened and her mother soothingly said, "Don't be frightened, little one. It is the fire god in the mountain taking a deep breath. Come outside and we may see his hot breath coming from the crater on the mountain."

They went out to the common area, where many of the villagers had gathered.

Nardania was one of them and she said, "Our fire god is getting restless. I can see flame as well as smoke this time. Many generations have passed since this has happened. I will record it in our ledger of historical events."

"Yes, maybe we should do as the ancients have done and offer a sacrifice to appease the fiery mountain," Cassania announced.

The villagers within earshot cowered. They had heard tales told by the ancient hags of the tribe. Human sacrifice seemed to be the preferred way of sacrifice when the mountain was active with fire and hot lava poured down upon them. Many turned away and scurried back to their huts, mumbling as they went.

The tremor stopped for the time being but the mountain still belched smoke and flame.

"The fire god has quieted. We can wait before we think about a sacrifice."

"I hope you're right," answered a shaken Nardania. "I've never seen it so active."

The village went about its daily activities but with a wary eye cast the way of the smoking volcano.

***

It was several days later when the shaman passed by the training area where Calida was deeply engrossed in a lesson of defense using a very sharp machete. She stopped and observed.

Nardania sharply scolded Calida, "No child, you must put your body into those jabs and thrusts. Swing quickly and snap your wrists."

Calida stopped and implored, "I'm tired of swinging at nothing. Can I go into the jungle where I can cut down brush and get the feel of what a machete can do?"

"I don't have time to take you out of the village and into the thick forest. I have other duties here. You must practice. You will soon be old enough to go on a real hunt."

The shaman stepped into the practice ring and suggested, "I am going into the forest to collect some roots that I missed the last time out. The child can go with me and will be a help in cutting a path to the deep part of the forest that I must visit."

"That will be good," said a relieved Nardania. "She is a persistent child but she is right. Cutting a path will strengthen her young arms. Please take her so I can work with the warriors who have healed from the battle."

Calida smiled, knowing that she would be getting more lessons on herbs, which she really enjoyed more than practicing warfare.

Chapter Five

It was a long and arduous trip into the jungle to find the healing roots. The trail took them through the thickest part of the rain forest and a half day of travel just to get to the area. Then another half day to find and dig up the roots. Calida got her share of machete work and her arms ached by the time they arrived at their destination.

She helped the shaman gather the roots and listened while she was instructed on their use. Learning about the healing remedies that Mother Nature provided was easy for her to remember and so interesting. She seemed to absorb all the instruction and craved for more.

"It is getting late, child. We must set up a place to spend the night. Gather some wood so we can start a campfire. If you are as good with that bow as you say you are, maybe we can have some fresh meat instead of the dried jerky in my pouch."

"Oh yes. I'll show you," Calida said as she strung her bow and tramped off into the bush after she had gathered enough dead branches to start a fire.

The shaman smiled and gathered the wood into a pile to get a fire started. After it caught and was blazing well enough to cook some meat, she patiently waited for her huntress to return. She was old and tired from a long day, so she dozed while sitting close to the fire.

Unknown to her, she was being stalked by a young jaguar. He was scouting for an easy prey to kill and drag back to his den where the mother jaguar awaited him. This stalker, though young and inexperienced, was strong and healthy. He was far from mature but still weighed over 125 pounds and was a natural killer. His hunting skills were inborn, and with some instruction from his mother, he was formidable.

Jaguars are stalkers and not like others in the cat family that chase the prey and with blinding speed catch and kill them. He slowly crept through the brush, moving away from the noxious smoke coming from the fire. His prey looked helpless sitting next to the fire with her head drooping forward and her breathing one of deep slumber. With stealth, he emerged from the protection of the rain forest brush into the edge of the clearing. Suddenly, he leaped and in one huge bound landed on the sleeping woman. With his powerful jaws, he crushed the skull of his prey with one gigantic but merciful bite. The old shaman didn't know what hit her. She was dead before she hit the ground. The raging young jaguar was fully on top of her body, her entire head in his mouth. He then dropped the head and tore into her chest cavity to devour the soft tissue, including the heart.

As his rapt attention was given to feasting on his prey, he did not hear the approach of another two-legged adversary, and although smaller than the one he just killed, this one was armed.

As Calida entered the clearing, she stopped short, dropped the game she had just killed, and gave a startled outcry. The young jaguar was also startled at this sudden intrusion. He slowly rose up on his haunches and gave a low growl, not quite sure if this was a danger to him or maybe an added prey. His hesitation proved to be his undoing. While he thought about an attack, his adversary acted.

Calida's long and intense training and her natural instincts for retaining what she was taught saved her from the same fate as the old shaman. She quickly took in the scene of slaughter as she dropped the game, swiftly removed an arrow from the quiver on her back, inserted it into the bow string, pulled back, and let the arrow fly, aiming it at the center of the jaws of the growling predator—all in one smooth motion.

Before the jaguar could crouch into a killing leap, the first arrow was true and struck him between his half opened jaws. He screamed in pain but this was not a killing shot. As he pawed at the projectile protruding from his mouth, he snapped the shaft in half and turned his body back to the intruder that caused this pain. As he raised his body to attack his foe, the second arrow was already in the air and this one was also true. It drove deep into his chest from this close range as he reared up to face the enemy. The sharp arrowhead slashed into his heart, ripping it in half. He was bewildered at this unknown adversary but he still attempted an impossible charge. He was a strong beast. Before he could muster the strength to leap, he took two short, painful steps and collapsed. As he lay, he twitched and tried in vain to rise up and face this strange enemy that he had never encountered before in his short life.

After pulling himself up on his front legs, he hissed, turned to look at the young girl that had flung the arrows, and then collapsed again for the last time. He would have been a magnificent beast had he lived.

Calida stood wide eyed at the carnage of the shaman and the killing machine that lay at her feet. She was now alone in the jungle, miles away from her village. She gathered the shaman's pouch and other belongings. There was no way that she could carry the dead woman back to the village. It was getting dark and too late to start back herself. She decided to stoke up the fire and spend the night tending it. She could keep the hyenas away from the dead body of the shaman with a fire blazing.

She struggled and pulled the dead jaguar out of the campsite. It may satisfy the hyenas and vultures. She covered the shaman's body with brush and leaves. If she left early enough she might make it back to the village in time to send someone to retrieve the body and hopefully it will still be intact enough for rites and burial.

It was a long night and strangely enough she thought she heard a rumbling sound. The fire god in the mountain must really be angry tonight for her to hear the sounds so far away. She was exhausted but she wanted to stay awake. As she sat by the fire, she listened to the sounds of the night. Animals were on the prowl and the deep rumble from afar seemed to increase and then recede. She nodded off. Her exhaustion overcame her young body. But she suddenly awoke with a start.

"I feel a tremor like the one in the village. Strange . . . I am very far from the mountain."

She stood and looked back to the southern sky. "The sky looks so strange with a red glow and it seems to be growing."

Suddenly the very ground under her feet seemed to move one way then the other way, then a violent surge that caused her to lose her balance and she fell to her hands and knees. Her campfire shook and flared up, sparks flying into the air and then the fire spread out to be reduced to glowing coals. It became dark without a fire lighting the campground and now the sky toward the mountain was blood red. Another violent tremor shook the ground under her as she tried to rise up from her hands and knees and fell back again. Then the ground was still, but the explosive noise from the direction of the mountain was so loud.

"Oh, what is happening? Are Mother and the others safe? If the tremor is bad here what must be happening at the village?"

She gathered the coals still glowing and piled some kindling on them. As she sat trembling in fright, she sobbed, and when an occasional tremor shook the ground under her, she cried out in fright.

The night sounds from the predators hunting for prey in the rain forest were now silent. They too were wary of this most unnatural occurrence that disturbed their hunt for food.

By morning the tremors were lessening. It was time to leave and make her way back home. She was frightened at what she might find. As she made her way through the jungle and got closer to the village, she encountered several huge trees that were toppled over, and the closer she got, the more she saw.

Finally, well into the afternoon she arrived at the cleft in the hillside that led to the village.

"That's strange," she mumbled. "What happened to the entrance? I know I'm at the right spot."

She climbed over a pile of rocks. She struggled over the rocks and boulders that were now in place of the entrance to the village.

"It's gone. Everything has changed."

She climbed back to level ground and walked both directions from the closed entrance but could find no way to get to the village. It was now getting dark. She was tired and beside herself. What should she do? She decided to make a camp and think about her next move. She had the shaman's pouch and her knapsack, so she was equipped to do so. She had passed an area that was sheltered and walked back to it. Little did she realize that this was the same place that the battle between the Amazons and the Yano-Matis took place.

She got settled in and built a fire. There was a strange smell in the air. It was a smoky odor and she noticed much dark ash on the trees and rocks. There was still a glow in the sky but not as intense as the night before. She couldn't see the mountain but she heard an occasional rumble from that direction.

She stoked up the fire and fell into an exhausted, dreamless sleep.

The trilling of birds woke her up just as first light found its way into the clearing. She groaned as she rose from the hard ground. Her body ached from the physical and mental stress of the past few days. She took some nourishment from both the pouch and the knapsack. She was famished and thirsty. The shaman had shown her the bush that held liquid to quench her thirst when a cool stream was not available.

She decided to explore. Maybe she could find a new way to get through the rocks and hills that blocked her way. The village was well hidden. Maybe the only way was to climb one of the foothills and go over the top. She spent most of the day traveling into the hills in one direction. It only got more difficult and she was farther rather than closer to finding a way in. She returned to her campsite. It was now well into the night and again she was very tired. She again spent the night in the same camp as before.

The next day she tried the opposite direction. As she traveled she saw more evidence of damage from the quake. Huge boulders were strewn about and more black ash was evident. As she traveled she could see that the huge rocks were flung from above and half buried in the ground. Others had landed at an angle and created a deep rut before they came to rest. Trees were destroyed when rocks rained down upon them. It was so much worse than in the other direction.

The acrid smell was getting stronger. As she rounded a bluff she came upon complete devastation. It looked like the earth had opened up and swallowed huge patches of trees and left others scorched. Then she saw why the noxious odor was worse. Smoking lava that had run through a new opening in the hill was lying in a hardened mass. She realized that the lava had come from the direction that included the village.

The hardened lava was too hot for her to climb over. Maybe she could make her way adjacent to it to find her way back home. She must try. She must find her mother. Tears streamed down her face as she called out, "I'm coming, Mother. I'm coming."

Chapter Six

The devastation was overwhelming. Calida found it very difficult to make her way over the hill. She clawed up the steep grade, slipping and sliding back when she did make a little headway. It frustrated her and it was painful, her fingers bleeding from scraping on the sharp rocks and singed from the hot, hardened lava. The hours flew by and she still wasn't close to making it over the hill. Darkness was creeping up on her.

"I must find a place to rest and spend the night," she muttered.

She spotted a flat area nestled between some rocks that looked like a place to stretch out and regain her strength. She slid into the crevice and was startled by a flurry of movement. Two furry little creatures scurried away when she entered the small sanctuary.

"I guess they had the same idea as I did," she said with a chuckle, "but it sure got my attention."

She settled in and groped in the shaman's pouch. "She told me that aloe was good for healing, especially for burns. Ah yes, here it is. She was always prepared. I miss her so much."

She applied the healing ointment on her hands and bleeding fingers. She also found the dried jerky in the pouch and hungrily chewed on a piece to appease the hunger pangs. Finally she lay back and rested. She was so tired. Her young lithe body had been running at top speed for days and it was starting to catch up to her.

"I've got to rest if I want to get over this mound of rock before I can get back home. Mother is probably frantic."

She closed her eyes and fell into a deep but restless sleep.

***

The next morning she was awakened by the sun shining in her eyes from an opening in the rock sanctuary. She stretched and had to reevaluate her situation, forgetting exactly where she was and how she got there. It all came back pretty quickly and she decided that she had better get moving. She had slept a bit later than she intended to.

It was a warm sunny day and might have been pleasant if circumstances were different. Climbing today was easier since she was getting to the top and it wasn't quite as steep. By noon she reached a spot where she could view the valley on the other side. She peered into the still smoking lava that lay in the valley.

"Where are the trees?"

She climbed down the hillside. Going was much easier on this side. It was downhill.

"This is strange. I think this should be the little vale beside our village, but it's so different."

She reached the bottom of the hollow and picked her way through the devastation. She knew that at the end of the flat area and down a short hill was home. She was excited and picked up her pace through the difficult terrain. She rounded the bluff that guarded her village and stopped short with baited breath. She peered out over an area devoid of any standing structure or tree or anything that resembled a village.

She called, "Hello . . . hello . . . is anybody there?"

There were areas of steaming lava and in other places there were huge fissures in the floor of the valley. She peered down into one of them and could see the remnants of an abode from the village. Calida was speechless. She looked around at what was once a thriving village of Amazons and now was smoldering ruins.

"I can't believe it. It's all gone. Did they escape? Where could they have gone?"

She tried to acclimate herself to where her house stood but it was all so different. Finally she got to the spot where she thought it was located and found remnants of the structure as well as parts of other houses scattered about. There was a terrible stench coming from direction of where the passageway to the outside stood. As she reached it, she screamed and raised her hands to cover her eyes. Decomposing bodies were lying all over the ground near the entrance to the passageway. Some were half buried with rocks that had fallen from above and some were at the entrance when it was closed off. The burned bodies were frozen in a position of clawing at the blocked passageway. She couldn't stay any longer. She had to see if anyone survived.

As she walked through the devastated village, the earth shook with a violent aftershock and dropped her to her knees. She heard a rumble from the place she just left, and when she turned, the noise got louder. The shock dislodged boulders on the hillside and caused a landslide. She ran as fast as she could to get as far away from the passageway as she could.

Soon it stopped and she was safe. When the dust cleared, she saw that all the bodies strewn about the entrance were now covered with rock and debris from the hill. They were finally buried. She walked through the rest of the village without finding another living human being. They were either dead or gone and she had grave doubts if anyone survived.

She climbed back to the hollow that led her to the village to set up a campsite and think of what she should do next. It was soon to be dark and she needed to rest.

***

The next morning found her back in the village once more to make sure there was no one left and to see if there was anything useful that she could use to build a shelter in the hollow. She collected enough to build a small shelter and passed a few days exploring the hollow and surrounding area. She found some spots hardly affected by the quake.

It was a bit more pleasant than the village area and was not quite so devastated. Some trees and bushes were left standing and she was able to find some fruit and berries. Small animals were now moving about, so her arrows provided her with some fresh meat.

Weeks passed and she had not encountered a living soul or even evidence of anyone. She was a healthy, strong, young teenage girl and had good survival skills. Her body was maturing and she was tall for her age. She had been taught well on weaponry, so food was not an issue. But she was lonely. She needed human companionship and had become very family oriented.

As she lay in her straw bed, looking at a full moon, she thought to herself, "I wonder if I could find my father, and what he would do or say if I could find him. Mother said he was a missionary doctor with the Yano-Matis tribe. How silly! I'd have no idea where that tribe is located. Or even if I did, how would I get there?"

She rolled over and fell asleep. She dreamed about a tall white man that smiled at her. She asked if he was her father and he laughed and said he was. But she couldn't make out his features clearly and then he slowly faded away, smiling and smiling.

When she awoke the next morning, she remembered the dream.

"I know it could never happen but maybe I should look for him. There is nothing here for me. My mother and all my friends are dead or gone if they survived. From the look of the village, I doubt any did live through the devastation. Yes, I must leave this place and find a village or town to live in. I'll prepare to leave and head north toward the great river Nardania told me about. From there I can go anywhere."

And the next day she struck out. She spent the next night in the spot she had previously camped in, the place where the encounter with the Yano-Matis happened and the place where, at one time, her father took shelter.

She dreamed about him again that night. Or maybe it wasn't a dream. Maybe she just thought she dreamed. Maybe she really was awake and he was deep in her thoughts.

Chapter Seven

Calida stayed in the campsite for the time being. It was beginning to feel like a second home. She felt a connection here but couldn't quite grasp the total meaning of why. The next step would take some planning, and in her well-organized mind she knew not to go off without a goal in mind. The ultimate goal was to find her father, but she needed short-term goals to succeed.

Game, wild berries, and fruit were plentiful here, so she was able to build up her strength and supplies. The lean-to she had put together served its purpose very well. She devised a travel knapsack to carry what she needed to set up camps along the way, as well as combining all of the shamans herbs and some spices for use while on the trail. Of course, her bow, arrows, and machete were necessary items to carry. They not only were a resource for food and making a shelter but for protection as well. She would be traveling through the dense rain forest and the encounter with the young jaguar stood out in her mind. There were many other dangerous animals to consider, as well as possible encounters with other tribes that may not be friendly. Nardania had told her stories about these tribes, as well as danger from snakes and insects. And when she reached a river or lake, a whole new set of dangers could arise.

It was not going to be easy. But what choices did she have? If only she wasn't so lonely. The last living person that she had seen was the shaman, several months ago.

***

It finally got to the point where she decided to start her journey. The planning was over. She readied her travel gear and slept in the lean-to for the last time. At first light the next day she hit the trail.

Travel through the rain forest was not easy. She attempted to pick the areas of the least amount of underbrush, which were usually in groves of the huge kapok or mahogany trees. But of course she must try to maintain the direction of the great river she had heard about.

She encountered several small streams and one formidable river but had no experience navigating them, so she decided to stay clear and to use them only to quench her thirst and not for transportation. In the larger river she caught a glimpse of the ugly caimans that lived in the water. There were other beasts like the caimans, only much larger. The reptiles had huge mouths and many jagged teeth. She was pretty sure she saw a big snake too with only his nostrils above the water, but when it turned and swam away enough of his body was visible to see that he was big and black. Other strange creatures were visible too.

She would use the river only as a guide. Surely if she followed the river downstream it would take her toward the fabled river she heard stories about from the ancient ones in the village. Could it really be as long and as wide as they described? The tales they told had it emptying into a great body of water so vast that it covered half of the earth.

She had plenty of time to think about this as she traveled. It was a long journey and there was no one to talk to.

Weeks passed. She pressed on, always in sight of the river. As she traveled, the river got larger and swifter, but it still was not the great river as described by the elders.

Suddenly she pulled up short. She could hear activity ahead. She quietly knelt on the riverbank and with her sharp ears listened to the sound of men talking. One of them was yelling loudly and some others laughed and spoke in a strange tongue not familiar to her.

She waited, still as a statue, until the sounds faded away. The men were leaving the area. She parted the bushes that shielded her from them and gazed at the river ahead of her. She saw several canoes with six or eight men paddling downstream away from her. She waited until they were around a bend and out of sight. She then slowly moved ahead. Something alerted her. All her senses were tuned to the highest level, so when she caught sight of a figure sprawled on the bank of the river, she pulled up short again. She quickly strung an arrow on the bowstring. She focused in on the figure.

"It's a man," she whispered. "He's lying very still. I wonder if he's dead."

She slowly approached the prone man. As she got closer, she could see that he was an old, wizened man dressed only in a breechcloth. She was now alongside the old man and peered at his half-naked body. There were bruises and cuts on his back. He appeared to have been beaten to death.

"AHHH," she screamed as the old man rolled over and attempted to rise but fell back on his belly. He moaned.

She backed off and started to run but stopped after only a few steps. There was no danger here. This poor old man was close to death or at least badly injured. Her nurturing nature arose deep inside her subconscious. She went back and spoke haltingly, "Hello. Can I help you?"

The old man turned his head and unbelievingly stared at this young girl with consoling eyes and a sympathetic voice. Even though he couldn't understand the words, the tone was such that he knew she wanted to help him. He rolled over and moaned loudly as his raw back made contact with the uneven surface of the riverbank.

"Oh," she said, "roll on your stomach. Let me see your back."

He didn't understand the words but he sensed the meaning and rolled over. She inspected the wounds as she put down her bow and then helped him sit up. She could now see his face. It was swollen and one eye was turning a deep shade of blue visible even with his dark skin. He obviously was a native tribesman.

She dug in the pouch she had salvaged from the shaman and removed the medication that she knew would help relieve some pain and promote healing. As she worked, she realized that this was not a one-time medication, he was going to need ongoing care. He was badly hurt and had other unseen injuries, possibly internal.

After treating him she cleared an area and made camp. She started a cooking fire and warmed a broth that she knew would help him sleep. He needed rest.

***

The old man had been sleeping for hours. His breathing was even and steady. She struck out on a hunt for some game. She was hungry and she knew when he awoke, if he was going to survive, he would be hungry.

After the hunt she fell asleep sitting up with her back against a tree. During the night she awoke with a start when her patient moaned. She carefully approached him, still being cautious.

He looked at her imploringly and said something she could not understand, but looking at his dry, cracked lips, she felt that he needed water. She scooped up a clam shell of water from the river and slowly fed it to him. Yes. That's what he wanted. After a few swallows, he closed his eyes and went back asleep. She too went back to her tree and quickly dozed off, feeling very satisfied with her situation.

Days went by as she gently nursed the ancient one back to health. Their spoken tongues were different, but they soon developed a sort of communication with sign language and she was able to discern what a few words meant in this different language.

As he got stronger she tried to get him mobile. He was now taking a few steps and trying to speak to her. He said, "Plata," and pointed to his chest. "Plata, Plata."

"Oh. Your name is Plata?" she asked.

He laughed and again said, "Plata," pointing at himself and then pointing to her and said a phrase she took to mean, "How are you called?"

"I am called Calida," she said. "Calida."

He tried to repeat "Ca-li-da?"

"Yes, yes. Calida."

"Calida?" he answered.

She laughed and said, "Yes, yes." It was so good to have another person to be around. She was happy and she took his hands and smiled at his beaming face. He was going to survive. She was healing her first patient.

Chapter Eight

The days turned into weeks and weeks into months. Plata's old body was as healed as it would ever be. The temporary camp had turned into a more permanent residence. Plata had constructed a formidable lean-to for his healer. He called it a *shabono*. He slept in the open on a bed of leaves.

Calida, with her quick wits, was able to pick up more and more understanding of the old man's dialect and soon they could communicate. He also must have had some contact with white men since he used some pidgin phrases and some Spanish slang, which she was also able to discern, but did not understand the origin.

He showed her how to fish in the river for fresh edible food and what aquatic creatures to stay away from, such as the piranha, stingrays, and electric eels, all in sign language and with sightings of the creatures. He called them by their tribal names but Calida was able to understand the dangers from them, also which fish were better to eat. Plata's village must be on a river or close by since he was so familiar with it.

Calida was growing into a strong, healthy teenager and had become very self-sufficient. She soon grew restless and recalled her goal to find her father. She sat with Plata, and in the best tribal dialect that she could muster, she asked, "Plata, do you know the great river that flows to the big water?"

"Ah, yes. White men call it the Amazon. It is very big, as big as a lake."

"How far is this . . . Amazon?"

"Many moons to go there, very far."

"Do you know how to go?"

"Yes, yes, go on river, in boat."

"Oh, well, we don't have a boat."

"Can get boat, my village have boat."

"Maybe you forget what your friends in the village did to you. We can't go there."

"Yes, yes, go at night, take boat."

"You mean steal the boat?"

"Yes, yes, steal. And I steal my blow pipe and darts."

"Oh, I don't know. Where is your village? How far?"

"We can walk. Take maybe three, four moons."

"Can't we build a boat?"

"Better we steal. Much easier."

The next two days were spent preparing for leaving the comfort of this camp and traveling to unknown dangers. They will try to steal a boat, and then, if successful, an arduous trip down stream.

Strangely, she felt safe with Plata. It was the first time in her life to have any association with a male. She was very lucky to find him. He was friendly and very capable despite his obvious advancing age. Several times at the end of a long day of travel she could sense his tiredness. Even so he did not complain and bounced back the next day with vigor that he dragged up from deep in that wizened old body.

He knew the jungle like the back of his hand and educated her on many things she never would have learned without him. But she too showed him some medicinal herbs as they traveled and harvested. It came as second nature to gather them for future use.

As they rested after a long hard day of travel, they feasted on a small tapir that Calida killed with an arrow from her bow. Plata marveled at this canny ability of the young maiden.

Calida lazily leaned back against a tree trunk and her eyes got heavy. She would be fast asleep soon. Suddenly her eyes popped open. She sharply breathed in and froze. She couldn't believe her eyes. Plata was stealthily coming at her with a machete raised in an attack position. She ducked as he swung the razor sharp blade, which whistled just over her head. She screamed, "Plata, no." She cowered as he reached behind her and pulled a headless but still wriggling snake from the tree trunk behind her.

The head from the snake was lying on the ground beside her. She jumped up and yelled, "What is it?"

"It is okay now, little one. I saw him getting ready to strike and my only recourse was to act immediately. You would have died if he struck. This is the most dangerous snake in the jungle. White men call it fer-de-lance. My people call it spearhead."

She was shaking from fright and she slumped to the ground. She put her hands to her face and cried. All the tension from the past tragic months came pouring out. She felt her cheeks both flush and drain. All senses seemed to fail and she seemed like she was falling. But within a moment or two, she started breathing normally again and all her senses rushed back.

Plata sat beside her and stroked her hair but he knew she had to release the tension in her young body. He arose and quickly disposed of the remains of the dangerous snake, the snake that he had just killed to save the life of the person who saved him many months ago. That person he now had a deep love for, just as a grandfather would have for a granddaughter, a granddaughter that he never had.

When he returned to the camp, Calida had settled down and he said, "We must sleep now. Tomorrow we will be close to my village. I will scout around to see how we can take a boat after dark."

She gathered and steadied herself and with clenched fist she said, "I'm okay now. I'll be ever grateful to you for what you did."

"I would be very sad if something bad happened to you," Plata replied.

They both fell fast asleep very quickly.

***

The next morning Calida arose from a restful night and saw Plata emerging from the jungle with an armload of fresh fruit for breakfast.

"Eat heartily, Calida, this will be our last sit-down meal for a while. We can eat sparingly as we travel, but this close to the village means no camping."

"I can do it, Plata."

They struck out and by late afternoon they could hear distant sounds of activity in the village.

"I am very familiar with this part of the jungle," Plata said. "My village is across the river, but it is not likely we will run into anyone. I would swim to this side and come here to go to my secret place when I was a boy."

"Where is this secret spot?"

"We will soon be there. We will wait until dusk and then I will leave you. I will swim the river and scout out a likely boat to take. I may also try to sneak in the village and find my blow pipe and some darts. If I'm lucky enough I may also find the poison potion for the darts. The shamans mix it and keep it secret. But if not I know how to mix a less lethal one."

They reached an unusual rocky place, well hidden by trees and brush. Plata used the machete to make an entry and they finally got to a small cave so arranged so it was hardly visible.

"We can wait here until I swim the river."

Calida asked, "Are you sure you can swim the river. It is very wide here."

"Yes, but the current is very slow, making it easier to do. Don't worry, I have done it many times."

"But you were much younger and stronger."

"I have gained much strength since I have known you, Calida. You have helped me regain what I lost when I was brutalized by the new chief."

"Why did the new chief brutalize you so?"

"Merely because I was an advisor to the old chief who was overthrown by the new one and his marauding followers. It was not good for my village. They killed many good men and stole their wives. My village is not a happy one now. I never want to go back even if I could."

"You should rest before you try to swim the river."

Chapter Nine

The night was very dark, perfect for what Plata planned. He slipped out of the secret place, into the jungle, and stealthily made his way to the river's edge. Calida was in a deep sleep and was not even aware of his leaving the hidden place of refuge.

When he reached the river, he looked toward the village directly across the slowly flowing water. The river was wide but shallow here, just before the big bend, which slowed it down. After the bend it picks up speed until it reaches the double falls many miles downstream. They will have easy going and be out of sight from the village very quickly but then, must portage around the falls.

Ah, yes, he thought to himself, *the village is quiet. Only a few cooking fires are still glowing in the dark. If I'm lucky I can locate all that we need and make the quick strike tomorrow night. We can be miles away by dawn if we move quickly. It all depends on locating what we need, loading the canoe, and silently floating downriver.*

He quietly swam across the river, using a breaststroke underwater so he wouldn't make any noise or create a splash. It was slow going but he finally reached the bank on the other side. He stopped and raised his upper body high enough to where he could look over the bank and into the village proper.

All was quiet. No movement was discernable in the village. He listened intently. The only sounds were coming from the jungle where the predators were looking for food.

He pulled himself onto the bank and slithered along the shore. He was happy to see the canoes were pulled halfway out of the water and would be easily and quietly launched when they needed to take one. That would be the easy part.

He rose to a squatting position with both hands hanging low to the ground. He duck-walked toward the long house. It was here that the shamans did their blending and compounding of herbs to make the poison used on the blow gun darts. There were several kinds. The lethal one would render an animal or a human unconscious immediately and dead within seconds. Others would work as quickly, would not be fatal, but temporary paralysis would make the subject helpless for hours or even days depending on the mixture. This ability was passed on from shaman to shaman and jealously guarded so that no one other than a shaman could compound the real poison. Not only the poison was stored here but also the blow guns and blow-gun darts themselves.

Plata didn't know the formulas but he was an expert shot with the blow gun. He could bring down a humming bird at 100 feet or a monkey at 200 feet easily. He needed a blow gun, darts, and some poison. With those items he could defend Calida and he could hunt animals to keep them in fresh meat.

He got to the long house and carefully scanned inside through a window. As always a guard was sleeping alongside the storage area of all the items desired by Plata. Only one guard was not a problem. Plata could quietly render him unconscious in seconds. If there were two, that may present a problem. He could see his favorite blow gun hanging in the wall with several others.

He slowly sank back to the ground. He knew what he must do tomorrow night. With a little luck and a dark night they could launch a canoe, steal the necessary blow gun paraphernalia, and be miles downriver before the village woke up.

He made his way back to the riverbank and slipped quietly into the water. Using the same method as when he crossed over, he returned to the opposite bank. He entered the well-hidden spot where Calida slept, and crawled on to his bed of leaves. He was asleep in minutes and Calida was not aware he had left and returned.

He slept well into the day, knowing full well that he must be awake and alert all night long. His old body needed the rest from the night of planning and the night of execution.

Calida awoke and assumed since he was fast asleep that he had accomplished his goal. She busied herself with preparation for the incursion and theft of a boat and whatever else Plata needed for the trip downstream.

He finally awoke well into the day. He said, "You must rest, Calida, it will be a long night. Gather everything that we have accumulated and take it to the river's edge. We will swim the river, pick out a good canoe. I will collect the blow pipe and darts while you stand by, ready to push off."

"What next, Plata?"

"When I get back from the long house, we must quietly paddle the canoe across the river and load up our supplies. Then we head downstream as fast and as far away as we can."

"I'll be ready. Must you take the chance and the time to get the blow gun and darts?"

"Yes, I must. If someone awakes, I will use the gun put them to sleep very quietly without arousing others. Also, as we travel I can provide us with meat very quickly. A dart travels very fast, and the sound is much like the buzzing of a mosquito."

She chuckled, "Well, with all the mosquitos here in the rain forest, I guess no one would notice a dart flying toward them."

"Very true, little one. When they realize it's a dart, it's too late."

The rest of the day was one of preparation and then rest.

***

Again it was a moonless night, and well into the darkness the unlikely twosome of a wizened old man and a young teenage girl silently paddled themselves across the slow-moving river.

Calida was apprehensive, well aware of the deadly inhabitants of the river. She kept her sharp blade in easy reach should she need it, although it would be useless against the onslaught of the red-bellied piranha. Attack from a caiman is unlikely, but the larger crocodiles possibly would attack. But then Plata told her the river here by the village was fairly safe. The village men tried to keep it free of predators by killing them on sight. Plata had also told her about the legend of the *boto*. This legend told by

41

many tribes tells of a river dolphin that turns into a man and seduces young maidens by the riverside. Now that really scared her. When she asked if he ever saw the man or knew of anyone who had seen him, he said, "No," and quickly walked away, smirking.

They reached the shallow part on the other side and crept up to the bank with only head and shoulders out of the water. Calida followed Plata along the river's edge toward the docked canoes. He stopped alongside a small but sturdy one and signed to her that this was the one he wanted. With one on each side, they slowly and as quietly as possible shoved the canoe into the river. Calida stood waist deep in the river and steadied the canoe. They had made a slight splash when the canoe slapped against the river during the launch. Plata signed to keep silent and stand still while he listened for any activity from the village. It remained quiet. No one had heard them.

Plata slowly made his way back up the riverbank, and as he did the night before, he belly-crawled to the long house. This time he went to the entrance and peered inside. In the gloom he could see the man left to watch over the blow guns, darts, and hollowed vessels containing the different poisons. He spotted the blowgun that he favored and a pouch of darts. The darts typically were already treated with poison and ready to use.

He inched his way into the long house, and using all the guile of a seasoned hunter, not making a sound as he removed the blow gun of choice and a pouch of darts. *So far, so good.* Now, could he grab a sealed vessel of poison? It was high on a shelf. He stood and reached over his head.

Suddenly he detected a movement below him. The guard rolled over and moaned. He stood very still, like a statue. A low snore came from the guard. He was still asleep. Plata slowly removed a small vessel and dropped it into his pouch. He quietly inserted a dart into the pipe, taking the precaution to be ready if he encountered a villager. He lowered himself back to the ground and without a sound he left through the same doorway.

He was only a few paces from the long house when he heard a bustling in the doorway and the guard came stumbling out and sleepily looked around. Taking no chances, Plata raised the blow gun to his mouth and let fly a dart aimed at the unsuspecting guard. There was a short buzzing sound and the dart buried itself on the side of the guard's neck. He stood wide-eyed for an instant, raising his hand toward his neck, but only got halfway as he silently slumped to the ground. Plata waited a minute. He could discern no other activity and dispatching the guard couldn't have been more quietly done.

He crawled back to the canoe where Calida impatiently awaited him. She jumped as he silently crawled onto the riverbank, appearing out of the darkness. He was in his element. He made not a sound. He motioned her to get into the canoe and sit up front. He steadied the canoe as she got in and then he expertly climbed over the gunwale, taking care not to tip it.

They slowly and silently paddled the canoe to the center of the river, and then more aggressively paddled across. They quickly beached the canoe, jumped out, and proceeded to load their gear and supplies. Wasting no time, they boarded the canoe and pushed off from the bank. They dug in with their paddles, and using speed over quietness they slipped through the water at a fast clip, trying to put as much distance as possible between their canoe and the village.

Chapter Ten

They paddled all night, only taking short rests while floating with the current and then back to long, steady strokes to eat up the miles. The current was getting swifter and they were seeing more and more signs of the wildlife that make the river their home. They also encountered some rapids, which meant negotiating around sharp rocks and through narrow openings with huge boulders on each side. It was precarious going but Plata grew up by the river and had many years piloting a canoe. He deftly steered the small boat around the rocks in the swift-moving current.

It was now getting light, with sunrise only moments away. He called to Calida, "We must leave the river soon. I'm going to beach the boat at the next good spot to land."

They rounded a bend where the current slacked off slightly, and Plata steered the canoe toward the shore. Ahead of them were impassable rapids and a dull roar wafted back from downstream. It was the double falls that Plata spoke of earlier.

They landed the canoe in a sheltered area. Calida jumped off in knee-deep water and guided the boat to a flat part of the beach, where she pulled the bow onto the shore. Plata jumped off and helped push the boat clear of the water.

He said, "We can rest here for a short time and then we have a long portage ahead of us."

As they stretched out, resting their sore muscles from hours of constant paddling, Calida asked, "How far is it to bypass the falls, Plata?"

"Many miles, little one. It will take all day but it's the only way. We will camp when we reach the end of the portage to sleep and rest our tired bodies. But we cannot waste too much time. It's possible that the chief will send a war party after us. The guard that I killed with the poison dart was one of his sons. He will be looking for revenge, especially if he discovers that it was me."

"I don't need much rest, Plata. I'm ready to go when you are."

"Be patient, little one. We have much traveling to do. It is best to conserve our strength for the emergencies that may come up."

"You are very wise, old one."

Plata smiled.

***

After a short rest, they chewed on some dried meat and drank from the river. They each hoisted a backpack, which left their arms free.

As they lifted the sturdy but lightweight canoe over their heads, Plata said, "Now you know why I picked this one instead of one of the larger ones."

Calida nodded and was thankful of Plata's foresight. He led the way, picking his path through the jungle, taking a route away from the river because of the river's direction change. As with many rivers in the Amazon basin, this one was far from straight and a trail through the jungle was the shortest distance around the falls. Plata knew this from past experience.

They tramped on, resting periodically. Plata's old body was beginning to show the weariness of this long portage and two prior nights of interrupted sleep. By late afternoon they reached the river at a spot below the falls. After laying the canoe on the riverbank, Plata literally collapsed.

Calida rushed to his side, "Plata, Plata," she implored, "are you all right?"

He opened his eyes, and with a half grin on his wrinkled old face, he answered, "Yes, little one. I'll be okay as soon as I catch my breath. We will camp here until sunrise and the push on. We have done very well." With that he closed his eyes and slept.

Calida took an extended look at the old man to make sure he was breathing and not in distress. He seemed to be resting comfortably. She realized that this old companion had found a way deep into her heart and she felt that he had the same mutual love and respect that she had for him.

She tore herself away and organized a campsite. They would stay the night. She too was tired, and her arms and shoulder muscles were sore from the intense paddling, but she noticed that it was paying off in added muscle and strength.

After organizing the camp she took her bow and arrows and headed into the forest for some fresh game and fruit. It didn't take long to forage both for the evening meal. She was sure Plata would soon be awake and as famished as she was.

***

The next morning, both were refreshed from a full night of rest and nourished with fresh meat and fruit from Calida's hunt. They packed up the equipment and launched the boat. The river was swift and Plata told her they would soon reach the part that he was not familiar with. They would be far beyond where he had previously ventured.

As the day wore on, the river picked up even more speed and soon they were encountering rapids. They were able to negotiate the first few groups of rapids but they were now approaching some more formidable ones. Plata yelled instruction to Calida, but his old voice was lost in the noise of the raging river. The rocks were huge and some were very sharp. The canoe was holding up well in spite of some very hard knocks while squeezing through ever frequent narrow passages.

A wall of rocks rose up ahead and Plata picked the best opening he could in the short time he had to make his decision. The opening was very narrow and very shallow. Calida screamed as they pushed their way through, scraping both sides of the canoe and making a loud grinding screech as it tore at the canoe's bottom.

When they exited out of the heavy rapids and into a calmer part of the river, water was gushing up through several holes in the canoe's sole. Plata grabbed a fur piece that he had skinned from one of Calida's kills and jammed it into the largest hole to stem the flowing water. That repair worked for the big danger but the smaller holes were still leaking river water into the fragile canoe.

"Calida, come bail out the water while I keep us steady. The current is still swift. See if you can slow down the other leaks."

She leaped right to it. She made headway with the water and was able to slow down the leaks with fur pieces and other debris.

"Okay, get back on your paddle. I see more rapids coming up."

Calida looked ahead and was taken aback at what she saw. She scrambled forward to the bow and grabbed her paddle. The rapids were huge. Among the first group was a huge but flat boulder with water pouring over it. It then dropped down six or eight feet. There was nowhere else to go. Jagged rocks were on either side, with roiling water pouring through them. The rock Plata chose was wide but the drop could swamp the boat if the bow dug in too deeply.

Over the rapids they went. Calida screamed as they plummeted down the face of the boulder. She dropped her paddle in the boat's bottom and grabbed the gunwale on each side, anchoring herself to keep from being ejected. The light canoe jumped and rolled, turning at an angle that put them in danger of capsizing. The stern was trying to catch up to the bow but Plata in his wisdom dug his paddle into the water and slowed the stern enough to keep the boat from spinning.

With the boat now straight again, the bow dug into the deeper water while exiting the boulder, sending water cascading into the boat. The force of the river water caught Calida and slammed her backward. She landed on the equipment lashed down in the center of the boat. The bundles broke her fall but she was breathing in deep gulps of water instead of the air she desperately needed. She was coughing and gagging but hung on as the canoe leveled off in deeper but calmer water. But now, it was spinning around and rolling from side to side, out of control. She looked at the stern and realized why they were out of control. There was no one guiding and steering. Plata was gone. She was alone on the boat.

She rose up and called, "PLATA, PLATA," scanning the river.

No answer.

She grabbed her paddle and crawled to the stern. She had seen how Plata steered and she attempted to straighten the boat. After several tries she got the idea and though the current was swift and the boat was skimming along she was somewhat in control. She could hear the roar of more rapids ahead, probably around a bend in the river just ahead. *Where was Plata?* She decided to try to beach the boat on the riverbank and search for him.

She deftly steered with her paddle, letting the swift current carry her. Suddenly she slammed into the shore in a small cove, so hard that she flew forward, and she again landed on the equipment amidships. Now beaten and bruised, she jumped free of the boat, grabbed a thwart and pulled it ashore, clear of the raging river. She collapsed on solid ground and sobbed, releasing the tension.

After a few minutes she composed herself and stood, gazing out at the river to hopefully see any sign of her mentor and companion. She saw nothing but rushing water.

She walked up river as far as she could while scanning the river. Soon she encountered heavy, impassable jungle growth.

I wonder if the current could have carried him downstream, she thought.

She turned back and trudged downstream until she reached the bend.

If he got this far, he would have made it to shore here at the bend.

She stood, and with her sharp young eyes, she scanned and scanned to no avail. She made her way back to the boat and pulled it farther out of the water. She unloaded the gear, which was soaked, and spread it out to dry. She would have several more hours of direct sunlight, so she decided to make camp, dry everything, and decide what to do.

She knew to survive she must eat and drink. After she pitched a tent, she sat and ate some dried meat and fruit. She didn't feel like hunting, so she'd make do with what she had. After building a fire she sat and contemplated her future and decided that the next morning she would attempt to see what awaited her downstream by walking to the rapids. She cried herself to sleep and dreamed about the wizened old man that probably saved her life by showing her how to survive in the jungle.

Chapter Eleven

The next day dawned hot and sultry. It was a typical day in the Amazon basin. Calida had awakened before dawn, and at first light had already eaten her morning meal. She had some exploring to do. Taking her bow and a quiver of arrows, she set out downriver to view if she could transit the rapids by herself. If she thought it too harrowing, she could make a short portage. Shooting the rapids would be quicker but more dangerous. A portage would mean at least two trips and maybe three to carry the canoe and all the supplies, medical pouch, and other gear. She had examined Plata's pouch and disposed of many items. Plata had given her a short lesson on the blow gun, but she knew she was not adept at it. Nevertheless, she decided to keep it along with the darts.

She made repairs to the canoe, so she felt it was now seaworthy. She again walked to the river bend, but this time on to the rapids. When she got there she could indeed see why they were roaring. They were formidable. But so much so that it held back enough water so that a natural bypass was created on the near side. She was able to inspect it closely, and although it ran swiftly it was fairly wide, with no rocky obstructions. As long as she could keep to this side of the river, she felt that she could navigate through. After the rapids, the river widened out and was without rapids as far as the eye could see while standing on a huge boulder. Her mind was made up. She hurried back to her boat and supplies.

As she got closer she could hear activity of some kind ahead. She pulled an arrow out of the quiver and inserted the bow string. She crept ahead carefully. As she got closer to her boat and stash of supplies and equipment, the noise got louder. She heard grunts and squeals and sounds of animals. As she burst into her clearing she saw five ugly piglike animals tearing at her bundle of supplies. They were fighting each other, trying to be first at the dried meat and other succulent morsels of food. She immediately let fly an arrow, and almost before it buried itself in the largest pig, she already had fired another arrow. The second pig screamed in pain before he fell to his side, pawing at the arrow in his head and squealing a horrid death requiem. The large pig with the arrow protruding from its side did not succumb so easily. He charged at his aggressor, foam dripping from his open mouth, showing his huge tusks and sharp yellow teeth, screaming loudly from the pain and anger. He was huge and outweighed Calida by a hundred pounds. He moved surprisingly fast for the great bulk of his girth.

Calida gasped. She hesitated only an instant. She recognized imminent danger and already had an arrow loaded in the bow. She drew back to the fullest and aimed at the ugly beast's open mouth. He was almost upon her. The arrow flew true and buried itself in the back of the beast's throat, burrowing through the soft pallet and tearing into the small brain. The pig took several small choppy steps, stopped short, and snapped his jaws closed, breaking the arrow at the shaft. Painfully he opened his mouth, now gushing blood, yellow teeth now shiny and red. He then fell on his side with a great thump. It seemed that there was a tremor when he hit the turf. He died, falling to the ground.

The other pigs watched this grizzly scene unfold before their eyes. Their monster leader had fallen along with his mate and the perpetrator was getting ready to do more damage to their pack. They couldn't move fast enough to get back into the forest, away from this killer. The largest of the three moved so fast that he knocked one of his companions off his feet. It was almost comical. The fallen pig was squealing and was so intent on getting back on his feet, he fell back down on his own. He finally got on all four legs and followed his brothers into the bush. They squealed as they ran and soon their concert of squeals faded into the rain forest.

Calida stood over her prey for a short time, staring at the carcasses with another arrow loaded in the bow. She didn't need it and she returned it to her quiver. At that, she started to tremble and sank to the ground, taking deep breaths.

Plata would tell me to relax. The battle is over and I will have fresh meat for my meal today.

There was more meat than she could ever eat or even smoke but she decided to spend a few days here and smoke most of the meat like Plata showed her. The pigs had devoured the dried meat stored in her pack. It would help to have it while traveling. With this new supply, she could eat while drifting in the boat, with no need to stop.

***

It ended up that she spent five days, which helped not only in replenishing her supplies but also healing her body from the beating she had taken while shooting the rapids. Also, she held out a slim hope that Plata would suddenly appear and rejoin her on their journey. But his frail body was nowhere in sight. Finally she decided that she must push on. She gathered her supplies and packed them in the boat as waterproof as she could get them.

She pushed off the shore again, looking around one last time for her traveling companion. She missed him. He was the only man that she had known in her short life and could not understand why her mother and the other warriors held such disdain for them. She stationed herself in the stern of the canoe and soon became adept at steering. She made a few errors at first but remembered all that Plata had shown her.

The current was swift and steady, so there was no need to paddle to make headway, just steer and adjust to the river bends. By the time she reached the rapids, she was doing fine. Now was the tricky part. She had to stay far to the right side of the river without going aground, and stay in the smooth-flowing bypass. No need to paddle here either. She was going much faster than she wanted but she had to go with the flow of the river. She was now halfway through. The only bad part was she was getting wet from the spray and an occasional dip of the bow since she was moving so fast. It was actually a thrill moving so quickly that she had to try to slow it down. But finally she was through and into the smooth, wide, slow current on the other side. Now she must use her paddle to make good headway.

She traveled well into late afternoon before deciding to stop for the night. After finding an ideal spot, she was very happy that things were going so well. She found a cove of calm water and completely out of the flow of the river. It was such that she was completely hidden and could not view the river from her camp.

As she lay in the gathering dusk, she heard voices. They were coming from the river. She crawled through the brush and looked out over the river. She saw two canoes with three men in each canoe. The canoes were similar to hers and the men wore the same type of garb as Plata. Yes, these men are looking for Plata and maybe looking for her too.

Chapter Twelve

Calida stayed well hidden in the deep brush until the two canoes were downstream and out of sight. She was very still and then very carefully scooted back to her campsite.

What should I do? I can't follow them downstream and I can't go back upstream. They probably will return going upriver before long. I think my best chance is to wait here until they pass, going back to their village. I have a good spot here, well hidden, and I'm sure there is game and fruit nearby. I will wait it out.

She pulled the canoe farther into the brush and made further camouflage for the campsite. It was impossible to see her camp from the river. She felt secure.

Late the next day, as she was skinning a small rodent that she would roast for her evening meal, she again heard voices. She crawled to the brush at the river's edge and peered out across the water. The same canoes were again passing by, but this time going upstream. She felt happy with her decision to wait. Perhaps tomorrow she can resume her trip. The villagers were far from home and probably felt that finding Plata was a lost cause.

She finished cutting up the meat and started a small cooking fire. It was getting toward dusk and she should prepare to leave in the morning. The roasting meat smelled delicious and she was very hungry. After she ate the very welcome hot meal, she started gathering her belongings that she had just unpacked for an extended stay. Little did she know how short her stay would be.

When the dark night closed in around her, she crawled into her tent to get some needed rest. Tomorrow would be a long day. She wanted to put as many miles between her and the villagers as possible. As she lay contemplating her future, she heard a noise, more of a rustling in the bush. She had experienced this many times, aware that jungle animals hunted at night. Her supplies were well protected and most were in the canoe ready for tomorrow's journey.

She was just dozing off when suddenly the small tent was jerked from around her. Two men grabbed her and pulled her to her feet. She gasped and before she could scream a rough hand was clasped over her mouth. Her arms were pinioned to her body by two huge arms. She caught the noxious smell of body odor and felt a sweaty body against her back. Two more men came out of the jungle and lit torches to give an eerie light to the camp. There were six men in all.

The one pinioning her arms flung her to the ground and the leader, whose muscular body and face were covered with tattoos, stood over her. He was spouting phrases in Plata's language but so loud and guttural she couldn't understand him. He again yelled at her and the only part she could grasp was "Plata."

"Plata is dead," she stuttered in a subdued voice. "Dead . . . dead."

He raised his foot and roughly kicked her, knocking the air from her lungs. She coughed violently and rolled on her side, gasping for air.

He turned to his men and yelled, "Pick her up."

Two of them grabbed her arms and jerked her to her feet. She stood with her head bowed. The leader grabbed her under her chin, lifting her face to look at him, and screamed, "Where is body?"

She tried to talk but he was holding her chin and she tried to say, "He drowned," but it came out garbled.

The leader released her chin but with the same hand he drew back and slapped her face with an open paw, knocking her back and buckling her knees. The two men pulled her back up straight. She whimpered.

"Where is body?" he again screamed.

With blood dripping from her cut and bruised mouth, she again said, "He drowned," this time more clearly.

Again he hit her. This time he understood but took his frustration out on the defenseless young girl and then he backed off. The side of her face was already starting to swell and would be purple by morning.

He called the two men that were crew on his boat. They walked to the edge of the camp and conferred in hushed tones. The leader then turned and gruffly barked, "Tie her. We will sleep."

One man stood guard over a bound Calida, lying uncomfortably on the bare ground. The rest slept in the open after foraging through her supplies and helping themselves to any and all of the food.

She couldn't sleep. The painful jaw kept her awake along with her frightening circumstance. The guard seemed sympathetic and offered her a drink of water, which she gladly accepted.

She asked, "How did you find me?"

He answered, "We smelled your cooking fire."

Her mother had taught her about abusive men and what the outcome might be if she was ever captured by uncivilized monsters. She vowed to fight them if it came to that. Nardania had taught her even more in the art of defense. She told Calida about the most vulnerable spot on a man, and how a well-placed kick could render him unable to perform, at least temporarily. She would use this defense, well aware that the circumstances could prove fatal for her, but they were not going to be merciful anyway. By morning her face was badly swollen and she tasted blood through the night.

The leader shouted orders to the men when they arose and they readied the canoes. They used all three boats, putting two men to a canoe and placing a bound Calida in the larger boat with the leader. After eating more of Calida's food, they bundled up the other supplies, as well as Calida's pouch of herbs and roots.

They launched the canoes and paddled upstream. The men were strong and made good headway against the strong current but it sapped their strength. By noon the leader called for a rest and directed the men to pull over at a convenient spot to beach the boats.

They rested and ate from the stored supplies. Fresh meat would be needed tonight. Soon the tattooed leader stood. As he was directing the men to launch the boats an arrow, whispering as it flew out of the trees, buried itself into the huge man's chest with a hollow sound. He moaned, and with a startled, unbelieving look on his face, he fell to the ground, grasping at the arrow. It was true and was buried deep in his heart. He was dead as he fell.

The other men scrambled, running every which way. They had no direction without their leader. They tried to pick up their weapons but the surprise attack caught them unaware. Two more fell from an onslaught of arrows, both dead. Another lay wounded and was trying to remove the arrow. The buzz of a poison dart dispatched another one as he fell screaming and clutching his neck where the dart was buried. Two were left, and as they ran to a canoe to escape this sudden attack, they were met by two near naked warriors with brightly painted bodies. The attackers wielded razor-sharp machetes, swinging them wildly and screaming a shrill war cry as they hacked at the two unfortunate canoers. Blood gushed from the wounds across their backs and arms that were raised for protection. Finally the painted warriors ended their suffering with mighty swings and both were decapitated.

The wounded villager watched this slaughter in horror as he lay on the ground. Sensing what was in store for him, he tried to crawl into the brush. One of the machete-wielding warriors saw this fruitless effort and with a deep guttural laugh he calmly walked up to the wounded man and loped his head off.

The other warriors stole out of the bush. All were brightly decorated with war paint, and all were trolling a victory chant. Suddenly one warrior stopped singing and yelled to stop. They all suddenly noticed a young bound white girl lying on the ground halfway into the brush. She was in the process of scooting further into the thick foliage to hide from her adversaries.

The large brightly painted wielder of the machete who had dispatched the wounded man and the obvious leader of the war party strolled over to the frightened girl. He chuckled and mumbled something that Calida didn't catch. The dialect sounded similar to the one she learned from Plata, and when she heard some of the others, she thought it sounded the same. She looked imploringly at the warrior standing over her with a razor -harp machete and in the language she learned she said, "Please don't hurt me. I was a prisoner."

"Who are you?"

"My name is Calida. I am trying to find my father. My mother was killed in an earthquake."

"You are hurt. Did they do this to your face?"

"Yes. I have salves and a poultice in my pouch there in the small boat. Those will relieve the pain and swelling."

The leader directed a man to fetch the pouch. When he returned, the leader examined the contents and showed it to one of the warriors. There was much mumbling and quiet talk among the men.

"Are you a shaman?" he asked.

"I was taught about the many cures from herbs and roots found in the jungle by a shaman."

"Can you cure jungle fever?"

"If you mean malaria, yes, I can help. I have bark from the quina tree."

"You come to village with us. If you make children well, you live."

"I will try. What is your name?"

"I am called Saurus. My father is chief. His two daughters have jungle fever."

With that the warrior rolled her over and cut the leather thongs that were used to bind her. He helped her stand. Even though she was not yet full grown, she was still several inches taller than all the warriors.

"You will be very tall when you are grown, and your hair is like the sun," he said in awe.

"My village had all very tall blonde women warriors."

The jabbering of the whole group was almost deafening. One of the men approached her and reached his hand to feel her hair and utter an exclamation. She had obviously made an impression.

As she applied the poultice to her face, they all stood curiously watching. They had never seen a white woman with yellow hair, let alone one who had a pouch of healing herbs.

"She said that her village had many like her. Was she from the fabled giant woman warriors?" a troubled warrior said.

Chapter Thirteen

The captors gathered up the spoils from their raid on the rival tribesmen. It included Calida's pouch and bow with the quiver of arrows, as well as Plata's blow pipe and darts. They questioned her on these items and she explained that the bow was hers but the blow pipe had belonged to her companion who drowned. They doubted that a young girl could be a danger with a long bow and a quiver of arrows— *little did they know.*

The marauders destroyed the canoes and laid the bodies in the brush covered with leaves to rot. Maybe a search party from their village will find the bones and have the proper ceremony to send them to the afterlife.

The warriors, along with Calida, struck out on foot through the rain forest for the two-day hike to their village. This river and the river alongside their village did not intersect, making an overland trip necessary. She was not bound, which made it easier to travel, but she was closely watched. She decided not to attempt an escape but to take her chances and try to cure the innocent children. Hopefully it was malaria and not dengue. Maybe they would release her if she was successful.

The rest of the trek was uneventful. Late on the second day they arrived at a bustling village located on the banks of a much smaller river than the one she and Plata had been on. As they entered the perimeter of huts, the villagers were very curious about the blonde white woman accompanying them. It didn't appear that she was a prisoner but she was under guard. A young warrior took off running to spread the word and to tell the chief what they saw.

The war party made their way to the communal grounds at the longhouse, where all the important tribal events took place. The raiders knew that the chief would be waiting there to see the prisoner. It was the custom that he inspected the spoils and take what he wanted for himself and his family. He also would hear details of the raid of the foreign tribe that entered their territory.

The communal grounds were crowded with curious villagers. The chief was standing in the center with arms folded across his chest in a defiant pose. He was a big man, and dressed in his regalia, he was intentionally very imposing. This attitude was customary when a stranger was brought forth.

As the crowd parted, the raiding party and its captive entered the grounds. They stopped in front of the chief. The leader of the raiding party announced, "Oh great chief, we bring many things from a raid on the tribe intruding on your domain. But most important, we bring a stranger who has powerful drugs and potions. She claims to have a drug to help your daughters who have contracted jungle fever."

The chief paused, eyeballing this young white girl who was strange in appearance and not like other shamans. He said, "Does this stranger speak our language?"

"Yes. She understands what we speak and her tongue is also understandable to us."

The chief turned to Calida and said, "Come forward and tell me how you are called."

She stepped forward and stood straight and tall, with head held high in front of the chief. She announced, "I am called Calida and I have a potion from the bark of the quina tree that can reduce the fever of your daughters. It will give them the strength to fight jungle fever if they have not had it too long."

"Are you a shaman?"

"No, but I was taught many cures by a shaman before she died."

The chief addressed the leader of the raiding party, "Do you know if this white woman speaks the truth?"

"I saw her treat the bruises and swelling on her face with potions from her pouch. She seems to be truthful."

The chief motioned to a woman in the crowd to come forward. He spoke to her, "Take this woman to our daughters. Watch her closely while she treats them."

The woman grunted and nodded her head. She turned to Calida and motioned to follow.

Before they left the chief said, "Treat my daughters, white woman. Their lives are in your hands. You will answer to me if more harm comes to them."

"I'll do my best," Calida responded. She retrieved her pouch from the spoils of the raid and followed the short, heavy-set woman to the chief's hut.

When she entered, she blanched at the conditions and odor coming from the enclosed hut with smoke coming from smoldering embers. Two young girls that looked to be five or six years old lay side by side covered with animal skins. Two women sat alongside, fanning the smoke over their bodies.

"Take the smoking embers away. Get some fresh air in here. Take the skins off of their bodies."

The mother said, "This is what the old shaman did for jungle fever. My daughters trembled from chills."

"We must give them the quina tree potion and cleanse their bodies with cool water. Send these women for cool water in the river."

She threw off the skins that covered the little girls. They moaned and started shivering violently. She then took the quinine derivative from her pouch and gave each girl a liberal dose. They choked it down. The two women returned with containers of water.

Calida addressed the mother, "Help me wash them with the cool water. If the quina tree bark is the right drug they will calm down shortly."

They cleaned the girls of sweat and soot from the embers. They still moaned and shivered from the high fever. When their bodies were cleansed and the hut cleared of the smoke, some progress appeared. The trembling was not as severe. Both girls seemed to rally and opened their eyes. A little later they stopped moaning and asked for water. Calida gave each a sip of water. They looked curiously at this stranger. Calida smiled at them.

It probably was two hours or so when the quinine fully kicked in and both girls stopped trembling and fell into a peaceful sleep. Calida heaved a sigh of relief. It was obviously malaria and not dengue fever. Quinine has no effect on dengue fever.

The mother grabbed Calida by the hands and announced, "You have cured my daughters. I will go and tell the chief."

"No, not yet. The drug will only work for a while. We must keep giving it until the sickness runs its course and goes away. The drug does not cure. It only makes the body able to fight the sickness. It is not over yet. It may take several days," Calida said.

"I still must tell the chief what you are doing. If I don't he will become very mean," said the chief's wife.

"Please come back then. I will need some help when the sickness starts again," Calida implored.

The mother left and Calida rested. She felt drained but she must continue to watch over her patients. The next twenty-four hours were critical.

When the mother returned, the girls were still resting comfortably and Calida had caught her breath and prepared for when they awakened again. The mother brought food with her and told Calida to eat. She obviously was thankful and felt comfortable with this strange young girl.

Hours later the two children awoke and were given water and a broth but soon started shivering again. The high fever returned and Calida quickly gave them another dose of quinine. They followed the same course as before.

It was late at night while Calida and the children's mother were sleeping at their side when again they awoke and more quinine was given to them. The next day was more of the same, and by this time Calida and the mother had become fast friends. Calida learned that her name was Miya and she was the oldest of the chief's three wives.

It was now early on the fourth day and Calida had only left the hut for the necessary bodily functions, the customary way, in the adjoining rain forest. It was obvious that the other villagers had been told not to communicate with her since all turned away when she passed them.

She asked Miya about this and Miya said, "The chief will wait until he sees how his daughters come out of this. Do not worry, Calida, I have been reporting to him and all is well."

The two little girls were now sitting up and taking nourishment. They were talking and laughing while Calida checked them for fever. She was very pleased that each seemed cool when she felt their heads. They suddenly quieted down when the huge body of the chief loomed over them. Calida did not hear him enter the hut. He stepped lightly for as big a man as he was. He knelt down between his girls and held out his arms. The two girls leaped into those heavily muscled arms. This was now their father and not the leader of the tribe that was embracing them.

He stood holding a girl in each strong arm, turned to Calida, and said, "You are a good shaman. You have given my daughters back to me."

Calida let out a deep breath. She hadn't realized that she had been holding it since she first saw the chief enter the hut. "Thank you, Chief."

"You will come to the long house with me when I leave."

She looked at the mother, who stood with eyes cast down but a smile on her lips. Calida answered, "Yes, I will come with you."

Chapter Fourteen

The chief was sitting on his makeshift throne when Calida entered the long house. He gestured to her with his hand to come in and sit on the ground in front of him. She did. She sat on her haunches and expectantly looked up at him.

The chief said, "Did Miya tell you about our old shaman?"

"No, all I know is that he died."

"He was training a young man to take over when he died. He had largely become dependent on a hallucinogen and it came to the point where he took a large dose and died an excruciating death."

"I have heard of this drug. I have never used it, nor would I want to," she answered.

"Shamans use this and other drugs when creating a spell or communicating with spirits. I do not like this and I do not take part, but a shaman is protected by these spirits and we tolerate them."

"Was he your only shaman?"

"Yes. We have an old witch doctor that can practice the rituals and other ceremonies when it is needed. He also has the ability to make the poisons for our darts. However, he is very limited on herbs and roots needed to cure illness, treat cuts and bruises, and repair damaged bones."

"I see," she said, now understanding why he wanted to talk to her.

63

He took a long and thoughtful pause. The chief was no stranger to the art of persuasion. "The young man that was being trained was chosen because of his desire to become a shaman. He was part of the family of the old witch doctor and has been exposed to these acts for most of his life. I have talked to the old man and he has agreed to pass on all of his knowledge to the young man before he dies. This process has already begun."

"Chief, I think I know what you would require of me. I had hopes that I could continue my quest to find my father."

"If you stay and act as our healer and pass on your knowledge of herbs and roots and train the young man on your knowledge of healing, we will aid you in your quest."

"How long would I be needed?"

"That depends on how quickly you are able to train the young man."

"Where will I live, and will I have a place to treat people?"

"You will have the shaman's hut and use it to live and to treat our people."

"Well, I guess I have no choice."

"Yes, that is right. You have no choice."

***

Calida became well established in the customs of the tribe. She had the inborn trait for nurturing. She was given the run of the village and was treated with respect because of her healing ability. Even though she was young, she had maturity beyond her years.

Time passed swiftly, and soon it was far beyond the two-year mark. She was busy and had lost track of the time. She matured quickly and grew into a beautiful young woman now in her late teens. She had almost reached her full height of six feet, so she towered over everyone in this tribe that adopted her. She was Caucasian with an olive cast to her skin, so even with a suntan she was several shades lighter than the tribe members. Her blonde hair was distinctive. Everyone else in the tribe had straight jet-black hair. But back in her home she would have been a smaller version of her mother and the rest of the Amazon warriors, many well over six feet tall.

The young apprentice shaman learned his trade well and was now treating more patients than she. She has been happy with this lost tribe of the Amazon. She learned that they were the Guato Indians and were a smaller tribe that had immigrated from the larger tribe in the Pantanal region. But she was again getting anxious to get along with her life.

From transient relatives of some villagers she learned of the cities located on the big river. One man that she treated for a strange lung disorder and had stayed in her clinic for days told her of a large city called Guajará on a huge river called the Amazon. She thought that this might be the place to start the search for her father.

She decided to talk to the chief and convince him to help her get to the Amazon River. The chief occasionally held council in the long house, whereby villagers would bring problems or requests. This was the only real access to him. There was no schedule, and as with other tribal affairs, it was as needed and no announcement was made.

She waited and kept an ear open to conversation that would alert her when this council occurred. She missed several. He avoided her. Finally, months later she heard two men talking on the way to the long house to counsel with the chief. She followed the men, and when they entered the long house, she scooted in behind them. The chief noted this, and when he finished the discussion with the two men, he halfheartedly waved the lurking girl forward.

She spritely strode to his chair, and facing him, said, "Good morning, great chief of the Guana tribe."

A slight grin played across his lips, but it quickly disappeared. He regained his composure. He nodded.

"It has been several years since I came to your tribe to cure your daughters of the jungle fever. You asked me to be your *shalyun* and teach the new shaman about drugs and cures. I have done that and I have no more to pass on to him. I'm here to ask that you help me get to the big river so I can continue my search for my father."

The chief paused. He still used the tactic of a long hesitation before answering any request. It sometimes brought an additional comment, making the request an easier one to answer. It was always for the better. But Calida was aware of this and she held her ground.

Finally the chief answered, "The young maiden is asking a great favor. You may remember when I asked you to stay I said you have no choice? You still have no choice."

"But, chief, you promised."

He suddenly jumped to his feet and loudly proclaimed, "I will tell you when you can go. For now you stay. We are moving the village before the rains start and you will go with us. I need you to tend to sickness and injuries that always happen in a big move."

"Where are we going?" she asked.

"Back to the Pantanal," he snorted as he turned and left her standing alone.

***

The Pantanal is 100,000 square miles of swamp. It is a great ecological reserve on the Brazil/Bolivian border and has the largest wetland in the world. It supports many known animal and fish species, including piranhas, anacondas, and alligators, as well as many predators and probably some unknown species of plants and herbs.

There are no towns or cities, nor even roads or highways. The two known large tribes are Guato and Ipicas and untold lost tribes, such as Machiguenga, whose culture haven't changed for a thousand years.

There are as many as fifty jungle tribes in the Pantanal and the surrounding area. The Brazilian government has placed many restrictions on miners and loggers in the Amazon basin. The Pantanal has been set aside for the aboriginal people that have inhabited the region for a thousand years or longer.

The rainy season was soon to start. It was time to move. All tribes of the Amazon basin frequently move according to weather or any other whim to make a move. By nature they are a migratory people. Each family's hut or lean-to is left in the old village and they usually transit by canoe and sometimes portage overland. It is done efficiently, with everyone taking part as they and their ancestors have done for generations past. Calida was amazed at the speed and cooperation of all the villagers. Each knew his job, including the children.

Weeks passed and finally word came down from the chief. The new village was established along a tributary of the Xeco River, which is a tributary of the Paraguay River. A hut or lean-to was erected for each family. It wasn't long before it looked much like the village they had just left.

This was slightly higher ground and less likely to be flooded during the rainy season, which was now upon them. The old village was flooded out several times and rebuilding was necessary.

The tribe experienced a very trying time after a flood, when a horde of Aedes mosquitos bred in the wet debris left when the water receded. This mosquito is a carrier of the dengue fever, which can be fatal and has no known cure. The first sign after being bitten, usually in the daytime when it is unexpected, is tiredness. This is followed quickly by a severe headache behind the eyes, then a mild fever that soon turns intense, with sweating, nausea, and vomiting. With the fever, the muscles in the calf and back begin to ache. Hallucinating is common. There is brutal muscle and joint pain, so bad that the tribes call it *break bone fever*. Then, after all other symptoms are present, a rash appears.

The fever may break for a day or so, but it usually returns with increased intensity. After a week, the infection wanes and the danger is gone. It takes a month or so of rest and liquids to return to normal. But that's a mild case. Dengue can progress into dengue hemorrhagic fever or dengue shock syndrome, both of which are sometimes fatal, especially to children and old people. A second attack is usually fatal.

Several children and one old-timer did not survive, but many others suffered through the fever and the month of weakness following the devastating illness. Calida had her hands full during this onslaught and thereby earned the respect of many former detractors.

She helped build her hut to live in, as well as to treat people until the new shaman established his area.

She was tending a minor cut when the chief appeared. This was unusual. She stood and greeted him.

He said, "I have made a promise to you and I intend to keep it."

"I am happy that you have made this decision, Chief. You are wise as well as fair," Calida said.

"As soon as we are better established, I will assign two warriors to take you by canoe to the Xeco River, and then on to the Paraguay River, where they can go no further." He continued, "It is at that point you must try to make contact with other white people on a *fazenda*, or a settlement, to board a *chalana* that can take you to a city."

"Will they understand my language?"

"You may find someone that understands our tongue. It is one used by many tribes but you may find difficulty. If you can find a missionary, they will help."

"I'll be forever grateful for your help, Chief."

"You have given of yourself here in my village. You are a good healer, a good *shalyun*."

Chapter Fifteen

The day finally came when Calida set off with her pouch of drugs and herbs, her bow and arrow, and a backpack with personal items in it. Two squat, burly warriors accompanied her in a canoe, complete with their blow pipes and darts. They were proud to be selected to escort the blonde *shalyun* to search for her father. It will take several weeks to complete the journey to the Paraguay River, maybe as long as six weeks depending on weather. And then the return home will be even longer, although lighter without her aboard, but upstream against the current. When they leave her, it will be another week for her to reach the cattle ranch called a *fazenda*. It is downstream from the confluence of the two rivers. With any luck she can catch one of the flat-bottomed supply boats called *chalanas* at the ranch.

Calida helped the men when she could. They camped each night and she insisted that she furnish the meat to cook over the fire. Each night she returned with a fresh kill. The men marveled at her skill with the bow and arrow. They laughed and said that she will be good protection for them in case of attack from men or animals. This was indeed very true. She was an expert with the bow and strong enough to use it well.

***

The small canoe with the two Guato Indians and the tall blonde girl finally reached the end of the Xeco River where it emptied into the Paraguay. It had been seven weeks of hard travel. The last duty of the men was to take her to the far bank of the Paraguay River. This was the place for her to leave them. The *fazenda* was on the far side. It's a wide river and the crossing was not an easy one, but they did it.

They beached the canoe, and since it was late in the day, they made camp. The evening was nostalgic. Calida was leaving the last two of the villagers that she had lived with for close to three years. They had treated her kindly and helped her with her quest.

In the morning the two warriors departed and she was on her own. All she knew was that by following the river downstream she would eventually intersect with the outer buildings of a cattle ranch.

She started her journey as soon as the canoe left. Travel along the river was easy in some spots but impossible in others. At times she had to detour into the rain forest to bypass an obstructed area. She camped each night. As previously, game and fruit were plentiful and she was more than capable of hunting.

It was on the fifth day that she spotted something different at the river's edge, and as she got closer, she saw that it was a dock. It was not a large one but adequate enough tie up a small boat on, like the flat-bottomed *chalana*.

As she got closer, she saw a small shack and farther offshore another building, but larger. This must be the ranch property. She cautiously approached. So far there was no sign of life. She slowly walked into the area of the ranch buildings and could see no one in either building. A weed-filled, rutted road led away from them into the surrounding trees. She contemplated whether she should follow the road or wait until someone came. Maybe even a *chalana* might show up.

She sat and dug into her pack for some leftover fruit. As she ate, she thought of her dilemma. Suddenly she became alert. Her keen hearing picked up sounds of voices. Definitely male voices and the *clop, clop* of an animal walking slowly.

She stood and stole behind the smaller building, making her bow ready for action if needed. Out of the thick tree stand appeared two young men, no more than teenagers, riding in a four-wheeled wagon drawn by an old horse. As they entered the small complex, Calida stepped out from behind the building with arms raised, a bow in one hand, calling a greeting in the dialect she learned while in the Indian village.

The boy with the reigns pulled back sharply to stop the horse, while the other boy stood and with wide eyes yelled, *"Caramba!"*

Both boys were speechless with surprise to see a young, tall blonde girl standing facing them with arms raised, speaking like an Indian.

One young man finally gathered himself, and in his native Portuguese, said, "Who are you?"

Calida didn't understand but could see that these two presented no danger. She lowered her arms and put the bow across her back. She approached them and smiled. The boys smiled back. The one who spoke jumped off of the wagon and said, "Do you speak Portuguese?"

Calida, not understanding, answered, "Ca-li-da, Ca-li-da" and pointed to herself.

The boy comprehended and replied, "Marcos," and also pointed at himself.

She nodded and in her Indian dialect said, *"Chalana."*

"Ah, *si, chalana."* He turned to his companion. "Juan, she waits for a boat."

Juan said, "She might be here a long time since the supply boat left yesterday and we'd better get busy loading the rest of the supplies."

"Okay," he said and turned to Calida. "We must take the supplies to the ranch. You can come with us. Someone might speak the Indian dialect that you understand."

She didn't understand what he said but his tone was friendly, and when they started taking supplies from a shack and loading them on the wagon, she got the idea of what they needed to do. She watched and waited.

Soon they were loaded, and through sign language they put Calida on the seat next to Juan. Marcos got in the back with the cargo. They started the long, slow, bumpy journey to the ranch.

When they arrived, Marcos jumped off and scurried into the ranch house. Very quickly he emerged with an unbelieving older gentleman and a pudgy, grandmotherly-looking woman. The woman was talking in very fast, unintelligible Portuguese.

"She doesn't speak Portuguese, Grandmother," Marcos said.

The woman then turned to Calida and in Spanish said, "Where did you come from?"

Calida stood dumbfounded at the torrent of foreign words that seemed to be so fast that no one could possibly understand them.

"She seems to speak an Indian dialect. I think she wants a *chalana*," Marcos added.

The older man said, "I think one or two of the hands speak some Indian. Juan, go check it out and bring someone back so we can communicate with this girl. Marcos, you can take the wagon and get it unloaded."

"*Si*, Papa, but shouldn't I wait here in case you need me?"

"I think we can handle this. You go unload," Papa answered.

Marcos grabbed Calida's belongings from the wagon and put them next to her.

Papa grabbed them and said, "Gisela, let's take her inside. I don't want the ranch hands ogling her when they hear about this."

Gisela took Calida's hand and led her into the house. Calida was in awe. This was the first time she had ever experienced a house like this. It was not palatial but was much more permanent than anything she ever knew. Even the hut she lived in with her mother was not like this.

Gisela seated her at the table and immediately, in the old country fashion, brought out food. It was mostly fruit and nuts but also wine. Soon Juan returned with two ranch hands both with features resembling some of the tribe members that Calida had lived with.

Papa spoke to them, "Will you boys see if you can understand this young lady?"

"*Si, señor*," said one of them and turned to Calida. He said, "What tribe do you come from?" in a dialect not familiar to Calida.

She replied, "I don't understand what you said."

The man shrugged his shoulders and turned to his companion. He tried a more common Indian dialect and this one was familiar enough to Calida that she could answer.

"I have been living with the Guana tribe for the last three years or so. Before that I traveled with an old Indian who taught me much about living in the jungle. Before that, I was with my mother in a village in the high ground."

"Why did you leave your mother?"

"She was killed in an earthquake along with the whole village."

As the ranch hand spoke, he translated so that Papa and Gisela also understood what she said.

"Where are you trying to travel to?"

"I am trying to find my father. He is a missionary doctor with the Yano-Matis tribe."

"That will be difficult. The Yano-Matis are way far into the bush and don't want to be found."

"I will go to the city and find someone who will tell me where the missionaries are. I have the names of my father and his wife. I will wait for a *chalana*," she firmly replied with a slightly raised voice.

"I think you have upset the child, Pedro. Tell her that she can wait here and we will help her catch a boat," Papa said.

He passed this on and she relaxed a bit.

"Tell her that it may be weeks or even months when the next boat arrives and we will give her a place to sleep," he added.

"Since she is very tall and a very light complexion, ask her if others in the village were like her. I am curious," asked Gisela.

He did so.

She answered, "There were many that were even taller as my mother was. She was also more blonde. They were the warriors of the village."

He translated and left, eager to spread the word about this lovely creature.

"*Mia Dios.* I thought so. This girl is an Amazon," Gisela remarked.

"Okay, Gisela, take her into the guest room and see if you can make her understand that she is welcome," Papa said.

Gisela took her by the hand and said, "Come with me, *querida.*"

When they got to the room, again Calida was in awe. There was no bed, just a hammock, but that was much better than the bed of fronds and leaves that she used in the jungle.

She felt very safe with Gisela, who treated her as if she were a grandchild. This feeling came through even though there was a language barrier.

Weeks passed and Calida became ingrained in the everyday life of a cattle ranch. There were always jobs to do and she was more than willing and a good worker. The two boys, Marcos and Juan, were very attentive to her, showing her on horseback how far reaching the ranch was. Riding a horse was another new experience for her. She opted not to use a saddle. The boys also attempted to teach her Spanish. They were fluent in both Spanish and Portuguese, but felt that she could more likely use Spanish in her travels. As before, she was very adept in picking up enough to have a limited conversation with those around her. When working with Gisela doing household chores, she asked the lady if she would also teach her the language. Gisela was able to cover many more facets of speaking Spanish than the boys did.

A supply *chalana* didn't touch their dock for well over six months. Neither Calida nor the ranchers minded. It turned out to be a pleasure having the young girl as a guest.

One hot, steamy afternoon, Marcos announced that new supplies were at the dock. He had asked if they had room for a passenger and they agreed to take the girl. Their course was to sail down the Paraguay River to the Amazon but would be picking up and dropping off freight. They will take her as far as Guajará, but it may take several months or more. They will require her to work for her passage. Calida agreed to work for her passage, and sleeping in a hammock was certainly no problem.

The day the boat got underway, the whole family came to the dock. Gisela hugged her over and over, and when Calida boarded the boat she cried. It was as if she was seeing a beloved granddaughter leave home, a granddaughter that she had never had.

As the boat chugged away Calida stood on the stern and waved until they were out of sight. She was now on her next adventure, continuing her quest to find her missionary father.

Chapter Sixteen

The *chalana* crew was led by the captain, who was also the boat owner. He was a veteran of many years as a skipper and crewmember of riverboats. He proudly owned his own boat and ran a tight ship.

The crew, aside from Calida, was made up of two young but experienced sailors who had also spent their lives on the rivers in the Amazon basin. Calida was fortunate to crew on this boat. There were others plying the many rivers in the basin that may not have treated her with the respect that a pretty young woman should get.

When she first boarded, Captain Hernandez took her aside and instructed her that his crew understood that no fraternization would be tolerated. He expected that she would live up to this rule. She explained that where she was raised *celibato* was indeed practiced. She also explained that she could protect herself if a man, any man, decided to try to take advantage of her femininity. He was impressed that she was so capable and yet so young.

The boat sailed down the Paraguay, stopping at a farm to pick up crates of fresh fruit, mostly green bananas. The fruit was for delivery to a dock downriver that was adjacent to an airstrip, where it was flown to market. Calida worked along with the crew, proving that she was strong and capable of holding her own. At six feet, she was taller than the stocky crew members, Ricardo and Carlos. Both of them treated her with respect but expected her to do her share of work. Captain Hernandez had instructed them so. They all got along well and it made for a happy crew.

At the airstrip dock they picked up another passenger, who was a pilot who had lost his job. The reason was not discussed, and since he paid for his passage, he did not work.

After they got underway, Calida, Ricardo, and Carlos took a break on the stern, enjoying some of the fresh fruit left over from the previous cargo. The pilot approached them.

"*Buenos dias*. Can I join you folks? That fruit looks good."

"Sure, help yourself," answered Ricardo.

He did, and then turned to Calida. "Well, this is a welcome surprise. What's your story, blondie?"

Calida noticed a slight slur in his speech and a strange smell on his breath when he spoke. She guardedly answered, "I have no story, sir, and my name is Calida."

He laughed and stepped back with an exaggerated expression. "Whoa, touchy, touchy. I guess you must belong to one of these boys, huh?

Ricardo stepped forward and said, "She doesn't belong to anyone, *senhor*. She's a crewmember just like us and likes to be left alone."

"Don't get tough with me, fella, I'm a passenger on this scow and I also need respect."

"No one's getting tough! You can talk to the skipper if you like. I've got the wheel watch now, so he's available."

Ricardo left for the wheelhouse. The pilot staggered away, mumbling as he left. Later, Captain Hernandez approached Carlos and Calida as they were stowing away the dock lines.

He said, "Ricardo told me about the altercation with the pilot. He's a paying passenger, so he should be left alone. He was also fired by the company he flew for because of his drinking problem. There is no doubt that he is still drinking, and I will address that problem with him. I can't do much except restrict him to his cabin, which is difficult in this extreme heat. Try to stay out of his way and come to me if he bothers you, especially you, Calida."

"I can take care of myself, sir, but *gracias*."

***

The voyage continued with no further incidents, until one very warm night, as they were steaming down a very wide and calm part of the river. Calida was in her hammock, which was topside, to try to take advantage of the evening breeze. There was none, only that created by the movement of the boat, and it was steamy. Hers was a restless sleep, waking occasionally to wipe the sweat from her brow.

She had just dozed off. In her shallow slumber she detected a movement beside her. She tried to wake up, but couldn't. Then she felt a hand groping her and she became instantly alert and instinctively pulled away. She was now fully awake to see a figure in the darkness next to her hammock, leaning over her. She quickly detected that telltale odor of alcohol coming from the hot breath of the man whose hands grabbed at her. She knew immediately who it was.

With an athletic move, she swung out of the hammock, away from the groping hands of the man, and had her dagger unsheathed before her feet hit the deck. She ducked under the hammock and leaped at the figure, catching his legs in a powerful lunge, hitting them just below his knees. The assailant's feet flew out from under him and he landed hard on the deck with a loud crash. A deep bellow came from surprised lips. Before he could right himself, she flung him flat on his belly with a strong move that belied the stamina of this feminine-appearing woman. She jerked his head back by his greasy hair, stretching an exposed vulnerable area. Now the sharp dagger was poised at his throat, just a fraction of an inch away from his jugular and death by bleeding out. He couldn't move because he was held in place by a strong pair of legs straddling him.

He screamed, "NO!"

"Wait, Calida," screamed Captain Hernandez.

She looked up and saw the skipper. He was holding a flashlight, illuminating the scene. Then Ricardo appeared, aghast at the girl holding a knife to the pilot's throat. His mouth dropped open in surprise. She slowly released the pilot's head and removed the dagger from his throat but stayed straddling him. His head banged on the deck and he heaved a sigh of relief.

She said, "Captain, he tried to assault me in my hammock."

"Yes, I can see that. Let him up."

Calida moved off of him and stood.

The pilot slowly rose to his feet and slurred, "What's wrong with her? I was just walking through here. I didn't bother her."

"Go to your cabin and don't leave it or I'll hog tie you so you can't move. We'll talk in the morning when you are halfway sober."

"I'm a passenger here," he slurred again. He started to say something further but changed his mind when he saw the aggressive demeanor of Captain Hernandez. He staggered away, mumbling unintelligibly.

The captain said, "I'm sorry, Calida. It won't happen again. I plan on dropping him off at the first opportunity. I don't put up with that on my vessel."

"Thank you, sir, but I doubt if he'll even think about it again."

Captain Hernandez smiled and thought to himself, *and no one else will think about it either.*

Several days later the passenger was dropped off at the dock of a *fazenda* where he could wait for another boat. It may be a long wait but he was glad to leave the boat with the crazy young Amazon on board.

The *chalana* sailed on, where more cargo was loaded aboard at a *fazenda* at the last stop in the Paraguay River. They would now travel on to the Amazon River to unload it and then possibly on to Guajará, which was downriver but far enough that more cargo stops might be possible. The everyday duties became second nature to her, and when a new mast light was needed she volunteered to climb up to change it.

Carlos would not have it. Though he kept his distance in respect, he was smitten. "No, Calida, I will climb the mast."

"I can do it, Carlos."

Ricardo knowingly laughed. "Let him do it, Calida. He wants to show he has monkey blood." He knew that Carlos wanted to show off in front of this pretty girl.

"Very funny, Ricardo," said Carlos as he started his climb. He easily moved up the mast on the rungs provided to do so. He was an expert at high work and not afraid of heights. When he reached the top, he removed the burned-out bulb and replaced it with a new one.

That done, he started back down and was about halfway when Captain Hernandez spied a huge log directly in their path. He screamed, "Hang on, Carlos." He backed down the engine full astern to avert a potential tragedy. The boat suddenly went bow down from the sudden change of direction. The extreme dip of the bow caused the mast to tip forward. The higher on the mast, the further the arc traveled. Carlos was over halfway up.

He did not expect such a surge but he hung on as the mast tipped forward and then it swung back when the bow rose. He still hung on, but his grip loosened slightly from the severity of the pitch. Alas, it was the roll of the boat, caused by its own wake, that pulled him from the mast and he tumbled down to land hard on the deck. He was out cold.

Ricardo and Calida rushed to his side. His head was bleeding from a deep, ugly gash. Calida took charge.

She said, "Ricardo, hold this pad on the cut to curtail the bleeding while I check him for broken bones."

She quickly checked his extremities for broken bones and found everything intact. The head injury seemed to be the only visible one unless internal injuries developed later. Captain Hernandez ran back from the wheelhouse. He had put the transmission in neutral and dropped an anchor.

"I had no choice. That huge log would have ripped out our bottom," he said.

"We know that, Skipper. It wasn't your fault," Ricardo said.

"Put him in a hammock while I get my medicine pouch," Calida ordered.

The men looked at each other with a questioning expression, and then did as they were told. When Calida returned she tied in three stitches and then dressed the gash. Carlos was still unconscious.

She said, "I will stay with him until he awakens, if that's okay, Captain."

"Yes, yes, by all means." He was again amazed at what this girl knew and could accomplish. He left her to get the ship underway again. Ricardo also went about his duties.

Calida checked Carlos' vitals periodically and found them to be well within reason but he was still unconscious. She waited patiently, using her herbs where needed. Later, Ricardo relieved the skipper at the wheel. The captain came back to check on the condition of his crewmember.

"What is that delicious smell?" the skipper asked.

She answered, "It's an infusion of the fruit from the *limon* tree. When a soul is in pain, a foul or cruel environment can drive it deeper into darkness. So light and soft-smelling airs may help lift his spirit, even when he is unconscious. My shaman taught me this."

"You are amazing, Calida," the captain said.

Chapter Seventeen

The flat-bottomed riverboat sailed on to its next port of call, another cattle ranch. Captain Hernandez checked with the farm's office. They asked if he would agree to move a load of supplies to a satellite outpost. Hernandez agreed, even though it was upstream in a shallow tributary off of the Juruá River, which in turn is a tributary of the Amazon. This will add another thirty to forty-five days roundtrip to this cruise. The tributary was noted for piracy and the high-jacking of boats for the cargo. But the transport fee was at a premium and the captain could use the money. Not many boats would venture into this region.

The cruise upriver was uneventful, and the Juruá River was easily located. The next leg of the journey was critical since the unnamed tributary was tiny and the entrance was well hidden. All hands were instructed to keep a sharp eye for the small waterway. They slowly crept upstream. All eyes were focused on the riverbank. The two sailors spotted the tributary at the same time and alerted the captain, who was at the wheel. He backed down and swung the bow into the confluence of the two rivers. An accumulation of sand and half-buried logs made for a careful entrance to this dangerously shallow waterway.

He called out, "Carlos and Ricardo, stay in the bow and watch for shallow water. We only need to go upstream about seven or eight kilometers to the dock. We can't run aground here. We may never get off if we do."

"Aye, Skipper," called Ricardo.

The boat inched along, oblivious to the eyes of two predators on the riverbank. A huge jaguar and his equally large mate were hidden by the thick jungle. They were watching their every move, and with the waterway so narrow, they were almost within striking distance. The two killing machines had tasted the succulent flavor of human flesh when they happened upon a rogue band of pirates in the recent past. They made short work of two of the sleeping men very quickly. Those pirates were not able to even attempt a defense. Two more ran off into the jungle without their weapons and they were quickly dispatched the next day. Humans were easy prey. The two sleek predators slipped through the thick foliage easily, well hidden from the boat slowly traveling up the shallow stream.

"There's a small dock ahead, Skipper. Is that where we're going?" called Ricardo.

"According to the chart, that's it. Make ready to tie up, Calida."

Calida scrambled to get the dock lines in place as Ricardo pulled the bow lines out of the line locker. Carlos stood ready to jump ashore as the skipper eased the boat slowly to the rickety dock. The flat bottom scraped along a submerged mud bank as they slowly bumped onto the dock, losing all headway from the gooey mud.

"Oh, oh, captain, are we aground?"

"It's okay, Calida, we'll be riding higher after we unload. It will probably make us float free, or at least enough to break us loose. Let's get tied up before we lose all light. We can unload as much as possible tonight before it gets pitch-dark, finish in the morning soon enough to get underway and back on the bigger river by dark tomorrow."

The three crewmembers worked together quite well and had half the cargo unloaded into the storage bin by nightfall. The two jaguars were waiting for their opportunity to attack after complete darkness had set in. It had fast approached that time. What the animals were not aware of was that the captain of the boat was sitting on the rail of the bow and had an AK47 balanced across his knees. The captain was no stranger to this part of the country and had several of these weapons ready for use against animal or human demons, whichever presented a problem to them.

He sat giving all his attention to the details during the unloading process. He peered into the surrounding jungle searching for any sign of activity whether from humans, be they pirates or natives, or be they animals, predators, or foragers. While finding their way upstream, he thought he felt they were under watchful eyes and he thought he saw movement ashore, but maybe it was just nerves. They were traveling awfully close to shore. He'd be very happy to be out of this place as soon as possible.

When it became too dark to see, he ordered the crew back aboard. He said, "Okay, guys, grab some chow. I'll keep guard until you are finished. Let's set up a watch overnight. Keep an automatic firearm with you at all times, men. Calida, you will do as well with your bow. If anyone sees any movement at all out there, alert me. Don't hold back. It could cost us our lives."

Everyone was nervous and jumpy. This was not a good situation. They were very vulnerable. Things settled down and only normal nightly jungle sounds were about. As she lay in her hammock, Calida could distinguish the flutter of wings from the hundreds of bats feasting on flying insects buzzing in the night. She listened for the grunts of the ugly pigs as they hunted in groups for rodents and other creepy, crawly, strange little beasts. She heard the chatter of monkeys swinging through the tress effortlessly looking for anything edible, and all the many other night sounds. What she didn't hear was the silent stalking of the two jaguars. They were quietly creeping through the thick jungle, looking for a spot close enough to the boat for the huge male to leap onboard and land on the man sitting on the stern platform. Meanwhile, his mate would also take one long bound, land on the deck, and quickly dispatch one of the crew who was lying in the swinging berth. They could then drag these bodies off the boat or kill more if it was needed.

It was Carlos who was standing watch when the sickening activity started. He stood with his automatic rifle in the ready position when he thought he heard a rustling on shore. Suddenly, out of the brush shot a black blur with eyes like two coals burning in a gigantic head. Its mouth was agape, showing huge yellow teeth with foamy white froth dripping from them. Carlos swung the AK47 around and pulled the trigger. A short burst flew into the darkness, hitting only the brush behind the charging demon. The gun clattered as it flew out of Carlos' hands. The jaguar landed on him and clamped his muscular jaws around this fragile human's head, crushing the skull like an eggshell. Poor Carlos died before he felt the killing blow. The huge animal then ripped open the chest cavity and feasted on another efficient kill.

As all this was happening, simultaneously the female followed shortly behind her mate, looking for another human to kill. She leaped aboard as the AK47 sprayed the rounds into the jungle. She bounded toward the swinging beds where she knew her prey lay. She roared as she landed. She saw movement as Calida and Ricardo swung out of their hammocks. Both had been awake and were ready to do battle. Calida cocked her bow as she landed feet first on the deck. Before she could fire an arrow, she heard the loud staccato of Ricardo's AK47. It was a long burst, and this one hit home as the female jaguar stopped short, stretched her neck forward, and opened those killing jaws one last time. She tried to step forward, to leap at this figure with the stick that belched fire and caused pain through her body, but another burst felled her. She would never kill again.

The male looked up from his kill, human blood dripping from his mouth. He was chewing on a huge chunk of Carlos' heart. When he saw his mate fall to the deck riddled with bullets and bleeding profusely, he dropped the human flesh out of his mouth and he roared, roared loud and long. It reverberated throughout the jungle. Those animals within earshot stopped and waited. These inferior humans had killed his mate.

He lowered himself to his haunches to make a gigantic leap. He would crush that brutal killer with the fire-belching stick that massacred his mate. But before he could complete his spring into a killing leap, an arrow from a strong bow only a few meters away buried itself deep into his chest. He moaned, turned his head to try to dislodge the painful arrow. He could not reach it. He roared. The arrow was true and the sharp arrowhead was lodged in his heart. Blood flowed from the large arteries surrounding the beast's strong heart. As he coughed, the blood traveled up his throat and mixed with the human blood in his mouth. Again blood dripped from the beast's mouth. His jaw quivered and his yellow teeth were now colored red from the mixture. He tried one last defiant roar that came out as a gurgling gasp. He then moved forward on shaky legs to where his mate lay. The magnificent beast stood over her slain body, gave an almost inaudible sigh, and then dropped dead, his head resting on her body.

Captain Hernandez had come topside with his AK47 cocked and ready for action. He was an instant too late and not needed. He stood there, unbelievingly surveying the bloody bodies lying on his pristine deck. Calida and Ricardo were already on the stern, kneeling next to Carlos' mutilated body.

"How could that cat do so much damage to Carlos in such a short time?" asked Ricardo.

"They are killing machines, Ricardo. I've seen it before," Calida answered.

"She's right, sailor. We are very fortunate that you two reacted so quickly or much more would have been done."

"What do we do now, sir?" asked Ricardo.

"Let's rig a block and tackle on the boom to get the two jaguars off of the boat. They are too heavy to try to move them without some help. In the morning we will dig a grave for Carlos and bury him. We have too far to go to take him home, and in this heat his body would deteriorate quickly. Gather all his personal items so I can pass them on to his family. This will not be easy."

They worked through the night, getting rid of the animals and cleaning the blood from the deck. After burying Carlos that morning and then unloading the rest of the cargo, they got underway for the return trip. When they reached the Amazon the captain was able to make contact with a warehouse to carry a cargo to Guajará.

In another month, Calida might be able to get some concrete information on the man she believed to be her father. He was her only living relative. She believed him to be a missionary doctor living with the Yano-Matis tribe. Plata had told her that there was a mission headquarters in Guajará. Could they direct her? It was a gamble but at least it was a chance. She was excited.

Chapter Eighteen

The *chalana* arrived at Guajará one crewmember short. This was not the home port for Captain Hernandez, but he docked here often enough to know the city very well. The boat will remain here for about a week. The captain will visit Carlos' family, who lived here, and explain the circumstances of his death. But first he must report to the Brazilian authorities and give the exact details of cause of death and burial, including the precise location showing latitude and longitude. He had already filled out the required paperwork that documented what he will verbally report to them. His visit to the family will not carry all the details of the violent death he suffered, to spare their feelings. But nothing will be held back in the report to the authorities. Ricardo and Calida will be given credit for killing the animals, thereby preventing further casualties.

On the long uneventful voyage down the Amazon, there was ample time to instruct Calida on life in the city. Although Guajará was in comparison a small town, it was an environment totally different from any that Calida had ever experienced. At various times in the past six months, one or the other of the men explained what she might encounter.

Captain Hernandez sat with her one balmy evening while Ricardo was on the helm, explaining again what she should expect. He said, "You have been an excellent crewmember, Calida, and although the deal was that you would work for your passage, I have decided to pay you a seaman's salary, especially since Carlos got killed. I'm sure you'll need it in the city."

"Thank you, Skipper, but what do I need it for?"

"As we have explained, you cannot hunt for food there and you cannot pick other people's fruit. You must buy it. You will also need money for transportation around town. After my boat leaves you will need a place to sleep, a hotel or boarding house."

"Yes, I understand. Thank you, Skipper."

"Now, when we dock, I have much business to take care of. Ricardo has no family here, so he will have time to help you find your way around. You can stay here on the boat as long as I am tied up. After that you are on your own."

"Yes, I know. I can take care of myself, Skipper," Calida said.

"I know you can, my dear, but the city is different. I'll make some inquiries for you before I embark. I pray that you will find what you are looking for."

When they arrived in Guajará, they tied up at the city dock. There was much activity and Calida was amazed at the buildings and throngs of people milling about on the dock. After securing the boat, Captain Hernandez left to take care of checking in with the local authorities.

Ricardo approached a wide-eyed Calida and said, "Would you like me to take you on a little tour of the downtown area? You should get acquainted so you won't feel lost when we leave."

"Yes, that sounds like a good idea."

They left the boat, and for the next few hours walked through the shopping area. Ricardo showed her points of interest, and she asked questions of things she had heard of but never seen. They stopped at a sidewalk café for lunch. Calida learned why she needed money to survive in the city.

Just to show her how it was done, Ricardo hailed a taxicab and took a short ride across town. Calida was frightened at first when the driver recklessly drove through traffic-filled streets at what, she felt, was a high rate of speed. It was a typical taxi ride, with horn blaring at other cars, motor scooters, bicycles, and even pedestrians. The entire trip was a medley of noise that Calida was not at all familiar with. Jungle noise was much more sedate, even when engaged in battle.

When they returned to the boat, Calida's head was spinning from the hustle and bustle of the city.

Ricardo laughed and said, "Don't worry, you'll get used to it."

The captain returned shortly after they got back. He told Calida that he did some checking on where to start her search here in Guajará.

"I find that there are several mission headquarters here. None are very happy about revealing information on the tribes that have a missionary, and where those tribes are located. They especially keep private the names and history of the missionaries themselves." He went on, "It seems that unscrupulous people have used this information in the past to establish their own agendas and profit in doing so. Many times, this has resulted in the exploitation of aboriginal people.

"Some of these tribes have been in existence for a thousand years without any contact with the outside world. Their lack of immunity to white men's diseases have, in the past, wiped out a whole tribe. And that is only one of the dangers for these aboriginals," Hernandez continued.

"The Brazilian Government has established laws, and has given assistance, by establishing designated protected areas for the lost tribes of the Amazon Basin. You must adhere to these laws."

The captain's friends suggested that she contact the local priest at the cathedral. "He is a good man, and has done much charity work with homeless children. He will guide you and can be trusted to lead you in the right direction. His name is Father Tom McCann," Hernandez said.

"What must I do to see this man? Is he your father?" she asked.

"No, he is no one's father. He is called that because he is a Catholic priest."

"Is he a shaman?" she asked.

"I suppose that would be the closest thing to what you have known, but a priest does not use medications. He is a member of the clergy, and he performs services called a mass."

"Is that when he prays to his god?"

"Yes, and he also does charitable acts, like establishing schools and orphanages."

"My mother once knew a man like this. He spoke a strange tongue when he said his incantations. He told her it was a language called Latin."

"Yes, Calida. That is the same as this man."

"My mother said I was named Calida, which in Latin means *fire* or *blazing*. She learned this and other words from this kind man."

87

"The man you will see is the same type of person. He is very old and has seen much in his many years as a priest. He will give you good advice. This is as much as I can do for you, Calida."

"Where can I see him?"

"Ricardo can take you to the parish office. You can make an appointment to see him. When you meet with him, tell him the truth and ask for help and guidance on where to start your quest."

"Thank you, Captain, you are a good friend."

"And you are a good person, Calida. I hope you find what you are looking for, and that when you do it is not a disappointment, or worse, a disaster."

"What bad things could happen? He is my father and I want to meet him," Calida said.

"It's still a long shot that you will ever find this man, and along the way you may meet predators like none that you encountered in the jungle. Human predators are the worst there is. Many will take advantage of unsuspecting, trusting young women. Always be on your guard, young lady, and if it sounds too good to be true then it probably is not true."

"I will be careful, Skipper, and I'll be forever grateful for what you have done for me."

***

The next day found Ricardo and Calida at the cathedral office door. She had marveled at the huge edifice of the cathedral itself with all its spires and a huge dome. They entered into a lobby of the office building next to the cathedral. Several women were at their desks behind the counter, typing or writing on documents.

One matronly woman stood and asked, "May I help you?"

Ricardo answered, "*Buenos dias.* I am with this young lady. Her name is Calida and she would like an appointment to see Father Tom McCann."

"I'm very sorry but Father McCann is not here. May I ask what she would like to see him about?"

Calida answered, "I would like his help in finding my father."

"Oh my, that sounds serious. I'm afraid that Father might not be able to give much help. He's now in the hospital. He's quite old, you know, and he may be forced into retirement. Can someone else help?"

"I was told that he might be able to direct me to the correct mission headquarters that my father might be attached to."

"Do you think your father is a missionary?"

"Yes, I was told that he and his wife are with the Yano-Matis tribe located somewhere in the Amazon basin."

The woman hesitated and said, "Are you sure about this?"

"I can only tell you what was passed on to me by my mother and her second-in-command."

"I'm very confused. Who was your mother?"

"My mother was the leader of a tribe of women warriors. Our village was very far from here, and was destroyed by the fire god in the blazing mountain by our home."

The other woman stood in amazement. She approached the counter and asked in a hushed voice, "Are you saying that your mother was an Amazon?"

"My mother and all of the women warriors were killed when the mountain spewed burning liquid rock out of its crater. Yes, I have heard that my people were called Amazons but I didn't know this name until I left and encountered other people."

"Please wait here while I talk to Father's assistant," said the first lady.

The second lady stared at Calida and said, "Well, you sure look like an Amazon."

They waited patiently until a young Hispanic priest appeared from an office door behind the counter.

"The *senhora* has told me your predicament, young lady. I'm afraid I can't help you. I've been here for less than a year, and I'm not that familiar with all the missionaries. Really, the only one to help would be Father McCann. He is in poor health but you might try to visit him in the hospital. I understand that he is now seeing visitors on a limited basis."

"Thank you, Father," said Ricardo, "we will attempt to see Father McCann." He motioned to Calida that they should leave.

She sadly said, "Thank you for your help." She turned and followed him out, more confused than before.

Chapter Nineteen

The two slightly depressed young people left the parish office. They stood at the bottom of the stairs in front of the building.

Calida asked, "What do I do now, Ricardo?"

"I'll go to the hospital with you, Calida. We still have time today. I hope Father McCann will see us. We will keep trying if he's not able today."

"Thank you, Ricardo. You have been very helpful."

"I want to help you, but I fear I won't be able to help much longer. I heard the captain hired another seaman to replace Carlos. He told him to be ready to get underway at first light on the day after tomorrow. That means that tomorrow is the last day I can be with you."

"Oh, I will miss you, Ricardo, and the captain too."

"I don't know if you'd consider it, Calida, but I'm sure that the captain would hire you to be Carlos' replacement if you wanted."

"But that would mean I would stop looking for my father."

"Is that so bad? Do you need this man? You don't even know if he'll accept you, or what his wife will say about his extra activities."

"Ricardo, please, the circumstances of my conception were unusual at best. My mother might have been at fault, but she was only practicing what generations in her tribe had practiced before. My father was an unknown participant. He may not accept me, but I must know and I must meet him. He is the only family that I have," she said.

"I'm sorry. It's just that I have become attached to you, Calida. We have been living in very close quarters for many months, and I have become very attracted to you. It has been so difficult to follow the skipper's orders on not fraternizing."

"Ricardo, I know. I am enough of a woman to realize that there has been an attraction between us. Maybe for that reason alone we should not continue as shipmates."

"I'm sure we could work out an agreement with Captain Hernandez if you would consent."

"I must continue in my quest. If I am successful and find that I then need to move on with my life, I will be free to do what my heart tells me. If you will still be on this boat, I'll find you and we can decide whether we need to move to the next level. Who knows? You may find someone else by then and I will be but a memory."

"I won't forget you, Calida. You are the best thing that ever happened to me," confessed Ricardo.

"Thank you, Ricardo. Will you take me to the hospital to see Father McCann? His answer may be all that we need for me to change my plans."

"Yes, I will take you."

***

The next morning dawned brightly and Calida just felt that this was the day she would get good news. They caught a cab to the hospital after Calida packed her gear. The boat was getting underway early the next day. She would stay in a rooming house from now on. Captain Hernandez had arranged a suitable one for her.

They arrived at the hospital late in the morning and asked to see Father McCann at the reception desk. The clerk looked on her roster and asked them to sit while she checked to see if he would agree to see them.

She returned shortly and said, "He will see you but he's presently with the doctor. It may be a short wait since they are performing a procedure."

They waited. The time dragged on. Ricardo went to the desk and inquired about the visit. The clerk said she would check. Sometime later she returned with the information that they should go to lunch and return later. The treatment was ongoing.

They walked to the cafeteria, another new experience for Calida. She enjoyed picking out her food from a variety. They returned and waited another hour. Finally the clerk advised them that they could see Father McCann in room 207.

They entered the room to see a perky grey-haired man sitting up in his bed. He smiled and beckoned them to come in. He said, "First let me apologize for the wait. When the doctors start probing, you think they'll never stop. Now tell me your names and why do I have the pleasure of your visit?"

"My name is Ricardo Ruiz, Father, and this is Calida."

"And is your last name Ruiz also, my dear?"

Both of the visitors blushed and together they said, "Oh no."

Calida said, "I have only one name, Father. After you hear my request you will understand."

"Well, that's interesting, but I'm only having a bit of levity with you, child, to kind of break the ice. My chief clerk visited me last night and briefed me on your pending visit. She told me that you are looking to connect with your father, whom you have never seen. Also that he is a doctor and a missionary serving in the basin with a lost tribe. She told me of the tribe where you originated, which I might add is very interesting. I do want to hear more, especially about the priest that your mother knew. Now please tell me, child, why do you think that this doctor is your father?"

"Well, Father, I can only tell you what my mother and her second-in-command told me, mostly what Nardania passed on to me. It was her job to train me, not only as a warrior but also in all the other things a young girl should know."

"Tell me what you know, child."

"There was a great battle with a tribe called Yano-Matis and—"

"Wait! Are you sure of that?" Father McCann asked.

"Yes, I am sure," she answered

"Go on then," he said.

"The battle took place because the doctor and his wife had been kidnapped by my mother's warriors. You see, it was the practice of the Amazon warriors to kidnap men and—"

"Yes, I know the stories about the kidnapped men. I may be a priest but I've been around a long time and I've heard it all."

"Well, I'm not exactly sure of all the details, but while the doctor was a prisoner of my people, my mother somehow tricked him into copulation."

"Details are not necessary, child."

"Anyway, my mother got pregnant. I was born and raised as an Amazon warrior, then a mammoth earthquake destroyed my whole village and killed every living soul."

"I'm so sorry, my child. It must have been traumatic. How did you escape?"

"I was traveling with the shaman in the bush, looking for medicinal herbs. I've been traveling for the last six years now on a quest, looking for my father."

"I see, interesting to say the least. I might be able to help you, child, but I cannot give you the information that you require. I have an idea of whom you speak, but I'm not at liberty to give you that information. What I can do is direct you to the mission society that has sponsored a mission with that tribe. I must say that I will be very surprised if this man is your father. However, stranger things have happened, and I have seen some strange things in my life. Now, what I will do is contact the mission headquarters, tell them your story, and let them decide if further inquiry by you is in order. Please contact my office and give them your contact information. They will be in touch to tell you whether they will see you or to tell you to please cease and desist with any further contact. Do you understand?"

"Yes, Father, I understand and I want to thank you, in advance, in case I don't see you again."

"You're welcome, my dear. I wish you all the happiness possible no matter what the outcome of this. Now, with your permission I would like to give you my blessing."

She looked inquiringly at Ricardo. He said, "It's okay, Calida."

She nodded her head, yes.

The priest made the sign of the cross and blessed them using the Latin phrasing. Ricardo blessed himself with the sign of the cross and Calida bowed her head. They left the priest feeling much better about the situation. Father McCann had that effect on everyone, kind man that he was.

They hopped a cab outside of the hospital. Since the boat was closer, the cabby dropped Ricardo off first.

"Will you be okay, Calida?"

"Of course, Ricardo. Please remember me."

"I will never forget you, and I can only pray that we meet again and can plan our lives together."

He ducked his head into the cab and kissed her. As the cab left, he stood and watched until it disappeared into the town.

The cabby turned around as he drove and asked "Do you mind if I make a stop? I have to pick up some drinks for my family."

"No, go right ahead," she said.

He drove on, leaving the main streets in the downtown area. She was deep in thought with what was coming next with the priest. Also, was she making a mistake not staying with Ricardo? He was such a good man and always protected her, even though she could protect herself as well.

It seemed like the ride was longer than she thought. She sat up and didn't recognize the area they had gotten into. She asked, "Driver, where are we? Shouldn't we have gotten to my boarding house yet?"

"Pretty soon now. Here, have a drink. It's a refreshing cola that my family likes. I'll open it for you."

She took the bottle and examined it. It looked refreshing and she was thirsty. She took a long drink. They rode on. She took another long drink. Strange, she suddenly felt dizzy and very groggy. She couldn't go to sleep here. She couldn't hold her eyes open.

Suddenly, it was black.

She slumped over in her seat. The driver pulled over, turned to look at her, and leered. He drove on with a satisfied smirk. Senhor *will be very happy.*

Chapter Twenty

The cab pulled up in front of a rundown stucco building in the most undesirable part of town. Several seedy-looking derelicts were standing in front, smoking hand-rolled joints. One was taking a pull on a pint bottle of unknown alcohol. He might be blind by morning—if not by sight, he would surely be blind drunk. This was as unsavory as you could get.

The short, stocky cabby grabbed two of the homeless addicts and said, "Get the woman out of my cab and carry her inside."

"Oh yeah! What's in it for us, Petey boy?"

"Just do it, you bum, or I'll kick you all out of here. You'll find a new place to sleep tonight."

Two of them grumbled and open the car door.

"Hey, Petey found himself a fine lookin' one this time."

They manhandled Calida, getting her out of the car, and carried her into the rundown building. Another one grabbed her rucksack and pouch. He dug into the rucksack to see what he could steal, but the cabby grabbed the bags out of his hands before he was successful.

"Keep out of there, you horse's ass." Petey followed the two carrying Calida into the building. "Take her into the back room and put her on the bunk."

They did so and then all left the room. The rickety door had a padlock on it. Petey snapped it closed.

"I don't want anyone bothering her. *Senhor* will be here in the morning to inspect the merchandise. This is *primo* stuff, and I expect to be paid well for this one."

"She looks good, Petey. You gonna sample it first?"

"No, stupid. I told you it's *primo* and I don't want her ruined by me or anyone else. YOU GOT THAT?"

"Okay, okay. Don't get touchy. Let's go, Raul."

As the night wore on, Calida didn't stir a muscle. The drug had taken effect throughout her whole body. Her muscles were useless. She was oblivious to the insect-ridden mattress. They were feasting on the blood under the tender skin of the young maiden. Several rats were chewing on the leather of her shoes. Fortunately, her pouch of drugs and herbs was sealed tightly against animal intrusion, so it was safe for now.

The sun rose in the east and shined through the narrow window of her cell. A bright sunbeam shined in her eyes and awakened her. She opened her eyes and tried to raise her head, which was splitting with pain from the potent drug. She lay her head back down and groaned.

Where am I? What happened to me? My head feels like someone beat me. She tried to think. *I was riding in a cab. Now I remember. That man gave me a drink. It was drugged. I was drugged.* She awakened slowly as the drug wore off. "Ahhh, there are bugs all over me," she screamed.

The rats scurried away as she became alert to her noxious, smelly surroundings. She tried to brush the bedbugs from her legs and arms. They seemed to have favored the right leg. It was covered with welts.

Oh, is that a rat bite on my ankle? She shuddered.

She pulled herself up from the filthy, ragged, thin mattress. When she stood, dizziness buckled her knees. She struggled to stand and clear her head, supporting herself with one hand on the wall. *What did he give me? I feel so weak.* She saw her rucksack and pouch on the floor by the door. She stumbled over to it and retrieved the pouch. *I have something in here to clear my head.*

She dug in the pouch and came out with a powder, which she sniffed, and immediately her head cleared. She still had pain, but felt that it would soon dissipate with a clear head. Now she could think without that fuzzy feeling in her brain. She tried the door. It moved slightly but would not open with the lock closed on the outside. She tried rattling it.

The door was not strong. Maybe she could break it and force it open. She slammed her body against the rickety door. It opened just a crack.

That's good. If I keep hitting it, I may break it.

She hit it again and again. She was making headway and suddenly it sprang open. But alas, it wasn't her abuse of the door that opened it, but the short, squat taxi driver.

"Hold it there, blondie, you're not going anywhere yet."

He grabbed her arm to fling her back on the bed. Big mistake.

Calida spun around and dislodged his grip, and as she completed her spin, she hit him on the side of his head with a double fist. She was at least a head taller than him, so her arms were shoulder high when her fist engaged his skull. This height was at the apex of her strength.

The one blow, with all her weight and frustration behind it, sent him crashing to the floor. He was still conscious, but severely woozy from this unexpected retaliation. He rolled to his belly and rose to his hands and knees. He shook his head like a dying fish and tried to stand, but he was knocked flat again by a well-placed kick in the ribcage. He let out a loud gasp as two or three ribs cracked under this long-legged kick.

He was laid out on the floor, panting and groaning, when two strong, burly men rushed into the room and pinned Calida against the wall. She tried to fight them off but these two were not the pushover that the short, squat cab driver was. One man pinned her arms against her side and lifted her feet off the floor. The other one helped the cabby to his feet, laughingly chiding him.

He chuckled, "What's the matter, Petey? Meet your match with this blonde bombshell?"

Petey moaned and painfully tried to breathe.

"Take her to the *senhor*. I'll be glad to get rid of her," he choked out.

"The *senhor* was going to come but we will take her. It's a good thing too. I think she had the upper hand."

"Just get out of here, I've got to see a *medico*. I can't breathe," said Petey.

"Let's go, Pablo, put her in the backseat and stay with her. She's a feisty one. I'll grab her bags," said the biggest thug.

They loaded Calida and her bags in the luxury sedan and pulled away. Pablo kept a tight rein on her. She was not going to escape from these two. They knew what they were doing.

They left the seedy part of town and eventually were in an upscale residential area. Calida tried to keep alert on her location but soon lost track with all the turns, and now they were in an area with large, expensive, gated estates. This was certainly out of her realm of experience.

They arrived at their destination by entering through an electric gate opened by the driver inserting a card into a slot. They proceeded up a long driveway and stopped in front of a large, palatial home.

"Okay, out you go, sister. Don't try any of the rough stuff here. It will only get you a lot of pain."

As they entered into the foyer they were met by a well-dressed and well-coiffed woman, who said, "So this is the *primo* stuff that Petey was so proud of. Well, we'd better get her cleaned up before the *senhor* sees her. For what he promised to pay Petey, she'd better be perfect."

"I'll say one thing, *senhora*, she's a spitfire."

"Okay, take her up to the guest room with the attached bathroom. I'll get her showered and smelling good."

When Calida was in the bedroom, the *senhora* came in and announced, "All right, *senhorita*, I'm not going to tolerate any monkey business. This is a stun gun and will make you very uncomfortable if I'm forced to use it. Just do what you're told and you won't have it so bad, at least for a while anyway. Do you understand me?"

"I can understand Spanish better than Portuguese," Calida said.

"That's fine, I'll speak Spanish. Get undressed and get in that shower. After you're clean and I get you properly dressed and that beautiful hair combed out, we'll look you over. I'll get rid of those rags that you're wearing."

"After I shower, may I get a salve out of my pouch to put on these bug bites from last night?"

"Yes, certainly. That animal shouldn't have taken you to that hovel he has in the red-light district. It's a miracle you came out of there unscathed."

After the shower and all the proper ablutions, the *senhora* said, "Okay, you look presentable. Yes, you are *primo*. Wait here while I see if the *senhor* is ready for you."

Chapter Twenty-One

The bedroom had more opulence than Calida had ever seen in her whole life. The bed was huge compared to what she was used to. A bathroom just steps away had fixtures she could only have dreamed of. Why was she here? What did this strange woman have in store for her? She could only wait and see. Escape at this time was out of the question.

The *senhora* returned. Calida sat in an easy chair, long legs crossed like blades of a folding instrument. She looked up, searching for answers as to the shape of things to come. When the *senhora* entered, she again reflected grace and definitely had an air of authority about her. She wore a tailored double-breasted jacket and skirt, all of it black, jet black, just like her boots and even her hair, which was perfectly in place.

"Please, can you tell me where I am and what is happening?" Calida asked.

"You are in the home of a very rich and influential man, my dear. He can do many things for you, extremely good or extremely bad, both very much dependent on your attitude," said the *senhora*.

"What am I to do?" asked Calida.

"For now, do nothing except look pretty. The *senhor* will take the next step."

They left the room, swept down the luxuriant staircase and into the beautiful paneled library. The library was a large room, well-appointed with expensive furniture. A mahogany desk with a black high-backed chair was the dominant feature. The room spoke of masculine elegance.

The two women were standing facing the desk when the *senhor* swept into the room. He was Hispanic, his age north of fifty. He also was well dressed and neat. His dark hair had grey through the temples. He was tall and thin, and was clean shaven to go with a handsome face. He might have appeared a pleasant Brazilian aristocrat except for his eyes. They were penetrating.

When Calida made eye contact, she quickly looked away and slightly shuddered. This was a "no nonsense" man. He demanded indisputable loyalty, and if he didn't get it, the penalty was final and swift. He paid well for what he wanted, but it better be worth what he paid. His was a business that could carry no emotion. A lucrative business where the lives of young women hung in the balance and decisions made with no remorse. That was the business of *white slavery.*

He sat at his desk, took a long approving look at the young woman brought in by his wife, and said, "Turn around, *senhorita.*"

She turned.

He stood and reached across the desk and felt her hair between his thumb and forefinger.

"Hmm, fine, like silk. Face me," he demanded.

She turned back.

He took her chin with his hand and gently turned her face to one side, then the other. He held her at arm's length, with a hand on each shoulder, again turning her body from one side to the other. "Yes, she has great potential, *elegante.* What is her history, Sofia?"

"The story told is that she came from a tribe of Amazon women warriors somewhere in the hills near Machu Picchu. She is in her late teens and she is looking to find her missing father."

"Is any of this true?"

"I can question her."

"Get everything that you can. I may use this one as a gift to El Toro. If I can get him to be indebted to me, it may bode well for me to buy in to his cocaine operation."

"El Toro? That animal? I don't like doing business with the likes of him, and do you know what he'll do to this girl? Let's just send her to Miami with the next shipment."

"It is not for you to say, Sofia," he sternly reprimanded. "I run the business, you run the house. If you don't shape up, I just may use her as your replacement. Now do as I say." He spun on his heel and stalked out of the room.

Sofia grabbed Calida by the arm and said, "Let's go."

As they walked out of the room and up the stairs, Sofia mumbled obscenities all the way and said, "He's so smart. He thinks he runs the business. Little does he know what I can do without him. Replace me? Huh! We'll see who gets replaced."

When they got to her room, Calida sat in a chair and the *senhora* said, "Well now, tell me your story. You may be just the piece of the pie to get me what I want. Too bad, I was getting to like you."

"What do you want to know?" Calida asked.

"Tell me more about the village of women that you came from."

Calida gave her what history she knew. She told her about the battle with the Yano-Matis tribe, her conception and birth.

"What kind of training did you get?"

She explained that she was trained to be a warrior and eventual tribe leader. She explained how the warriors captured men and used them. She explained about how she was to remain celibate until a chosen time.

"And what happened to the village?" asked the *senhora*.

Calida explained about the volcano and earthquake, also about traveling with the shaman and learning about herbs. She went on about Plata, learning how to fend for herself in the jungle, and living with the lost tribe.

"How did you end up in Guajará?"

She explained about the trip downriver in the *chalana*.

"Well, that's quite a story. You seem like a very capable young woman. If I taught you the social graces and how an educated young damsel acts, you could be very valuable to me. Yes, I think I'll change tactics with the boss man."

"I'm very tired. Can I rest before we eat?" Calida asked.

"Yes, Calida, rest while I do some thinking. I'll be back to get you for the evening meal."

She left and Calida used this time to explore and get the layout of her room. She had all her wits about her now and knew that her only chance was to play along until an opportunity presented itself. She tried the window in her room, which faced the rear of the property. It would not budge, and there was a heavy mesh over the glass. She tried the door. It was locked. The small window in the bathroom was also bolted shut. But there was slight movement when she tried it and the outside bolt rattled when she tried to raise the window. There were marks around the edge where someone tried prying it open. Someone preceded her here. If she could locate a pry bar she might do some good here. It looked like the outside mesh covering the window was askew. It was a small window, but big enough that she could wriggle through. She searched the room, but was unsuccessful in finding a pry bar.

Several hours later, the *senhora* returned.

"I've brought a new outfit for you to wear. The old tyrant wants you to have dinner with him, and interrogate you for information."

After Calida was dressed, the *senhora* briefed her on how to act at dinner. She said, "Keep an eye on me and I'll guide you through. Your biggest hurdle is keeping *senhor* from getting irritated. He can sometimes be volatile under that austere front that he gives. He prides himself on the formal dinner fiasco. He's come a long way from where he started, when he had a string of three girls he pimped out of a taxicab."

"How did he get so rich and become so proper?"

"Huh! That's where I came in. When he met me, he swept me off my feet with his sweet talk. I didn't know what business he was in. My family left me a fortune and he used that to build a bigger business shipping women to the US. I taught him how to put up that polite facade that he uses today. Before I met him, he was a buffoon. Now, he insists that everyone have the same manners that he does. He thinks I don't know about that luxurious apartment that he keeps in Manaus. That's where he goes to take care of the shipment of girls from all over Brazil. He keeps a few of the *primo* girls there for his use and the use of his business friends."

"You don't sound happy," interjected Calida.

"The one thing that he still remembers from the old days is how to beat a woman. I've learned my lesson and now I just go along with his idiosyncrasies. But it will soon be over. By the way, you will probably end up in Manaus sooner or later."

"What do you mean?" Calida asked.

"It will not be pleasant. You are virtually a prisoner and you won't know who you will be sleeping with from night to night."

"But what did he say about giving me to El Toro? Who is he?"

The *senhora* shuddered. "That's even worse. El Toro is a nickname because he acts like a wild bull. He runs a cocaine operation in Columbia. He is a masochist. He uses up women like they were disposable. You will wish to die if you end up with him. But if the *senhor* uses you as an incentive for his own profit, it may even speed up my chance for freedom from this monster. You may be the best thing to complete my conspiracy."

"I don't understand."

"Just do as I say, young lady, and maybe we'll both come out of this thing unscathed and much farther ahead. Come on, let's go down to dinner with the master of the house."

As they entered the dining room, they saw that four places had been set.

Senhora Sofia softly said, "Hmm! I wonder who he has invited."

They stood waiting for the *senhor* to enter. Suddenly the large double doors swung open and he swept in along with a dapper young man dressed very conservatively.

"Ah, Sofia and Calida, this is Lieutenant Ramos Gomez with the *federalista*. He has recently been assigned to the office in Guajará and stopped by to introduce himself. I invited him for dinner."

Sofia seemed flustered, and quickly said, "It is our pleasure to meet you, Lieutenant. Please, let's sit. Can we offer you some wine?"

"Thank you. Yes, some wine before dinner would be very pleasant. Your companion is quite lovely."

"Thank you, sir," said Calida as she sat, really confused now.

Chapter Twenty-Two

The dinner was served by a butler and two maids. Conversation was light. The *senhor* asked the lieutenant where he last served.

"I spent my time in Brasilia at headquarters after I got my degree," he answered.

"Aha, you may have become acquainted with my brother, who owns a restaurant downtown," said the *senhor*.

"I have heard of this very fine restaurant, but I am not among those who can afford it, *senhor*," Gomez said.

"Well, maybe we can help," the *senhor* said, barely audible.

Senhora Sofia quietly gasped. A sly grin came to the lieutenant's lips. Calida listened intently, but while all others were attentive otherwise, she slipped a butter spatula into her shoe.

The *senhor* dominated the rest of the dinner conversation with facts about the town of Guajará directed at the guest. The butler approached him in the middle of a description of a landmark. The *senhor* turned to face him with an annoyed look. He then sarcastically uttered a blunt, "Yes?"

The dignified butler cringed and stuttered, "Omar sent me, sir. He . . . he needs you. He . . . he said it's very important."

The senhor harshly threw his linen napkin down on the table, jumped to his feet, and then quickly composed himself. He grimaced, forced a smile, and said, "Please excuse the intrusion. My staff seems to need my guidance at any time of the day." He hurriedly left the room.

Omar, one of his bodyguards, was waiting for him outside of the library.

"What the hell do you mean by disturbing me when I'm entertaining a government man?"

"I'm sorry, *jefé*, but your *contador* notified me to disturb you. He said you will understand when you talk to him."

"What could that bean counter have that is so important? Where is he?"

"He's in the small office with the encrypted telephone."

The *senhor* suddenly got attentive. He briskly walked to the rear of the large house, where the office was located. When he entered, the *contador* handed him the phone and said, "It's El Toro. He insisted on talking to you."

The *senhor* softened his demeanor. He took the phone and said, "Yes, *amigo*, you must have gotten my message."

In a crisp tone, El Toro answered, "I'm very interested in your gift, *senhor*. When can I inspect the merchandise?"

"I leave for Manaus in the morning, and I will return in three or four days. Would you like me to bring the package, or can you travel safely now?"

"Yes, I can travel. Anything is possible if you grease the right palms. I will plan on one week from today. I will have two of my *manteners* with me. Will you have a car pick us up at the airport? I'll be in my Learjet."

"Yes, of course. Call when you leave your base and give us an ETA. You can call on this line and coordinate with my *contador*."

"I will plan on it. I'm very anxious to see the *primo* stuff that you spoke of. I am very much in need of something different than the *pasatiempo* that I have now."

"I guarantee that you will be pleased," answered the *senhor*.

"If I am that pleased, maybe we can discuss other business."

"That will make me very happy, El Toro. I'll see you in a week." The *senhor* hung up and hurriedly returned to dinner.

***

Immediately after the *senhor* had left the dinner table, Lieutenant Gomez caught Sofia's eye and motioned with his head toward the butler. Sofia correctly took this to mean that Gomez wanted the butler gone.

When the three of them were alone, Gomez looked toward Calida with a question in his eyes.

"She's okay. What's going on? I didn't expect anyone so soon," said Sofia.

"Our government has heard you, Sofia. The agent that you talked to has convinced the right people that this may be the break we need. We hope to stop some disturbing criminal operations, not only here but also in some of the neighboring countries."

"What should I do?" Sofia asked.

"Get any information that can help us, especially on movements of merchandise and travels in the drug trade. I must engrain myself with the *senhor* and get him to think that I'm on the take like *agente de policia* here in Guajará."

"When will you get back to me? I've got a feeling that he's not happy with me," Sofia said.

"Very soon. Let him get comfortable with me. Just wait and listen," Gomez answered.

They heard footsteps and hushed up.

The *senhor* briskly entered the dining room. He took his seat and said, "I am very sorry, but it was an important business matter." He signaled the butler and nervously said, "You may serve dessert now." He bantered and made polite small talk. Sofia smirked.

"Lieutenant, will you join me in the drawing room for brandy and a Cuban cigar?" the *senhor* asked.

"I'll be happy to, *senhor*," Gomez answered.

"Please, my butler will escort you. Sofia, may I see you in private?"

Lieutenant Gomez left with the butler and the *senhor* turned to Sofia. He said, "Leave with her now and retire. I am leaving in the morning for Manaus and returning in three or four days. I want her trained to perfection while I'm gone. El Toro is coming, and I intend to make him very happy."

"When will he be here?"

"In one week, and with any luck, soon after I will have a nice interest in his cocaine trade. *Mucho reais* are in my future."

"Will he bring anyone with him? How many are coming?"

The *senhor* suspiciously eyeballed her. "Why do you ask? What does it matter to you? Our servants will accommodate them."

"Oh, nothing, nothing. Just a woman's curiosity."

"Just do what I told you and leave the business end up to me like I've told you. You are becoming much too curious lately." He spun on his heel and left for the drawing room.

***

"Ah, Lieutenant, I see my man has served the brandy. Does it suit you?"

"I'm sure this is a vintage bottle of brandy, *senhor*. It is very smooth."

"And a fine Cuban cigar to accompany it will also hit the spot. Will you join me in one?" the *senhor* asked.

"My pleasure, sir. This has been a fine evening, one I didn't expect."

"When I have an important guest, they get only the best."

"Well, I certainly didn't expect this. I am only a lieutenant."

"I was told that I would receive a visit from an important government *policia*. You may only be a lieutenant, but I understand you are held in high regard."

"Thank you, but I am limited," Gomez answered.

"I also understand that you like the finer things in life."

"Hmm, you seem to have some personal information."

"Don't be naive, Gomez, and let's get down to business. I know that you were sent here to investigate organized crime. I also know that the *agente de policia* here in Guajará have briefed you on what you can expect as far as additional income."

"Well, *senhor*, I must do my job here in this one-horse town so I can get back to the big city where the real action is. I will report what I see," Gomez answered with a sly grin.

"And if you suddenly have a blind eye on certain operations and on certain people, is that possible?" the *senhor* carefully quizzed.

"I suppose I could skip a few paragraphs if an incentive to do so were present," Gomez said while sipping on vintage brandy.

"I raise my glass to you, Lieutenant. I'm sure we can make life easier for both of us," said a beaming *senhor*.

The lieutenant smiled, raised his glass to the *senhor*, and sipped some brandy. Gomez said, "I start my investigation tomorrow. When can I look forward to our next meeting?"

"I go to Manaus tomorrow for three or four days on business. After that we can meet," answered the *senhor*.

Gomez said, "Very well, I'll be in touch with some initial findings and perhaps some questions."

"That may be a good time to provide you with a *pagar lo debido*."

"I can see that we have similar thoughts, *senhor*."

"As I said, Lieutenant Gomez, I know how to treat important guests."

"Thank you, sir, and I bid you a good night."

"Goodnight, Lieutenant."

As Gomez was leaving, he turned and said, "One more thing, *senhor*. I'm very curious about the beautiful tall blonde woman at the dinner table. I tried to engage her in conversation and she was very polite but she also seemed very hesitant about what she said. Is she a guest or perhaps a relative of yours or Sofia's?"

"If you are a regular guest here, Lieutenant, you may see beautiful women occasionally. I like having them around. This one is very special, and is one of the items that should be overlooked in your report."

"I see. Well, it was a pleasure being in her company, even if only for a short time," Gomez said. Gomez quickly took his leave and purposely left the briefcase that he came with.

Later, the butler gave the case to the *senhor*. He examined it and found generic government documents that an investigator would carry: a brief summary of crime statistics in Guajará and surrounding areas, a listing of his *per diem* expenses. There was nothing of any real significance or informative. He called the butler, gave the case back to him, and said, "Send word to his office that he left it here and that he can pick it up at his convenience."

Chapter Twenty-Three

The *senhor* left the next morning. He instructed the security, which consisted of three quite large, muscular men, to keep a sharp eye on the *senhora* and the young girl in her charge.

"Should we allow them to leave the house, *senhor*?" Omar asked.

"Only to visit the garden. If they want to leave the compound, stop them."

"Will the *senhora* object?"

"Certainly, you idiot, but she is not in my good graces at this time. And if she objects, just tell her you are following my orders."

"Okay, *patron*."

With that, the *senhor* left for the airport.

Senhora Sofia was within earshot while these instructions were given to Omar.

So the old goat is getting suspicious. I should have done something long ago. I can only blame my own selfishness for having waited this long.

She quietly left and climbed the stairs to the second floor. She unlocked Calida's room and entered. "*Buenos dias*, Calida. Sit down. I want to discuss something with you."

Calida sat and waited expectantly.

"Things may be happening in the very near future that might be very helpful in saving you from a life of hell."

"Please help me, *senhora*. I don't want to become a prostitute, nor do I want to be El Toro's doll to be trifled with. Help me to escape."

"You would only be caught, and the consequences could be fatal. Human life, to these people, means nothing, and I'm ashamed to say that I've closed my eyes to this for years."

"What can I do?"

"I have contacted the *federalista,* and they have responded with Lieutenant Gomez. I want to wait until our next contact before we do anything rash."

"I think he likes me," said Calida.

"I don't doubt that one bit, my dear. Now, let's you and I work on a few things that will help you in any situation."

The instruction began while activity in the large house was at a minimum. It lasted well into the late afternoon. The two women dined alone that evening. Calida received instruction on proper table manners and dinner conversation.

The next day started much in the same manner when Omar knocked and announced that the lieutenant had come to retrieve his briefcase. He would like to pay his respects. The two women composed themselves and joined Lieutenant Gomez in the drawing room. Omar was standing by as they greeted their guest.

Senhora Sofia turned to him and announced, "That will be all, Omar. I will call if I need you."

"But, *senhora*—" he tried to respond.

She glared at him, "I said that will be all. I will call if you are needed."

He shuffled out.

Sofia's shoulders slumped in relief, a bead of sweat appeared above her upper lip. "Whew," she gasped.

Gomez smiled, "Easy, *senhora*, I have the situation under control. We must now move quickly."

"*Mio Dios!* I don't know if I can take much more. How soon can you get us out of here?"

"Very soon. The really big fish that we want to catch is El Toro, and the egotistic bastard is going to fall right into our hands. Hopefully, the bait has been cast."

They both looked at Calida.

She squirmed. "I don't like being the bait. I would rather leave here now."

"Please don't do that. This is the first time in years that he has left the protection of his compound. He's getting very brave, and feels secure because of the lack of enforcement in the past. That is now over and we will bring him to justice," Gomez lectured.

"What can we do to help, Lieutenant?" the *senhora* asked.

"Go ahead with your instruction of the girl so the security does not become suspicious. I will be in touch as soon as a concrete plan is in place, but rest assured it will happen while El Toro is here."

"Yes, we can do that," Sofia said.

"One thing you can do is to tell the *senhor* of my visit and that I requested that he contact me upon his return. I will also tell Omar that I asked you to do this. By that time I hope to have a plan in mind. Men from my main office and men from the Columbian Feds are due in tonight. They both have some additional information I may need to be successful in this sting."

"I am frightened. I have seen things and heard of other things over the years that make me cringe. It has gotten even worse lately."

"We will need your testimony on that. Now, play along. It will soon be over. I'm leaving now, *senhora*, but I'll be back. *Adios*, Calida."

He left the ladies and hurriedly departed from the room. He encountered Omar in the foyer and said, "I told the *senhora* to have your *patron* contact me. Make sure that he does without delay."

Omar said, "*Si*, Lieutenant."

As Gomez left through the door, Omar gave him the one-finger salute.

The next few days passed without incident.

***

The *senhor* returned with a flourish. He seemed revitalized when he walked through the door. *Senhora* Sofia met him in the entry.

She said, "You seem to be full of vim and vigor. Your concubine must have treated you well."

He stopped short and answered, "Be quiet, you jealous hag. I'm invigorated with the prospect of my future business prospects. The thought of amazing profits has me flying high."

"Well, some of that profit may be leaving you soon. Gomez wants you to contact him as soon as you return."

"Ah yes," he sighed, "the cost of doing business. All right, I'll call."

***

Dinner that evening was a very quiet, sedate affair with just the three of them. The conversation consisted predominately of the training of Calida.

"Well, Sofia, it seems that you have done an adequate job of teaching social skills to our young lady. Let me ask, have you also shown her some of the skills a woman should acquire to satisfy a man?"

"You are very crude, *senhor*. I will not take part in seeing any satisfaction from that horrible animal El Toro."

The *senhor* laughed loudly. Finally he said, "I should let him practice on you. I understand he does amazing things with his whip. His subjects beg him to do his bidding if he stops."

"You are as sick as he is," Sofia screamed. She jumped up from the table. "Come, Calida, let's leave this animal to his own filthy thoughts."

The two women left the dining room to his loud, drunken laughter.

***

The next morning, as the two women were eating breakfast, the door chimes rang and Lieutenant Gomez was announced to them.

Sofia told the maid, "Show him in and go wake your *patron* out of his drunken stupor. I will serve the lieutenant breakfast while the *senhor* makes himself presentable."

The maid left and soon returned with the lieutenant in tow.

"Please join us, Lieutenant. Would you like a cup of *cafezinho*?"

"I'd be delighted. *Buenos dias, senhora* and *senhorita*."

They waited until the maid left with her duty to alert the *senhor*.

"Have you any good news for us, Lieutenant?" Sofia asked.

"*Si*, all my men have arrived. We are ready. Now we must wait until the big fish arrives," he murmured softly.

"I heard Omar tell his men to be alert when El Toro is here. He arrives tomorrow afternoon. The *senhor* has planned a big celebration for that evening, with a seven-course dinner and a string trio to play

112

while dinner is served. He has pulled out all stops for this deviant," she answered defiantly.

"The more confusion, the better it will be for us. I'm planning a raid during dinner. You are a big part of the plan. Listen quickly before he comes," he instructed. Gomez quickly and concisely laid out what she was to do and what would happen after that. He had just completed when the *senhor* walked in.

"Ah, Lieutenant, I didn't expect you so early. I slept a little later than usual, being tired from a long flight."

"The ladies kept me entertained, *senhor*. How was your trip?"

"*Mucho gusto,*" he answered alertly.

The maid entered and asked, "*Cafezinho, patron?*"

"Yes, very strong," he replied on a less alert tone. He turned to Sofia and softly said, "My dear, would you excuse us? We have business to discuss."

Sofia rolled her eyes and said, "Of course. Come on, Calida." They quickly left the room.

The *senhor* removed an envelope stuffed with reais from his jacket pocket and slid it across the table to Gomez.

"Thank you, *senhor*. I shall put this to good use," Gomez said.

"I'm sure you will, Lieutenant."

"The word on the street is that someone big is coming to town in the near future. I hope this is something that you, and as a result, I can look forward to," Gomez said.

"There is no big deal that happens in this town that I am not a part of. You were very astute in recognizing that and becoming a part of it, young man."

"*Gracias, senhor.*"

"You must understand that you cannot be a participant in this gala event, Lieutenant. There are those that would feel very uncomfortable if you were present," the *senhor* advised.

"I understand. And with that, I will leave you. Thank you for returning my briefcase," Gomez nodded and said.

"*De nada*, Lieutenant."

Gomez rose to leave, stuffing the envelope into his inside coat pocket. While leaving, he thought, *this will go a long way for the youth soccer program back home in Brasilia.*

Chapter Twenty-Four

The two women left the dining room and climbed the staircase to the second floor. When they got to Calida's room, Sofia said, "I have some preparation to do for the lieutenant. I will leave you for a few hours. Please don't attempt to leave."

"I'm very confused. What is going to happen to me?" Calida asked.

"Just try to be patient. You heard the lieutenant."

Sofia turned on her heel and hurriedly left the room, locking the door behind her. As she stood outside the door she thought, *I hope it goes well, but if it doesn't, she could be my bargaining chip. I want to come out of this with enough to last me for my lifetime.*

***

It was late in the afternoon the next day when a jet-black stretch limo speedily entered through the gate of the estate and screeched to a halt at the front entrance. Two burly, very obvious security men quickly and simultaneously exited the car, one from the front seat and the other from a rear door. Their oversized jackets bulged with the automatic weapons secreted under them. After a scan of the area, one opened a rear door while the other stood back and scrutinized the surroundings.

A dapper Hispanic man climbed out of the opened door. He was of medium height, with slicked-back jet-black hair. A pencil-thin hairline mustache graced his upper lip. As he stood surveying the surroundings after exiting the car, the front door of the estate sprang open and an exuberant *senhor* bounded down the steps.

"El Toro," he greeted, "welcome to my humble—" He pulled up short. With a puzzled look, he said, "Wait a minute. What the hell's going on here? Where's El Toro?"

As the *senhor* was questioning the farce in front of him, a similarly black Cadillac Escalade wheeled in through the gate. It sped up the long driveway. As it screeched to a halt, the passenger door flew open and a muscular *vaquero* leaped out, his cowboy boots hitting the ground the instant the car stopped rolling. He guffawed loudly and rudely bellowed, "*El Senhor!* Why the puzzled look? Did you really think I would come unprepared? I brought my bean counter with me just in case there was a reception committee to greet me on the way here. I thought he could stand in for me for anything not expected. There are two more men in the limo, as well as my driver in the Caddy. I believe in being prepared."

"I didn't expect so many, El Toro, but it is no problem. I have a big house."

"Another change in plans. We will leave immediately after we have conducted business. I don't like to stay away from my compound too long. I owe my longevity to that and the fact that no one knows my schedule except me."

"But, *mi amigo*, I have prepared a banquet for us. We can accommodate everyone that you have brought."

With a steely look El Toro said, "We will go inside and I will tell you my new schedule. If you don't agree, my Learjet is prepared to leave in a moment's notice."

"Of course, of course, let's go in. I have a choice wine for you."

After entering with two of El Toro's bodyguards, they were seated in the paneled library, each with a drink of their choice.

"All right, *senhor*, the first thing I'd like to do is inspect the gift you have offered me. Then we can discuss our other arrangement."

"As you wish, *mi amigo*." He rang for the maid. When she came, he said, "Notify *Senhora* Sofia to bring Calida here to the library right away."

She scurried off.

The *senhor* said, "I'm sure you will be pleased with my choice for your pleasure, *amigo*. But I am disappointed that you will not partake of the meal I have planned for you."

"I will consider it," he replied.

As they refreshed their drinks, Sofia and Calida entered the room. El Toro stood as they entered. Calida was gorgeously resplendent in a gold gown picked out for her by Sofia. Her long blonde hair and her olive and tanned skin highlighted the shimmering gown.

El Toro set his drink down, approached Calida, and said, "Well, well, this is beyond what I expected. Yes, *mi bella*, you will do quite nicely."

"I'm glad that you approve, *mi amigo*," the *senhor* said with a smile.

"Perhaps if you can accommodate all my men we can stay to break bread with you, *patron*," El Toro murmured.

"Yes, by all means. There is plenty," the *senhor* agreed.

"But we must go immediately after the meal. I won't have it any other way. No lingering," El Toro emphasized.

Sofia's ears perked up at this. She asked "Will you still be serving the full dinner, *patron*?"

"Yes, but we will start earlier so our friend can get a good start."

"How much earlier?" she asked.

"Enough questions, Sofia. I will let you know. Now, if you please, El Toro and I have business to conduct," the *senhor* admonished.

El Toro was standing facing Calida, his hands supporting her arms. She was slightly taller than him and he was leering as he looked up at her face. El Toro spoke, voice dripping with lust, "I'll see you later, bella mia. We have a long plane ride to get to know each other."

Calida turned, hiding her revulsion, and quickly left the room with the *Senhora* Sofia. When they reached the bedroom, Calida, now in a panic, said, "*Senhora*, what are we going to do? I can't go anywhere with that perverted animal."

"Be quiet and let me think. I must get in touch with the lieutenant and move things up. Fortunately, they will stay into the evening. We may still be able to work this out." Sofia left the room in a rush.

As soon as the room was empty, Calida reached under the mattress where she had hidden the butter spatula. She had secretly stolen it at dinner previously. She found it and hurriedly went into the bathroom. She started working on the locked window, prying it loose.

I know I can't escape now in the daylight, but if I can get everything loose I might get a chance after dark. Thankfully sunset is early now.

She pried and almost had enough room to reach the bolt on the outside of the window, but the spatula bent from the strain.

Oh no, now what can I do? Maybe I can straighten it if I stick it in this crack.

She forced it into a small crack and bent it back.

Yes, that did it.

She slowly worked it and worked it. Suddenly the bolt popped back from the window sash. She tried raising the window but it was hard to move. She put the spatula under the window and pried. It gave way past the tight area. But the spatula was now broken. Nevertheless, she could now raise the window.

The steel mesh was loose from the window and easily bent back to provide an opening, a very narrow opening, but enough for a slim, athletic girl to wriggle through. As she stuck her head out to survey the escape route, she saw two of the security men smoking outside of the rear door.

I'll have to wait until dark. I hope I'll get a chance before dinner but they'll probably miss me if I don't show up. Oh what should I do?

She went back into the bedroom after lowering the window. Senhora Sofia had allowed her to keep her pouch of herbs, but the rest of her belongings were confiscated. She dug in the drawers and found pants and a blouse, an outfit more suitable for climbing than the dress they had her wear for show time in front of El Toro. The only thing to do now was wait. Sunset will be in about an hour.

She nervously paced the floor. Time passed slowly but twilight was now upon them. Suddenly she heard the lock snap open on the door. She held her breath and thankfully it was *Senhora* Sofia that entered.

"I was able to make a very abbreviated telephone call to Lieutenant Gomez. His men are already in the area but will need my help in gaining entrance to the property and to filter into the house undetected. He wasn't expecting to encounter this many men."

"Can they save us?" asked a nervous Calida.

"Oh, you silly child, this may be a bloodbath. God only knows who will be saved now. Get out of those rags and get back into the dress that I picked out. As soon as I get you presentable, I'm taking you down to the dining room. There, you will do your best to entertain the *senhor's*

117

criminals, who have been imbibing all afternoon. We can only hope that the alcohol has slowed their reactions."

"What about the men that El Toro brought with him?"

"I've seen to it that they've also had an ample supply of alcohol this afternoon. Fortunately, they must have built up a thirst on the trip here. I tried to create a party atmosphere like Gomez instructed me. Of course, it was easy to feed alcohol to El Senhor's men, the gluttons."

"Must I go, Sofia? That man makes my skin crawl."

"You will go!" Sofia announced adamantly. "They would suspect something if you don't. With you there acting coy and friendly it will create the diversion needed when I leave the table. I will let the Feds in through the back door. I know how men think, and you must try to overwhelm them with your charm and beauty."

"I will try, *Senhora* Sofia, but I'm scared."

"You have a natural ability, my child, use it," she assured Calida.

Sofia helped Calida primp and get ready. They left the room for the dining room.

Chapter Twenty-Five

The two women approached the ballroom where the men were enjoying cocktails. The raucous laughter of inebriated men toned down to a murmur when the young Amazon, escorted by the lady of the house, entered with a flourish. The intent was to create a diversion, and she did. All eyes were upon her.

El Toro, with all the aplomb that a drug lord could muster, sidled over to her. He clumsily took her hand and kissed it in a failed attempt to appear as a gentleman. He slurred, "*Buenas noches*, my dear. You are ravishing this evening."

"Thank you, *senhor*," she cooed.

Sofia knowingly smiled. She worked the room like an experienced hostess. Sofia approached El Toro and said, "I know you are anxious to depart, so with your permission I will notify the kitchen to serve dinner."

"You are very kind, *senhora*. An early departure is appreciated."

She excused herself and left the room. After advising the staff to prepare to serve, she discreetly exited the kitchen through the rear outside door. She entered the garage and quickly jumped on an electric golf cart used for quick movement around the grounds. She covered the distance to the front gate swiftly, and upon arrival she aroused the guard, who was sitting in his chair in the guard house. The rum she had given him earlier was taking effect.

She said, "Pablo, it is I, the *senhora*."

He quickly jumped to his feet. "Ah, *Senhora* Sofia, I just finished checking the wall and was resting."

"Don't worry, Pablo, I'm not checking on you. Everyone is celebrating. You should too. Take the cart and go to the kitchen. Cook will give you what you want to eat. Bring it back and enjoy. I will wait and watch the gate until you return."

"*Gracias, senhora,* you are very kind." He hopped in the cart and was gone.

She waited until she could no longer hear the drone of the cart. She then activated the electric button to open the gate. Lieutenant Gomez and his contingent of agents were discreetly hiding outside of the wall. As soon as the gate opened and they saw the signal from Sofia, they poured in through the open gate. They melted into the darkness, camouflaged by the official-issue black night-battle gear.

Gomez said, "Okay, Sofia, we will hunker down behind the house and wait for your signal to enter through the kitchen. Please be cautious."

"I will, Lieutenant, and I'll try to have the guards as docile as possible."

"We'll be waiting," Gomez said.

She waited until Pablo returned and then quickly returned to the house. When she entered the kitchen, she advised the butler to announce that dinner will be served and for the guests to please be seated.

She entered the ballroom minutes before the butler made his announcement. It was not a moment too soon, the men were getting restless. The entourage entered the dining hall and Sofia skillfully but discreetly assigned the seating. Of course, the *senhor* was at the head of the table, with El Toro in the seat of honor to his right. Next to him was Calida, with Sofia directly across the table from El Toro. She spaced El Toro's entourage as far from each other as possible and as close to the wine as possible. She instructed the maids to keep the men's glasses full at all times.

It was an elegant dinner and proceeded without a hitch. El Toro was ogling and casting sheep's eyes at Calida during the whole meal. It bordered on being sickening. Calida was uncomfortable but hid it well and tried to be as coy as well as she could muster.

After the dessert of cherries jubilee, Sofia asked if El Toro would like to congratulate the kitchen staff on a job well done. He agreed, somewhat reluctantly. He wanted no distractions from his clumsy attempts to impress Calida.

Sofia left the room to fetch the staff from the kitchen. They soon appeared and lined up at the head of the table where the *senhor* stood and did the honors of congratulating them. His ego demanded that he always be in the forefront, so a drawn-out congratulatory address was in order, just as Sofia anticipated.

While attention was elsewhere, she discreetly slipped out of the room and dashed to the now empty kitchen. She quickly opened the rear outside door and signaled the awaiting force. They quietly filed in with Gomez in the lead. Sofia had previously supplied Gomez with the floor plan, so all the federal agents knew exactly where they were strategically stationed. She slipped back into the dining hall just as El Toro announced that the evening was now over. He stood and instructed his men to make ready for the departure.

That was the signal for Calida and Sofia to take cover and try to exit the room. Sofia gave Calida the high sign. Calida discreetly moved away from El Toro. He took notice and grabbed her arm.

"Where are you going? I like you close by," he said, agitated.

She looked at Sofia, panic stricken. Sofia approached the couple and said, "All right, young lady, I told you that it was time. Now let's go to your room and collect all your belongings." She pulled Calida's arm away from El Toro and said, "Please, *senhor*, let us get her ready to travel."

He reluctantly released her and said, "Don't screw with me, *senhora*. I have already been here too long."

Calida implored, "Please, *senhor*, I just—"

The doors all flew open and three percussion grenades exploded, sending a blinding flash through the room. Federal agents dressed in black and wielding automatic weapons poured into the room.

Gomez yelled, "FEDERAL AGENTS, SHOW ME YOUR HANDS."

Gunfire erupted. Both El Toro's men and the *senhor*'s local guards got off a few rounds but were quickly cut down with automatic fire. El Toro skillfully hit the deck and rolled under the table. He brandished a weapon and fired a fusillade of shots toward Gomez, who ducked but not quickly enough. He was hit and fell back against the wall and then down on his knees. Two rounds hit him square in the chest. The impact taken up by his flak jacket. Not fatal, but the velocity knocked the wind out of him. He struggled momentarily. In his hazy vision, he saw El Toro taking a firing position and aim toward the women. Gomez, in his stupor, was slow to react.

El Toro squeezed off two more rounds, aiming at Sofia and at the same time yelling, "You bitch!"

Gomez fought the dizziness and fired an instant later. He was able to put a round between a surprised El Toro's eyes.

El Toro, wide-eyed, turned toward the man he thought he had just killed. His last breath escaped his lips as he slumped to die on the costly Persian rug that graced the opulent dining room.

Gomez ran to Calida, who was kneeling over the prone body of a profusely bleeding Sofia.

"Sofia, Sofia, speak to me," begged the crying young girl.

Sofia was bleeding badly from a double chest wound. Both rounds had hit home. Sofia was still barely conscious and failing fast. Gomez grabbed a napkin from the table and applied pressure to the gurgling, gaping hole in her chest to try to stem the flow of blood. It was a futile effort. These were fatal wounds and he knew it.

Sofia looked at Calida with dimming eyes and struggled to say, "Run, child, run away from this place." She gurgled and took her dying breath. Her sightless eyes looked at the ceiling.

Gomez lowered her head to the floor and closed her eyes. He said, "I'm sorry, Calida."

One of the agents approached Gomez. "We've got them secured, sir. Should I call headquarters and report?"

"Yes, and have the medical teams that were standing by come in and take care of the wounded. Do we have casualties?"

"Three men with wounds, sir, two minor and one might need some blood."

"Okay, how about them?"

"Four dead, counting El Toro, two with bad wounds and two more with minor ones."

"What about the *senhor*?"

"He's okay. We found him cowering behind a table in the corner."

"He's going away for a long time. Where's the girl?"

"She was here a minute ago, sir. I don't know."

Gomez then got busy with the badly wounded man, directing the medical teams that arrived and taking charge in general. Calida scurried off up the stairs undetected after she saw that Sofia had died. She wanted to get away as far as she could. She went to her room, changed clothes, and collected her rucksack and her pouch of herbs. She stole into the bathroom where she had prepared the window for an escape. She would now put her plan into action.

I don't know what anyone has planned for me, but I think I'll take my chances on getting away from here. I'll make it back to town. I've had enough of this kind of life to know that I'd rather be in the jungle.

She climbed up on the sink to the small window. She pushed on the window but it was stuck. Frustration built up and she banged at the window, trying to break it. Being quiet was no longer a factor. She was unsuccessful because wire mesh was embedded in the glass, making it shatterproof, although banging on the window seemed to loosen it to where she could now raise it. She reached through and bent the wire guard away so she now had an opening large enough to wriggle through.

First she pushed her bags through and they hit the ground below. Next she climbed through headfirst and pulled herself through all the way. She was on a narrow ledge and could shuffle to a down spout, where she could shinny down to the ground. When she hit the ground, she grabbed her two bags and broke into a trot toward the front gate. When she got within sight of the gate, she caught a glimpse of the guard. But wait, that's an agent. She could tell by his black uniform. He must have replaced the guard.

He'll probably stop me from leaving. Hmm, maybe I can trick him.

She hid her bags in the brush and very openly walked down the driveway, humming a song to herself.

The guard came out of the shack and said, "Halt, who are you?"

"It's me, Calida. Lieutenant Gomez sent me to tell you to report to the house for other orders. There's been a change in plan. Another agent is coming but he wants me to stay until he shows up."

"That doesn't sound right to me," he said.

"Well, okay, I'll go back and tell him, but he's awful busy. I hope he doesn't get mad. It's not my fault." She turned and started back toward the house.

"Wait a minute. Get back here. Are you sure he wants me?"

"Now why would I lie?"

"Okay, okay, but I'm going on the double." He left, running up the driveway.

When he was out of sight, she grabbed her bags, opened the gate, and quickly ran down the road.

Chapter Twenty-Six

The night was almost as bright as day, with a 95 percent moon shining at its apex. The cloudless sky added to the brightness by allowing the full complement of stars out in addition to the bright moon.

The road leading to town was lightly traveled. She walked along the side of the road. Several cars and a pickup truck zoomed by. She ducked into the brush as one car screeched to a halt down the road after passing her. The car made a U-turn and slowly came back. It reached the spot where, hiding off the road, she was well concealed in the brush.

She could hear several young voices calling her and laughing. She stayed very still, and soon they tired of their little game and made another U-turn, burning rubber and sped off. She trudged on, staying a little further off the road.

She had been walking for several hours when a military-type vehicle approached and slowed to a halt. She quickly dove into the brush again. She ventured a glance back and saw a man exit the vehicle from the passenger side. He walked around the vehicle and stood within a stone's throw of where she was hiding.

He called, "Calida. Calida. It's me, Gomez." He waited. She did not respond. "Come on, Calida. I know you're there. I saw you. Please come out. I want to help you."

She answered, "I don't want your help."

"I can assist you in finding your father if you'll let me. We are grateful for your help in breaking up the white slavery ring and ridding our country of a notorious drug lord."

"I don't want to go back to that house."

"You don't have to. We will take you into town and find some safe lodging for you. If you got in the wrong area it could be dangerous."

There was a delay in conversation.

Calida stood and said, "I think I can trust you. There is a priest in the city that I talked to before. Can you take me to him?"

"We will try to find him. I have several contacts that I can use. Get into the truck and we will go into town and find some decent lodging. I promise that tomorrow we will try to help you."

She walked toward them and got in the truck.

He asked, "Do you have reais?"

"Yes," she responded. "I have some reais in my rucksack. I earned it on the *chalana* coming to Guajará."

"Very well, I know a nice, quiet hotel where you can spend the night. It has a small restaurant where you can have breakfast. I will meet you there in the morning."

"Thank you, Lieutenant."

***

It was, as Gomez had said, a respectable, quiet hotel with a small homey place to have breakfast. She ate a light breakfast and awaited Lieutenant Gomez. He entered, dressed in civilian clothes.

"*Buenos dias, senhorita*. It is more comfortable traveling as a civilian. Some people get intimidated by a policeman's uniform. I did some checking, and from what you've told me, I believe the priest you talked to was Father Tom McCann. He has been released from the hospital. His assigned parish is the cathedral downtown, where he has established a home for abandoned children. He probably was a good choice to start with. I've made an appointment to see him this morning."

"I'm ready," she answered.

"Relax for a few minutes," he said with a chuckle.

She sat back and heaved a sigh. "I'm sorry, but I've been seeking my birth father for so long. This is the closest I've been to a clue of who he might be."

"Can you tell me a little more about yourself and where exactly you came from?"

Calida explained her story of her village and all the subsequent travels for the past five or six years. He was amazed that this young woman had survived all that she had, seemed to be in excellent health, and very determined to continue with her quest.

"Let's walk to the cathedral. It's only a few blocks away and it's a beautiful morning."

They left the restaurant and soon reached the parish offices, where they asked to see Father McCann. After a short wait, they were shown to his office.

Father McCann greeted them as they entered *"Buenos dias*, Lieutenant. And I'm happy to see you again, young lady. I understand that you've had a very trying experience."

"Yes, but that's over now and I'd like to resume my search."

"Of course, I can certainly understand that. I gave some thought to what you told me while I was in the hospital and did a preliminary check. When you didn't return, I stopped my research."

"I'd appreciate anything you can give me, Father."

"I have several ideas but one in particular stands out."

"Can you tell me what you have found?"

"Not at this time, child. We are very restricted on giving information on missionaries and where they are stationed. It is for the protection and privacy of both mission people and the lost tribe they are living with. Also, you must understand that this inquiry is a very sensitive one. Proving paternity can be devastating, and could cause untold problems in a marriage."

"But how can I know without information?"

"First, I must contact the mission headquarters and tell them about you and your quest. They may want to meet you and interview you for further information. Then, they must agree to contact the mission and pass on your request. The missionaries then must agree to further inquiry from headquarters or directly from you. Both the mission headquarters or the mission people can deny further investigation if they so choose."

"When can I find out?"

"I'm afraid it will be a lengthy process. There is no communication with this aboriginal tribe. The only way to send or receive a message is by *chalana*. This only happens every six to nine months, when supplies are delivered. It's conceivable you could wait several years before finding out anything concrete, or if headquarters chooses to deny your request, you may never find out."

She was devastated.

"Don't despair, young lady. Let me talk to the director at the mission that I have in mind. Can you come back in a few days?"

"Yes, Father, I can do that. Thank you for your help."

***

Several days later, Calida took the short walk to the parish office to talk further with Father McCann. She entered his office and he greeted her.

"*Buenos dias*, Father. I got the message that you had information for me."

"Yes, I do. In my conversation with the director he agreed to make a preliminary inquiry on this matter. I gave him the basics and he is very doubtful that the mission couple with the Yano-Matis would be the ones that you seek. However, he is willing to hear you out. And if he can be of help in directing you elsewhere, he will do so."

"When can I see him?"

"I have made an appointment for tomorrow. Can you come here first thing in the morning? I will take you there and introduce you to him."

"Yes, I'll be here bright and early."

***

That next morning, Calida and Father McCann traveled by car to the headquarters of the Mission Society of the Universe. They asked to see Director John Nash and were ushered into his office. He stood when they entered.

"*Buenos dias*, Father McCann. It's always a pleasure. Is this the young lady with the monumental task that we discussed?"

"*Buenos dias*, John. Yes, may I present Calida, who has been trying to locate her father for quite a long time now."

127

John Nash grasped Calida's hand in a firm handshake and said, "The good father has told me of your travels to try to locate the man you feel is your biological father."

"Yes, sir, that is right."

"Tell me, young lady, do you have a certain amount of reliability to accuse a missionary of this?"

"Oh, *Senhor* Nash, I'm not looking to make trouble for this man. It's just that he would be my only living relative. My mother was killed in an earthquake and I have no siblings."

"And if you found him, how would you prove such a thing?"

"I have no way to prove it except to tell him the circumstances under which my mother conceived me."

"Would you tell me exactly what these circumstances were?"

Calida repeated what was told to her by Nardania and confirmed by her mother.

"Hmmm. That's a story that has an awful lot of conjecture."

"I don't understand," asked Calida.

"That means forming an opinion without sufficient evidence."

"I don't know what evidence I could come up with other than asking if the mission couple was kidnapped by an Amazon tribe for the sole purpose of creating offspring. And if the Yano-Matis warriors battled the Amazon tribe. If before the Indian tribe rescued the couple there was a circumstance that would have put the doctor in the position to copulate with my mother."

"How did you know that he's a doctor?"

"My mother's aide, Nardania, told me that I inherited my healing skills from my father who was a medical doctor."

"These healing skills, where did you learn them? Did you attend a school?"

"No, I have no formal education. My skills just came to me as I grew older. I also learned about herbs and roots from the shaman in our tribe."

"I have reservations, but what you are telling me might have some merit. I am very close with a couple, a doctor and his wife, who may have had a similar circumstance years ago. How old are you, young lady?"

"I'm not exactly sure, but I think I have had nineteen or twenty cycles of the seasons."

"Hmm. That could fit time wise. But it doesn't fit with the people involved. I'm going to have to study on this."

"Director Nash, I can see where this might be farfetched for you to comprehend and maybe I'll never find my father, but I must try."

"Give me a few days. There is a man here in the city that has been close to the couple in question. I'd like to confer with him and get an opinion."

"When can I see you again, Director?"

"I will be in touch. Can I reach you through Father McCann?"

"Yes," she answered.

She and the priest left the building.

When in the car, Father McCann asked, "Whatever way this plays out is going to be very lengthy. Have you enough reais to last a while?"

"My hotel room will take up more than I can afford for any length of time. I will need some work and a more reasonably priced place to stay."

"Let me ask you about your healing skills. Would you be interested in working in the infirmary at our children's home if they proved suitable?"

"That would be wonderful, Father. How would I do this?"

"I will take you to Mother Superior. She runs the home and she will interview you. It's possible that since you have no lodging and we can't afford to pay a high salary, some arrangement on room and board could be worked out. We have done this before."

"You have been a great help to me, Father."

"I'll do what I can but Mother Superior will decide whether or not you can work with the children. She is very protective of them, and rightly so."

Chapter Twenty-Seven

The next day the director welcomed Quito into his office. Quito was a mature older gentleman that was no stranger to mission headquarters. He was the owner of a small shipping company that operated a fleet of *chalanas*. He founded the company over thirty years ago with one boat. He was owner and captain. The company had grown to over a dozen boats. Quito's son, Quito Jr., runs the everyday operation of the company with Quito, the founder, overseeing the administration and taking care of public relations. His client contacts were priceless.

"*Buenos dias*, Director Nash, it is always a pleasure visiting you here at the mission."

"*Buenos dias*, Quito. I see you are exuberant as ever. How is your health?"

"It couldn't be better, my friend. Business is great and Quito Jr. is taking more responsibility every day. Life is good."

"I'm happy for you, Quito. Now, I'd like to discuss a very sensitive situation with you, and I must ask that you keep our discussion today strictly confidential."

"Of course, John, you can trust me. Our conversation will not leave this room."

"I was pretty sure of that. It involves one of our missionaries who is an old mutual friend of both of us, as well as someone else who became very close to you."

"I'm intrigued. Please go on, John."

"It involves the mission at the Yano-Matis tribe village in the Amazon basin."

Quito perked up. "You mean Dr. André and Mrs. Caroline Clark. *Mia Dios*, I hope they are all right."

"It doesn't involve their health. As far as I know they are fine and still doing a wonderful job with the tribe they've lived with for the last several decades."

"Then what is it?"

"Do you remember an incident about twenty years ago when Caroline Clark was kidnapped by a tribe of women reputed to be Amazons who had been living in that area for centuries?"

"Yes, of course I do. The doctor and men from the tribe rescued her. I believe there was a terrible battle and the Amazons were pretty well defeated. I don't know the details but I guess both she and the doctor came out unscathed and went back to the village to continue the mission. I never did hear what happened to the Amazons. Was it really a tribe of huge women like the legends say?" Quito asked.

"Oh yes, and every legend you've heard about them is pretty accurate. Dr. Clark delved into their history and found that they in fact were a tribe of warriors who could outfight most men. There were several tribes spanning centuries and on several continents, but this one was the last surviving one here in the Amazon basin," Nash said.

"Wow! Are they still out there? How can they continue if they have no men? Do they really kidnap some men, use them, and then kill them? That seems pretty ruthless, if you ask me," Quito said.

"Yes, Quito, it is and that's kind of why I asked you to stop by."

"Now I'm really intrigued. Please go on."

"I'll give you a little more detail on the kidnapping of Caroline twenty years ago," Nash continued.

"Please do, I know I didn't get it all at the time," Quito said.

"Not realizing how close they were to the Amazons, the doctor and a few Yano-Matis men camped outside of the village. During the night, two of the women warriors stole into the camp and slaughtered the guard. They placed a pad of some sort of drug over the doctor's nose and mouth that knocked him out immediately. They then carried him back to their village without waking the others."

"So both Doctor Clark and the *Senhora* Clark were prisoners?"

"Yes, Quito, quite true. Later the couple found out that the plan was to integrate them into the tribe, using them to propagate and strengthen the birth line, which had deteriorated for several generations. They needed new blood, and the Clarks were prime candidates because of their size, lineage, intelligence, etc. Caroline Clark would have children and the doctor would act as a breeder to her and to other Amazon women."

"That's almost unbelievable," said an amazed Quito.

"Well, as it turned out, the Clarks were rescued and returned to the campsite. A fierce battle then ensued, and with reinforcements from the tribe, the Yano-Matis prevailed. The Amazons pulled back into their village in the foothills."

"So why are you telling me this, John? Are the Amazons rising again and creating a problem? Do you need my boats for some supplies? Tell me why I'm here," Quito asked.

"That's only part of the story. You'll understand when I finish. In the last few days, I have been paid a visit by a young lady. She's about twenty or twenty-one years old. She is a very attractive blonde with an olive complexion. She stands slightly over six feet tall and is very capable of physically defending herself. She was brought here by *chalana* and referred to Father McCann, who brought her to me. She claims to be of Amazon lineage, and was born in the village we just discussed. She said that when she was in her early teens an earthquake destroyed her village and killed her mother, along with every other person in the village. She escaped with the shaman, the only other survivor, because they were in the rain forest gathering herbs. The two lived in the forest for a time after that and then the shaman was killed. The girl decided that her only alternative was to find her birth father, her only living relative," Nash continued.

"She knew him?" Quito asked.

"She has never met him, and in fact does not even know his name. She only knew what she was told as a child by her mother and another warrior that was teaching her Amazon skills. She was told that her father was a tall Caucasian doctor who was a missionary with a lost tribe, probably the Yano-Matis."

"*Mia Dios!* I think I know why I'm here. Are we talking about Doctor Clark?"

"Yes, Quito, and I'm in a quandary. What do we do now?"

"I don't know, John. Are there any facts to prove her claim?"

"Only her verbal recollection of what she was told," John answered.

"He is such a good and moral man, I guess the doctor should have a say-so in this. What's your opinion, John?"

"Absolutely, he should tell us his side. He is not the only Caucasian doctor in the Amazon. But I will say this, the girl is very convincing."

"Where is she now?"

"Father McCann has sent her to the mother superior at his orphanage to work with the children. I understand that she is very nurturing and has an understanding of medicine, although no formal training. She has a natural ability that transcends what is learned in medical school."

"You didn't send for me just to tell me this story, John. What do you have in mind?"

John chuckled. "I can't pull the wool over your eyes, can I, old friend? Yes, you are correct. All this is very sensitive. A matter such as this could ruin many lives if misconstrued or used to create gossip and scandal. It must be handled with kid gloves and by a minimum of involvement by others. Would there be a possibility that you could visit the Yano-Matis village and talk to Doctor Clark?"

"Hmm. As you know my *chalanas* travel to the village every six to nine months with supplies. Quito Jr. has made many of the runs but he has slacked off due to family obligations. I have not made a boat run for years. The next supply run is probably due within the next thirty to sixty days. We have just hired a very capable young man who has recently received certification to run the rivercraft as a captain. He is experienced but not on this particular run, and as you know it is a very remote village and takes extra care to reach. I could go but only as the navigator. My days as a working captain are long gone. I could not last other than as a passenger with knowledge of the river route. I will require as much information as I can get. May I interview the girl?"

"Yes, in fact I was going to suggest it. It will give you a better insight to the situation."

"I also want to talk to Father McCann. He can give me some words of wisdom on how to approach such a matter with the doctor. I have known them since they first came to Guajará. I was captain of the boat when we found the remote village. The Yano-Matis people had only seen a few white men in a thousand years. They only knew of them in the stories as told by the ancients. Wow, this is not going to be easy."

"Not easy for me either, Quito, I'm the one who must take the outcome to the board if it in fact comes to that. That is why, my friend, I have picked you to be my emissary and to bring back to me the most accurate information that you can."

"You can count on me, John."

"I know, Quito, I know, but I have an uneasy feeling about this."

***

It was several months later when a *chalana* left Guajará heading upriver with a cargo of supplies bound for the remote Indian village of the lost tribe of Yano-Matis. The *chalana* had its usual crew of a captain and two seamen. Also on this trip was the owner of the company. Quito was a passenger but would act as navigator when they reached the hinterlands and traversed the less-traveled tributaries and lakes. The captain was newly commissioned, and although extremely experienced in river travel, this was his first in command of a ship and his first traveling to the remote region of the Yano-Matis tribe.

The first day on the river was one of getting everyone acquainted with their duties and settling in with the new captain. The captain, Ricardo Estaban, was on the wheel during a very calm part of the cruise. The two seamen were going about their duties as assigned when Quito felt that it was a good time to set up a rapport with the new skipper.

"*Buenos dias*, Skipper."

"*Buenos dias*, sir."

"Please call me Quito and I want you to forget that I own the company. I am a passenger who will help in the navigation when needed. This is your command, and you are as responsible for this ship and its cargo the same as if I were not aboard. My son and I checked into your background thoroughly and found it to be excellent. Do we have an understanding?"

"Yes, Quito, we do and I will not disappoint you."

"Very well then, let me ask you, how is my good friend Captain Hernandez?"

"He was well the last that I saw him. Do you know him well?"

"Oh yes, Ricardo, he is one of the reasons we hired you. He gave you glowing recommendations."

"Yes, I served with him for several years. We had some real adventures at times."

"I heard about the hassle with the pirates and the loss of a crewmember, but got no details."

"That was something. It was a good thing that Calida was aboard or we may not have survived."

Quito stood slack jawed with bulging eyes. He finally blurted out, "Did you say Calida? Tell me about her."

"She is a wonderful young girl that came aboard as a working passenger. She has been on a quest to find her father after her mother, who was leader of a tribe of Amazons, was killed. I had lost track of her, but I found her again. She is now working at an orphanage. She's still searching and I'm hoping to help her when I earn enough money."

"You know this girl well?"

"Yes, Quito. I hope to see more of her after she completes her quest."

"Ricardo, you and I are going to have a very interesting cruise together," Quito exclaimed.

Chapter Twenty-Eight

The voyage up the Amazon River was typical, long, and uneventful. The difference on this one was the connection between Ricardo, the new captain; and Quito, the owner of the shipping company. Ricardo was able to give Quito the human side of the girl who claimed to be of Amazon decent.

"You must admit, Ricardo, the description of this girl's journey and from where she came is pretty hard to comprehend. Those facts alone without the claim she is making as to the man that sired her make for an unbelievable saga of events."

"Yes, that is so, but just being with her constantly for several months convinced me that she is as genuine as anyone could possibly be. She has a knack for intuitive perception without being a know-it-all."

"Is her knowledge of healing as prevalent as I've heard?"

"I don't know the depths of her medical experience but I saw her in action, and if I were hurt or sick I would trust her diagnosis or her treatment without hesitation," Ricardo said.

"Where did she learn this?" asked Quito.

"A shaman from her village taught her about the herbs, roots, and other medicinal substances that are found in the wild. She also taught her the proper use of them. Calida said she just seems to know what to do and learns from each experience. She's a natural," Ricardo answered.

"Hmm, that's very interesting. Is she as adept with a bow and arrow as they say?"

"She's better with it than anyone I've ever seen. That's not all either. An old Indian taught her how to use a blow pipe and how to make darts that can incapacitate an animal, or for that matter, a man."

"Yes, now I have a better understanding of how she survived all those years in the jungle," said Quito.

"She is very nurturing but can also protect herself in almost any situation."

***

When they entered the Purus River, Quito told Ricardo that if they took out the curves in the Purus it would be the longest river in the Amazon basin. He wasn't far from wrong.

After several weeks on this curvy giant, Quito instructed the crew to be observant for a landing at a certain *fazenda*. They could stop here, where Quito was very friendly with the owners. As well, this was close to the entrance of the tributary that would take them on the next leg of their cruise.

Sure enough a ramshackle dock was spotted and they made a landing. Tying up was a problem, but enough dock was available to make the boat fast. Quito assigned one of the crew to hike to the farm house and tell the owners that his boat was here with a few supplies for them.

Hours later, the seaman showed up riding in a wagon being pulled by an old nag of a horse, with a young farmhand at the reins.

"*Buenos dias*," said Quito, "I was hoping your *patron* would come with you. Is my friend Valasquez in good health?"

The surly young man answered, "*Senhor* and *Senhora* Valasquez are no longer at this *fazenda*."

"I was not aware. Who owns it now?"

"A very large corporation. No more cattle. They are timber people."

"*Caramba!* That is not good news," answered Quito.

"Not for us either," the farmhand said. "Can you stop on your return trip and take a few passengers? My brother and I want to leave this place. We can pay."

"Of course we can take you. I will return in three or four weeks, be ready. We will stay tonight and leave at first light."

"I will tell the foreman. He said I was to give you these reais for the supplies."

The farmhand turned the wagon and slowly ambled up the dusty path and out of sight in the gathering dusk.

The next day they left the dock and entered the narrow tributary that would take them on the more difficult part of their journey. As they got farther into this stream, more and more wildlife was prevalent. Crocodile and caiman basking on the riverbank were common. Since the water was shallow, several anacondas were spotted with just their nostrils above the surface. This is the world's largest species of snake. The part underwater could be twenty feet long. It is very nerve-wracking when these nostrils follow a boat for hours, waiting for the opportunity to squeeze a prey to death.

Unseen underwater were the dangerous piranha, but you know they are there. A school of these devils can strip the flesh off of a deer in minutes. And even more dangerous are the freshwater stingray. It typically lies in a sandy bed, half hidden and almost invisible with its mottled camouflage. A man walking unaware can stumble across one. The ray's tail flicks up with a poisoned barb and strikes human flesh. It will cause acute pain, delirium, and oftentimes death.

These are some of the dangers in the water, but even more are prevalent on shore. Because of the many rapids, shoal in the water, blind curves in this small river, it is necessary to anchor or tie up overnight. This makes predatory animals also a danger and necessitates a watch. The crew and captain take four hour shifts overnight.

Aside from the obvious danger from a jaguar, more numerous are the white-lipped *queixadas*. This animal defies description. It is similar to an ugly wild boar but even more deadly. Strong and squat, herds up to 400 can attack anything and anyone. They have scissorslike canines that can slice any flesh. They will sever the Achilles tendon of men, horses, and even jaguar.

The only side benefit of abundant wildlife is the opportunity to hunt for fresh meat. The peccary, a wild pig, tapir, and deer are easily killed for food. There are also 110 species of rodents, from the three-foot capybara, which is a staple to many Indian tribes, to the small ones on the forest floor. There are seventy-five species of monkeys and some are hunted and killed for food with a blow gun by many tribes. An Indian hunter prides his accuracy with a blow gun and claims to be able to hit a flying humming bird at twenty paces. Poison from the dart can kill or paralyze instantly.

The small river became a narrow stream and ended in a shallow lake. The shallow draft *chalana* was built for this type of travel. Quito remembered this part of his first journey here when he could not find the outlet stream on the other side of the lake and almost turned around and called off the search for the village of the lost tribe. He now had a chart that showed the location of the outlet stream and they soon were in it. Now they must look for one more tributary to the location of the new village.

As typical with many tribes, villages are moved depending on flooding, or sometimes the opposite, a receding stream caused by interference by timber harvesting or sometimes mining. This has been a real problem in the past. Large corporations devastate the rain forest with no regard for the aboriginal tribes that have been here for centuries. An example was the demand for natural rubber in the late 1800s. In the 1860s, approximately 3,000 tons of rubber was being exported annually out of Iquitos, Peru. By 1911, the annual exports had grown to 44,000 tons.

With the influx of foreign workers that brought white men's diseases, approximately 40,000 native Amazonians died. This was only a fraction of what devastation was brought about by indiscriminate mining and deforestation. Many tribes were wiped out by marauding soldiers and even more were devastated by diseases, such as the flu, measles, small pox, and many more that the Indians had no immunity for. It is estimated that 15 million Indians in the fifteenth century now number about 350,000 to 400,000. The federal governments of Brazil, Peru, and Bolivia now have assigned protected areas in the rain forest for Indian tribes. Even so, some abuse still prevails.

***

The *chalana* reached the point in the very shallow tributary where it could go no further. They were now very close to the village.

Quito said, "Launch the skiff. It's either walk to the village or go by skiff with an outboard motor. My choice is the skiff."

After the skiff was in the water and the medical supplies loaded in with Quito and Ricardo, Quito instructed, "While Ricardo and I go to the village, you two get the cargo ready to unload. Several canoes will show up with men to help unload and they will ferry it to the village. I'll need the both of you to stay here to guard the boat from both men and animals. We will relieve you in a few days."

They shoved off and carefully motored upstream to the village. As they rounded the bend, they saw and heard the villagers standing on the riverbank, eagerly awaiting them.

Chapter Twenty-Nine

The skiff motored to the riverbank to the cheers and laughter of the Yano-Matis villagers. They knew that the arrival of the supply boat would bring provisions not seen for months. They crowded the shore and secured the skiff on the bank. Some of the old-timers recognized Quito, whom they hadn't seen for years. They laughed and jabbered as they patted him on the back.

Quito was overwhelmed by the reception he was getting. He tried to remember the dialect of this tribe, which was an unusual one, so he stumbled over the words.

"What's the matter, Quito? Did you forget how to talk?" came a response in English from a smiling tall white man who stood next to an equally tall white woman with a glowing smile.

Quito turned and quickly embraced the man, saying, "Dr. André, you don't know how happy I am to see you."

The doctor responded, "I'm happy to see you too, old friend."

Quito backed off from the doctor and turned to Caroline. "*Senhora*, you are still the beautiful woman that I brought to these people many years ago."

She laughingly melted into his arms. "Quito, I could always count on you to give me a lift. Thank you, my faithful *compadre*, and I am so happy that you are here."

The crowd suddenly quieted. From the center, they parted, creating a pathway from the long house to the reception area. Parading down that pathway was Xetana, the chief, in full regalia. He walked slowly and regally to officially welcome the men of the supply boat.

He stopped, faced Quito, and in a booming voice, gave the official greeting, welcoming Quito and his crew. Later Quito would meet with him in the long house in a much more casual setting and they would renew an old acquaintanceship. In front of his subjects, Xetana would be the stoic, formal chief.

After the greetings all around were completed, Quito arranged for a village work crew to canoe to the *chalana,* help unload the cargo, and transport it to the village. He then introduced Ricardo to the doctor and his wife, and explained, "Ricardo is partially why I am on this trip. Quito Jr. had other obligations and Ricardo was unfamiliar with this run, so I volunteered to show him the route."

"Welcome, Ricardo, we hope to see you on future trips here."

"Thank you, Dr. Clark. I plan to do just that."

Quito added, "André, I must do my duty and meet with Xetana in the long house. After that I will meet you in the clinic and deliver the drugs that you ordered."

"We'll both be there, Quito, and look forward to a long visit."

***

It was now later in the day. Ricardo motored back to the *chalana* to supervise the unloading of the cargo and to spend the night on the boat. Quito finished the obligatory meeting with Xetana and now walked to the clinic where André and Caroline awaited him.

"Please come and sit with us, Quito. Caroline has poured some cold drinks for us. We've got a lot of catching up to do."

"It's been a long time and I now have grandchildren. I must tell you about Quito Jr. He now has three boys. In fact, he is very busy with them, and that is why he couldn't make this run."

"Did you bring pictures?" asked Caroline hopefully.

"My wife would not have allowed me to leave without them," he answered.

The next several hours were spent with three old friends reminiscing about the old days when they all were much younger.

"Well, Quito, would you like to rest before the big celebration tonight?" asked André.

"*Mio Dios*, I forgot this always happens when the supplies arrive. Yes, please, and maybe tomorrow André and I can have some time to go over the drugs that I brought. Some are new and need an explanation. I'm sure this would not interest Caroline. Also, she has her own list of supplies that she and I will go over when the men arrive with them."

"We can do that the first thing in the morning before I see my patients. Now, it will be a long night, so we all should rest a bit. I saw some of the men gathering wood for a huge fire, and I know there will be plenty of that fermented drink that they are so proud of."

***

It was indeed a huge celebration that the whole village took part in. There was plenty of food and even more plentiful were the drinks. Quito was nursing a bad headache when he and André met for breakfast.

"You're moving a little slow, Quito, maybe a strong cup of *cafezinho* will help ease the pain," offered the doctor.

"Yes, please, I had forgotten how strong that drink is. A *cafezinho* will hit the spot."

"Let's go over the drugs that you brought. I'm really short on penicillin and other antibiotics."

"I have that and also these other new ones that I cannot pronounce. These are the specifications on them. I'm sure you can better understand them than I can."

André took the sheets and read them thoroughly. Quito waited patiently while he studied the sheets.

"Yes I'm somewhat familiar with these drugs. There were several articles in the last batch of medical reports that Quito Jr. brought me."

"Good, because I'm sure that I couldn't explain them."

"Okay, Quito, now maybe you'll tell me why you really wanted to meet with me alone. I knew the drug explanation wasn't ringing true."

"Yes, you're right. I never could hide things well."

"Is it bad news?"

"It is very troubling, my friend, and not easily done."

"Please, it is just you and I. We've known each other too long to be troubled by this. What is it?"

"John Nash asked me to be his emissary on this since I've known you ever since you arrived in Brazil. I would like to start by asking some questions and creating some history as a background."

"I'll answer as accurately as I can."

"Back about twenty years ago there was an altercation between the Yano-Matis and a tribe of reputed Amazon women. Do you remember this?" asked Quito.

"I remember it vividly, and I can verify that the tribe of Amazon women did in fact exist. Caroline had been kidnapped by them."

"Yes, and I understand that you also were captured in the process of trying to rescue her," Quito said.

"Yes, that is true."

"Could you describe what happened when you were captured?"

"Of course. While we were camped very close to the entrance to their village, two of their warriors drugged me and carried me off to the village. I was unconscious, so I don't remember much until I awoke trussed up in a hut. I was alone and very confused. I had some very disturbing dreams and confusing nightmares while I was under the drug. Strangely, there were times when I felt at peace and had a warm pleasant feeling." He went on, "Some of the Amazon warriors were guarding me, and I think the leader looked in on me. They finally allowed me to join Caroline, who was in a room close by. She was not hurt and they had treated her well. She had gotten the information that we were to be used to propagate and strengthen their birth line. It was a crazy notion, but to my knowledge it was not a new experiment with them. Men had been used in this respect for hundreds of years with this exclusive woman culture."

"Were they successful in progressing with this plan for you?" asked Quito.

"Do you mean did I have coitus with them? Hell no!" said Dr. Clark emphatically.

"I must ask, André. When were you rescued?" Quito softly asked.

"Xetana and Jonha were successful in breaching their defenses and miraculously saved us. We quietly stole out of the complex and were able to make it back to the camp. The Amazon warriors went on the attack and would have defeated us had not the rest of the Yano-Matis, led by Xeta, joined the fray. After a fierce battle we wore them down. The Amazon leader put up a fight like none I've ever seen, but she finally succumbed due to sheer numbers. The warriors that survived carried her off, a bloody, beaten mess. I think she still was alive but probably died in the village."

"Was that the last you saw of them?"

"Yes, we had no contact after that. There were a few reports that some of the warriors were seen in the foothills, and we heard of the capture of some men of other tribes, but not ours. We've heard nothing for years now."

"I can add to the saga. It has been reported that the leader did survive. And in fact she even delivered a child. It was a girl. There were many warriors lost in the battle, and the leader tried to instill a program to increase the population. They might have been successful after several generations but disaster stepped in. The volcano miles away from their village erupted and created a devastating earthquake. The entire village was wiped out except for two survivors. The shaman and a young girl were in the rain forest hunting for healing herbs, plants, and roots. They returned to find the devastation. The shaman was killed, which left this teenage girl to fend for herself."

"That poor child, how did you come about all this information, Quito?"

"That child not only survived but she grew into a strong, capable young woman who set a goal to find her father. She turned up in Guajará several months ago, seeking information," Quito said.

"I have an inkling that's part of why you are here, Quito."

"Yes, the girl is obviously Caucasian. She is an attractive, tall, blonde woman and has natural skills beyond what you would expect out of an uneducated woman who spent her life in the Amazon basin."

"Does she know who her father is?" André asked.

"She was told that her father is a tall white missionary doctor with the Yano-Matis tribe."

"QUITO, ARE YOU OUT OF YOUR MIND?"

"André, I was sent here by John Nash to find out what you know of this accusation."

Chapter Thirty

André was stunned. He looked at his old friend in disbelief. A different set of emotions then coursed through his body.

"That's ridiculous, Quito. How could John think that of me after all these years of devotion to my wife, as well as the countless sacrifices that we've both made dedicating our lives to the Yano-Matis and the betterment of this mission," Dr. Clark admonished.

"Please, André, don't think badly of John, or for that matter, of me. John was forced to investigate this matter. It is known that you are not the only Caucasian male in the Amazon basin. The woman has only hearsay to back her up but she has a possibly believable story. John had to hear your side," Quito said.

"Well, you got the basics. Are there any more questions?" asked Dr. Clark.

"Let me get it clear. The only time you were alone was when you were under some sort of sedation after you were captured at the campsite, is that correct?" Quito asked.

"Yes, when I awoke from the drug or drugs, I heard Caroline calling from the room where she was confined. Soon after that, they allowed me to join her."

"The two warriors that captured you put you under sedation by clamping a drug-soaked fur piece over your mouth and nose, much like you'd use ether or chloroform. You said drugs, do you think they used an additional one?"

"There was a time when I was kind of in a state of euphoria. I could hear talking but it was a strange sound, like an echo. I was very confused . . . yes . . . I believe someone gave me something to drink. I choked down a bad-tasting liquid. At first, I thought I was going to awake, but then I spiraled into a dark place."

"Did you awake after that?"

"Well, not fully. I remember now, I started to dream pleasant dreams where before I had nightmares. I tried to open my eyes when someone lifted my head and gave me another drink. I was thirsty, so I gulped this one down. It had a sweet taste, not bitter like the other."

"Did you go under again?" Quito asked.

"Not completely, kind of suspended in between. This was when I felt warm and secure. I dreamed I was with Caroline and we made love. Can you believe I had an erotic dream while I was confined?"

"André, do you understand what you just told me?"

André sat with a puzzled look on his face. He took a deep breath and blew it out through pursed lips. He said, "Oh my god, Quito, do you think . . . could it be possible?"

"There are many drugs now being used by civilized man that have been known to the shamans of these tribes for hundreds of years. Given the history of how the Amazon women used the men that they imprisoned certainly adds credence to your experience."

"Quito, What if I'm . . . ?"

"I'd say there is an outside chance."

"What should I do? How do I explain to Caroline? Quito, I've never cheated on my wife."

"We can't be sure, André, until tests are performed. I'm not sure how we should approach this. Why don't we step back and give this more thought?"

Suddenly the two engrossed men were startled by a bubbly entrance. Caroline bounced lightly through the door. "Oh my," she said, "you two are in some serious discussions. You didn't even hear me come up the path."

Both men were speechless.

Caroline stopped short and said, "This really is serious, isn't it? Maybe I should come back later."

André stood, approached her, and facing her, he took her hands in his and said, "No, dear, please stay. Perhaps we should bring you into this. It certainly involves you and you should give some input."

"Please sit, Caroline, I'd like to start from the beginning," Quito said.

Quito spent the next hour giving Caroline the complete history before he ended by saying, "Given all that I've learned from John Nash, Calida, and now, digging into the far reaches of André's memory, there is enough to warrant further tests and investigation. My job was to come here and gather all the data possible and report back to John."

Caroline sat through the explanation without comment. It wasn't until the end that she sat up straight and said, "You said that I was involved in this and that I should give some input. Do you want it?"

"Yes, of course," said both men together.

"When our captors allowed André to join me in the room where I was confined, I was overjoyed. We discussed our dilemma, not aware that a rescue was going to happen. If we were to be captives, we both knew what was expected of us in order to survive. We accepted this. We were more in love at that instant than ever. He told me in detail about the erotic dream that he had, and we laughed about it. I commented that I was happy it was me that he dreamed about. I'm not sure what all happened during his confinement, but I'm confident that he was true to me. If the young woman is a result of his confinement, then I feel the erotic dream that he had makes her as much my child as his. Let's find out if it is, in fact, true and then move on from there."

André took Caroline in his arms, looked her in the eye, and in a husky, emotional voice said, "Darling, you don't know how much I needed your strength at this moment, and you came through with all your heart. I love you more every day, Caroline." And he kissed her.

She drew back and smiled. "Well, I'd say it was worth it, Doctor."

Quito stood watching with a lump in his throat and teary eyes. He said, "Looking at you two makes me proud to be your friend."

"Thank you, Quito, but we still have a mystery on our hands, and the scientific way to proceed is for me and the young lady to have our DNA tested."

"I was going to ask if you would be willing, André."

"Of course. In fact, I would like to accompany you to Guajará. I feel that I should meet the young lady, and I also feel that I should visit John Nash. I'd like to know the position of the board on this matter."

Caroline spoke up next, "I too would like to go, if you have room for me, Quito. I'm as involved in this as anyone. If André's job is on the line, then so is mine as far as I'm concerned."

"We can make room for you, *senhora*. Can the mission get along with both of you gone?"

"They have survived for hundreds of years without us. I'm sure that four or five months won't matter."

"Okay," said Quito. "Let's plan on leaving in one week."

Chapter Thirty-One

The *chalana* got underway a week later, empty of cargo but full of passengers. Quito was joined by Dr. Clark and his wife Caroline. Accommodations were made for Caroline to give her as much privacy as possible. It was a small boat with five men aboard, including the three crewmembers. André and Caroline had made this trip several times over the years. They knew what to expect as far as living conditions.

The initial part of the cruise through the small stream and subsequent lake was filled with the usual too close sightings of hungry amphibious residents. When anchored for the night, there was a very nervous encounter with a curious young jaguar. As it turned out, the youngster was more frightened than the humans. He roared when he suddenly awakened five very loud men and especially a screaming woman. Then he turned tail and ran when the man on watch fired a penetratingly loud, ear-bursting round from a .12-gauge shotgun.

Since it was close to dawn, they decided to have breakfast and get an early start for the day. As they started moving they were surprised to see a convoy of five or six crocs slide into the river. The hungry crocs had set up quarters for the night right alongside the anchorage. Fortunately, no one had decided to take a walk during the night.

The rest of the trip on the Purus was uneventful, other than the many curves to contend with on this very crooked river. The confluence with the Amazon was a welcome sight.

Caroline was disappointed that a stop at the *fazenda* was no longer on the itinerary. On previous trips, it was a needed stop to rest and relax before the long run down the Amazon. She had become close friends with the *senhora* whose husband owned the cattle ranch. She would miss the visit with her.

It was long and boring to be confined to this small craft when the end of the trip in Guajará was fraught with unanswered questions. Both Caroline and André spent some sleepless nights thinking of what awaited them in the city.

On one quiet, moonless night, André sat on the lazarette on the fantail, smoking his pipe and turning his thoughts over in his mind. With the constant drone of the boat engine and his gaze directed into the darkness, he didn't hear the approach of his barefoot wife.

She slipped up behind him and whispered, "Hi, sailor, ya wanna talk?"

He turned with a broad smile and said, "Sure thing, lady," and he hugged her lovingly and firmly.

They sat together, both now wide awake, and talked for hours on the sudden turn their lives had taken. What awaited them in Guajará? Would this young lady be receptive? Was she, in fact, the child of Dr. André Clark? If so, what did she expect of them? And then, there was the attitude of mission headquarters. What action would they take if the child proved to be his? Would they dismiss them after the many years of hard but successful labor in the Yano-Matis village? Their whole lives could change with this one unforeseen event. The one unshakeable decision for both was that no matter what happened they would face it together. Their love would remain as it always has, whether the future continued as before or what other direction it may take.

They reached Guajará very late in the day and tied up at the shipping company's dock with the other company boats. Since it was late, André and Caroline decided to stay on the boat for the night with the crew. Quito left for his home, which was close by. It was another restless night for the married couple, but both finally fell asleep.

Dawn came quickly, bright, hot, and dripping with humidity. All aboard awoke at about the same time. Caroline had galley duty, so she put on the coffee and dug out the few scraps of cheese and flat bread left in the cupboard. Provisions were scarce after a long trip.

They packed their belongings and made ready to leave the boat and book a hotel close by.

Quito arrived as they were leaving. He said, "I notified Director Nash that I brought both of you back with me. I told him that I would rather he got the information directly from you. He agreed, and asked that you come to his office after you've booked your hotel and freshened up."

"Thank you, Quito, and thanks again for your concern in this matter. We appreciate your support," answered André.

They then left, walking to a nearby hotel.

***

After showering and a change of clothes, the couple took a cab to mission headquarters. Upon entering the building and encountering some old faces and many more new ones, they both felt an uneasiness in their reception.

Caroline whispered, while they sat waiting to be ushered into the director's office, "André, do you get the same feeling that I do?"

"If you mean do I notice discomfort among the troops, yes, I do."

Fortunately the wait was soon over. The director's secretary entered the lobby and asked that they follow her to the office of John Nash. As they entered, Nash stood, smiled broadly, firmly shook their hands, and said, "Please sit and relax. I want you to know from the start that no one has prejudged either of you. The board is aware of your fine reputation and cognizant of the many years of hard, unselfish labor you've given to the mission. This situation, though unusual, will be fairly investigated and then brought to fruition. Now first of all, tell me how you've been and give me a briefing on the mission. After you've relaxed we will bring up the other matter."

André and Caroline gave a sigh of relief. Just knowing the attitude of fairness from their employer was all that they could expect.

The next hour went quickly with the conversation directed at the business of a successful mission at the village of a lost tribe. When the director was satisfied with the status of the mission, he said, "We can get into more detail later on the needs of the village. Now I've got to ask you, André. Do you have any input on the claim of the young lady called Calida that you may be her father?"

André sighed and quietly answered, "Yes, John, I do. Caroline and I have mulled this over, time and time again. Although a bit farfetched, there is a remote possibility that I could be. You may have cause to wonder about the scenario I'm going to give you. I wonder about it myself, but nevertheless it's the only one I can come up with."

"I'm intrigued. Please go on," Nash said.

André then launched into the story of the kidnapping of Caroline by the Amazon women, the attempted rescue by André, and of his capture by the women warriors. He then, carefully and as close in detail as he could remember, told the most important part that happened during his confinement.

"Are you saying that you were in a drugged state and the leader of these women seduced you?" Nash asked.

"There was no known seduction on my part. As far as I was concerned it was an erotic dream. The same as any normal, healthy man could have," André said.

"Well, you said it was going to be a farfetched scenario. It certainly is." Nash hesitated and said, "I may require that you repeat this to the board. I'm not sure that I can."

"If I may, John, before we go to the board, can we meet the young lady and see if she is willing get DNA testing done?"

"Yes, of course, I planned for that already. We have discussed DNA. She agreed and we have her results already. We now need yours and can proceed with that this morning. It will take several days for the results on an expedited basis," Nash said.

"Great, I'm ready," anxiously answered André. "Now when can we meet her?"

"Let me check," John said as he picked up his phone and hit the intercom. He spoke into the phone. "Has Calida arrived yet?" He waited and said, "Yes, thank you," and then hung up. He took a deep breath and said, "She's here. I've agreed that she be brought into my office."

They all stood as the door slowly opened.

Calida entered. She was dressed simply in the clothes she wore as a medical assistant in the parish children's home. She wore her hair pulled back into a ponytail. As always, even though she didn't wear makeup, the bone structure of her face highlighted her natural beauty.

John said, "Come in, Calida. I want you to meet Dr. André Clark and his wife Caroline."

She confidently stepped forward, extended her hand to André, firmly grasped his hand, and said, "I'm very happy to finally meet you, Dr. Clark. I have heard many compliments on your skills as a doctor and your pleasant personality."

"Thank you, Calida. I have heard that you also have healing skills that are beyond what a young person should have."

"My skills are minor. I have no formal training," Calida said. She turned to Caroline and grasped her hand. "It is also a great pleasure to meet you, *Senhora* Clark. My mother told me about you. She admired you greatly."

Caroline was aghast. After gasping, she sputtered, "I didn't expect that at all. It was so long ago but I remember your mother very well."

The two women stood eye to eye. Both were exactly the same height. There was an immediate connection. An unspoken bond was bridged between them as they stood facing each other.

"Director, would it be possible for me, Caroline, and Calida to have some time by ourselves for a discussion?" André asked.

"I think that would be a good idea. After you give your DNA sample, go into the conference room and join Calida and Caroline, who can go there now. I'll have some lunch sent in a little later, and we can meet again this afternoon to discuss the next step."

As André left the room, he turned to look at his wife and saw her walking with Calida hand in hand with a peaceful, contented look on her face. He now knew that however this turned out, it was going to be okay.

Chapter Thirty-Two

The two women were chatting to each other when André entered the conference room. He stood and observed for a moment before he spoke and disturbed them. He waited. Caroline was speaking.

"The last time I saw your mother was at that intense battle between the Yano-Matis warriors and the Amazon warriors. She fought gallantly but was severely outnumbered and fell to her knees, badly wounded. But amazingly she continued the fight from a kneeling position and slayed several attackers before she finally fell. I thought surely that she had perished."

"So did all her fellow warriors," Calida answered. "When she fell, it took the fight out of what was left of them. They stopped battling, and when the chief of the Indians saw that victory was imminent, he pulled his men back. He showed great respect for the gallant, beaten women who were still standing, and allowed them to remove my mother's body."

Caroline added, "It was inspiring to see those wounded women gently lift her body and carry her away. But obviously she survived. It must have been a long and hard recovery."

"According to Nardania, who was my mentor, it was even more amazing since she was pregnant with me at the time."

Caroline took pause and then said, "I'd like to hear more about that, Calida. What were you told?"

A sudden chill penetrated the room.

Calida felt the change and haltingly said, "Well, my mother only told me that my father was not among us. I wondered about that. When I questioned her, she was hesitant. She went on to tell me about being an Amazon warrior without men, and that someday I would lead the Amazon warriors as she had."

"How then did you determine that André might be your father?"

"My best information came from Nardania, who was my mother's second-in-command and her closest friend. Nardania told me that my father was a Caucasian missionary physician with the Yano-Matis tribe. He was captured during an encounter with the tribe and was held in the village with his wife for a short time. He escaped with his wife. We've already talked about the battle that ensued shortly after."

"Was there any discussion on the conception?" Caroline asked.

"No, but I imagine it was done in the standard way."

Caroline couldn't help but smile at this innocent quip. The levity helped to relieve the chill in the air.

Calida felt the relief and grinned as she dropped her eyes.

André had quietly stood aside and heard the bulk of the conversation. The women were too engrossed to notice his presence. He said, "Sounds like you two are hitting it off. Can I get into this conversation?"

"Of course, André, Calida and I understand each other, I think. Why don't you sit with us? I'd like Calida to tell us the intriguing tale of her years of travel from the destroyed Amazon village to Guajará. Start with the part where you went back and discovered the ruins of where you had lived."

"Yes, it was a terrible experience finding not a living soul. I was devastated," Calida said. She went on to review her experiences with the shaman and the old cast-out Indian. She reviewed her time in the Indian village, the boat trip, and her pleasant meeting with Father McCann.

Hours later all three were very comfortable with each other. Calida asked that André and Caroline explain their history with the lost tribe of Yano-Matis. She wanted to know about the mission. She was curious about the training Caroline had, and what she had taught the tribe. She asked about the Christian religion. She had become interested while working at the children's home that was run by the diocese.

All too quickly it was the end of the day. John Nash had not disturbed them earlier since it appeared that it was going well. He entered the conference room and said, "I'm very pleased to see the bonding that appears to have happened. And you can continue here tomorrow if you wish, but it's time to close the offices."

"Thank you, John. We would like to continue with Calida, but I'm not sure what her responsibilities are at the children's home."

Calida spoke up, "Father McCann told me to take all the time that I need to meet with the Clarks. So I would like to return tomorrow."

"That's fine," said Nash, "perhaps they can drop you off at the home on the way back to the hotel."

"We'd be happy to, and pick her up in the morning. We'd like to say hello to Father McCann while we're there."

"Sounds like a plan," said Nash.

***

André and Caroline were back in the hotel room after having a relaxing dinner. They were very tired with the lasting effects of the long journey and the stress of the past few days.

"I'm really bushed," muttered André. "I think my age is catching up with me."

Caroline chuckled. "You're not the only one, Doc. I'm just behind you in years."

"It's kind of humorous that on our thirtieth wedding anniversary we might become parents," he said with a grin.

"You know, in spite of the circumstances, I really like her. She seems so genuine and unspoiled," she said.

"I'm not sure if it was mostly hereditary or environmental, but she seems to have gotten the best of both," he added.

"I wonder about this healing ability. Do you feel she has a gift?" Caroline asked.

"I plan on delving into that tomorrow. We haven't even touched on it. I'm curious too," André answered.

"Let's hit the sack. It'll be another long day," she said while yawning.

***

The next day went well, with more questions and answers on both sides. As they were about to call it a day, John Nash entered the room. He announced, "I just heard from the lab. They have put an expedited status on the DNA test and feel that they will have an answer for us tomorrow morning."

"That's wonderful," said an excited André. "Should we go to the lab tomorrow?"

"No, I told them that I would like it sent here, to my office, and that André, Caroline, and Calida will all be present for the results. That way we'll all find out at the same time."

"We'll be here bright and early," Caroline said. She turned to Calida. "The doctor and I would like you to join us for dinner, Calida. It should be a little more relaxing than sitting around a conference table. Can you go?"

"Of course, I'd like that very much," she answered.

They again dropped Calida at the children's home with instructions that they would pick her up later for dinner.

***

That evening, after eating and a relaxing bantering of small talk, André asked, "Have you made any plans for your future, Calida?"

"No, I had my goal set to find you, and I've not thought beyond that," she answered.

"None of us can be sure of the results that we will hear tomorrow. It is possible that it can go either way. Caroline and I have discussed this and we would like to be a part of your life if you want us to be, no matter what the DNA results are."

"I would like that very much, André," she said with moist eyes. "I have felt closer to you two than anyone else since my mother died."

Caroline reached across the table and squeezed her hand.

"Calida, in our conversation today, I questioned you on your medical knowledge. You have basic knowledge and an uncanny ability without any formal training. You have that nurturing quality that is so important in the medical field. Would you consider furthering your medical knowledge and becoming a physician or a nurse practitioner?"

"How could I possibly do that? I have no resources. Doesn't that take money?" Calida asked.

"There are scholarships and grants available for gifted students and we would like to help as much as we can," he said.

Calida hesitated. "All this is so . . . I'm . . ."

Caroline leaned across the table and whispered, "Don't worry, dear, we have all the time in the world to talk about this. We just got caught up in the moment."

"Thank you, Caroline. I'm sorry but I just got overwhelmed."

"Certainly, let's wait until we know more."

***

The next day found the same three people in the conference room. The conversation centered on the herbs and roots that Calida carried in her pouch.

"I haven't had the chance to replace what I've used since I need to go deep in the rain forest to find many of them."

"Since we've been living with the Yano-Matis for the last thirty years, I'm somewhat familiar with many of the herbs that you are using. It still amazes me."

As they sat around the table, somewhat relaxed, the door opened and John Nash entered with an elderly gentleman. He announced, "Let me introduce Dr. Enrico Perez from the Brazilian National Laboratory. He has the DNA results."

Nash turned to the doctor and nodded.

"Good morning. I will speak in English for your better understanding. The results of the DNA test of André Clark and Calida, with no family name, is a 99.9 percent match. There is no doubt that he is the biological father of the child."

The room was shrouded in silence. A long sigh escaped from André's lips. He sat up straight and said, "Well, I guess that answers it."

Even though it was almost a foregone conclusion of the outcome, it was now a reality and the finality was like a thunderclap. The rest of the group sat in silence as André stood, walked to where Calida was sitting, and she stood as they embraced, tears flowing from her eyes.

Caroline then stood, approached the father and daughter, who gathered her in for a group hug.

Chapter Thirty-Three

The clerk in the parish office announced, "Father McCann will see you now. Please follow me and I'll show you to his office."

The three of them rose and followed her. When they entered Father McCann's office, he stood and greeted them, "Come in please. Aha, three of my favorite people." He extended his arms and Caroline was first to get a warm hug. Next, following her, was André with a manly embrace.

"Calida, I am so happy that you have completed your quest, and I'm sure that you are very happy with the outcome and with these wonderful people."

"Yes, I am, Father. Even in my dreams I didn't think that I would be so lucky as to find two such wonderful people to call my family."

"Please sit and let's hear what you plan next."

André said, "We want to get your input, Father. As you know, Calida has a nurturing gift and a basic knowledge of medicine. We think that this gift should be expanded upon but we're not sure of the next step."

"Hmm, let me ask. Calida, is it your choice to further your study of medicine with a formal education?"

"Yes, I think I would, Father," Calida answered.

"Are you aware of the sacrifice, of the study time, let alone the expense involved to do this?"

"My love of medicine and healing will take care of lengthy studying time and the sacrifices. I have no money, but I'm willing to work to help pay."

André spoke up, "Father, Caroline and I have saved a bit of money during the time we have lived with the lost tribe. Also, Caroline had a small inheritance that has remained untouched for the last thirty-five years. We're waiting to hear from the attorney that handled the estate to determine what it is worth now. We're willing to give as much as we can afford to fund her education."

"Well, here in the diocese we have a scholarship fund for deserving young students. I can submit her name and her circumstances to the scholarship board. They determine who and how much a student receives. I can give a recommendation, but my influence ends there," Father McCann explained.

"Is there a school that you prefer if some help is granted?" asked Caroline.

"We have used the University of Miami for medical students. The board of regents works well with us," Father McCann added.

"If granted, is there an obligation by the student to the diocese after the student graduates?" André asked.

"We, of course, would prefer that the student return here to practice or agree to spend time with the aboriginal Indians here in the Amazon basin. But we don't make that a binding agreement. It is a decision made by the student after graduation."

"That's more than fair," added Caroline. "Can you wait until I hear from the attorney of my parents' estate before you submit her name? The money has been invested in blue-chip stocks and some high-interest bonds, so they tell me. All dividends and interest have been retained. I'm not sure of the value, but it may have appreciated some."

"I'll do that. How long are you and André going to be here in Guajará?" asked Father McCann.

"We've asked John Nash for an extended leave of absence and he has agreed. We've rented a house on a six-month lease and Calida will move in with us. She would still like to work with the children as long as she's here, if those arrangements can be made."

"I see no problem with that. I'll talk to Mother Superior."

The trio stood, shook hands with the elderly priest, and said their goodbyes, promising to check back in several days.

***

161

Later that day, after they bought a disposable cell phone, Caroline called the attorneys in her hometown to check on the value of the inheritance.

After a short wait, the attorney handling her parents' estate came on the line. He said, "Thanks for waiting, Caroline. I was getting a final figure from our broker on the value of your investment. I'm pleased to report that it has grown a considerable amount in the last thirty-five years or so. Total value is well over a million. I can mail or fax a total breakdown if you give me where to send it . . . Are you there, Caroline . . . Hello . . . Hello?"

"Yes, I'm here. I was so surprised . . . I guess I was speechless."

"Well, I can understand that. Where can I send this breakdown?"

Caroline gave him the address of the rental house and hung up the phone. She sat for a moment, collecting her thoughts before finding her husband to tell him the news. He walked in as she sat there.

"You looked dazed, dear. Are you okay?" he asked.

"André, I just found out the value of the inheritance."

"Uh-oh, that doesn't sound good. What's the damage?"

"No, no, just the opposite, it's worth over a million."

"Oh my god," he exclaimed. "How could that happen?"

"He's sending a breakdown, but I imagine it's a combination of dividends, interest, and growth."

"It's obvious that you made a good decision to let it ride with them," he added.

"I think that Mom and Dad would like nothing better than to invest this money into the future of a young person with Calida's potential in medicine," said a dazed but happy Caroline.

***

Several days later, Calida and the Clarks had finished dinner and were discussing the funding of Calida's education. Caroline was reading from a document sent from the estate's attorney. She said, "The Miami law office has contacted the University of Miami. They have explained the circumstances of accepting a student with no prior formal education except for hands-on experience in the jungle. The university has agreed to send multiple documents to be answered, as well as questions to test her knowledge and experience. If they feel these are acceptable, they will send additional tests and questions. And if these are acceptable they will require a personal, in-depth interview on their campus. They will provide room and board, if paid for in advance, for a one-week stay."

"I didn't realize that it would be so complicated," said a discouraged Calida.

"Yes, they are very particular of who studies in their school," explained André, "but don't lose faith. I have also written a letter to a friend who practices in Miami. I've asked for his input."

"I already called the lawyer in Miami and asked that the first packet of documents be sent overnight, FedEx, as soon as possible. They returned my call late today and said that it will go out tomorrow," Caroline said.

"Are you ready for this, Calida?" asked André.

"Yes, I am," answered a determined Calida.

Chapter Thirty-Four

FIVE YEARS LATER

"The ceremony's going to take place without us if you don't hurry, André," said a disgruntled Caroline.

"Okay, okay, don't forget I'm not as young as I used to be. That was a long flight. I don't see why they take us from Guajará to Manaus to Caracas, then to Mexico City and finally to Miami. Maybe we should have come by boat," answered a harried André.

"Quit complaining and get ready. You had a good night's sleep. I ordered a cab to be here in twenty minutes."

***

Several hours later, after the graduation ceremony for premed students, André, Caroline, and Calida were attending a reception for several chosen students and the staff from the school. They were approached by the head of the department, Dr. Dominic Casey.

"Dr. and Mrs. Clark, allow me to introduce myself. I am Dr. Casey from the university here."

"Our pleasure, Dr. Casey. Yes, we have heard many good things about you from Calida. Thank you for giving her your time and extra instruction these past few years."

"It was very refreshing, Dr. Clark. Your daughter has more insight and medical knowledge than any student that I've encountered in my career."

André beamed with pride.

Caroline gushed, "Oh, Dr. Casey, you have no idea how pleased we are to hear that."

"I understand the circumstances, Mrs. Clark, so I imagine it is doubly satisfying."

Calida added, "Dr. Casey thinks that I can bypass some of the hospital work because of my past experience, and also since I want to get into lab work."

"Yes, I think I can work something out and I have a connection at a large experimental laboratory that would love to talk to Calida about her experience with the herbs, roots, and other medicinal cures found in the rain forest."

"Are we a little premature on employment, Dr. Casey?"

"Yes, I'm just thinking ahead, Dr. Clark. There must be a year or two of hospital work before I can approach that."

"Even so that is much sooner than we expected," said Caroline.

"Ordinarily that is so, but as I said, you have a very talented daughter. I will make all the arrangements and keep you up to date, Dr. Clark. Now I must smooze the guests. Have a safe trip back to the Amazon."

Caroline turned to Calida. "We're very proud of you. You've made both of us so happy. Let's have some dinner, then your father and I need to turn in. We have an early flight in the morning."

"You are the best mom and dad that anyone could ask for. I want to work with experimental drugs and help find a cure for the horrible diseases mankind is faced with. I hope to repay you by working with an experimental laboratory."

"We've dedicated our lives to bringing God and good health to the aboriginal people of the Amazon basin. Finding you has been a blessing to us and brought us untold joy. That's payment enough for us. Use your skills to benefit others less fortunate."

"Thank you, Mom and Dad," she said as she embraced them.

They then left the hall to enjoy a celebratory dinner. As they boarded a taxi and pulled away, an expensive dark-colored sedan fell in behind them. In the sedan were two Hispanic men.

After the taxi discharged the three passengers at a high-end restaurant, the expensive sedan rolled to a stop. One of the men spoke Spanish into a cell phone and then hung up.

The driver asked, "What's next?"

"The boss said to follow them and find out if the girl is going back to the dorm or somewhere else. We're not to do anything until he tells us."

"*Caramba!* I think we should just snatch her now and get it over with," exclaimed the driver.

"WHAT! You outta your mind? The boss would hang you by the gonads. Besides, what makes you think we're going to snatch her?"

"Ain't we?"

"Hell no! The boss wants to meet her and talk. Somethin' to do with this lab that he took over. Some kinda drug stuff."

"Ya mean like pot or coke."

"NO! Don't be stupid. The boss is goin' legit."

"Okay, okay, I know. I just get anxious."

They sat and waited for the next several hours listening to salsa music. When the three Clarks left the restaurant, they followed, confirmed where Calida was staying, and then pulled away.

Chapter Thirty-Five

"Did you get settled into the dorm, Calida?" asked Caroline.

"Yes, I did but I wanted to ride to the airport with you. It's going to be a long time before we see each other again and I have a question for you."

"Okay, is something bothering you?"

"Oh no, Mom, it's about a tribe in the Amazon. Is your Yano-Matis tribe in any way connected with the Yanonami tribe?"

André thought about this and then answered, "If I'm not mistaken they are a tribe just on the other side of the Venezuelan border. I think I heard some of the ancients in our tribe discussing them. They may be an old, old offshoot of our tribe, but I don't think there has been any recent contact, at least not while your mom and I have been there. Why are you asking?"

"I've been doing some research on the health of the aboriginal tribes of the Amazon along with the cures from herbs found in the rain forest. I found a very interesting phenomenon with this group. A study has found that those in this isolated village have a very diverse colony of bacteria in their bodies. We all have these beneficial bacteria in our bodies but they have trillions more. A study of this isolated group could prove very beneficial to nutrition and medication."

"Wow! It sounds like you're already beyond what I have studied, young lady. I'm amazed."

"I'm on a different course from yours, Dad. I'm on the research end of the medical profession. You're out there curing people."

"Well, I'm proud of you. When we get back I'll find out what I can on this remote tribe."

"Thank you, Dad. I hope to be back in the Amazon before too long. I'm still hoping to work for a lab that will station me doing research in the rain forest."

"Your mom and I are both hoping for that too, but you may not have a say-so in that respect."

"Well, Dr. Casey seems to think that I have the background that will bode well in an Amazon basin assignment. Not everyone wants to live in a jungle outpost. During my teenage years, that kind of living would have been a luxury."

"You are very unique, Calida," Caroline said.

***

While André and Caroline worked their way back to the Yano- Matis village, Calida worked in the university hospital. As with typical interns, her hours were long and free time was scarce. But also, as with all young people, she found some time to socialize. She worked with another intern that asked her to have a coffee with him at the local Starbucks, and since she noticed this young man's approving glances in class, she happily accepted. They walked together, slowly strolling through the campus after a pleasant hour having coffee.

"Your background is so much different from my upbringing, Calida. I hadn't been more than a couple of hundred miles away from our farm in Iowa before I came to school here in Florida."

"Tell me about it, Jonah. Were you born on the farm?"

He laughed. "No, it wasn't quite that bad. I was born in a fine hospital in Des Moines. My mom was visiting my grandparents when I happened kind of unexpectedly. We were back on the farm in a few days." He went on to explain about farm life and growing up with a younger brother and an older sister. "My grandfather on my dad's side is the local doctor in the little town closest to the farm. It was because of his input that I was able to get a partial scholarship here at U of Miami."

"Do you want to go back to Iowa to practice medicine?" she asked.

"As with you, Calida, I'd like to do some research. I think the stories I've heard you tell in class about the herbs found in the rain forest are so intriguing."

"There's so much more to it than that, Jonah. I didn't get into the many quack cures given by charlatan medicine men that try to pass themselves off as shaman. Also, even the real shamans can make diagnostic errors. And even with a correct diagnosis, the wrong dosage may be harmful or even fatal. I only covered the good stories."

"Yes, I see what you mean, but there have been those kinds of circumstances with educated doctors also."

"I'm sure that's true, but believe me, Jonah, there is much work that can be done in the rain forest, especially in the Amazon basin."

"I hope to be a part of that, Calida. Maybe we can do it together."

She blushed as he held her hand walking through the campus.

***

It was at a fraternity sponsored dance that Jonah asked Calida to attend and meet him there. She agreed if she could come with another young lady. The two interns entered the gymnasium where the dance was being held. Jonah spotted them and he quickly advanced with another young man before the two pretty young maidens got overwhelmed by his fraternity brothers.

"Hi, Calida, this is my friend Zach. Is that Jennifer that you brought with you?"

"Yeah, Jen's in our chem class. I'm glad you remembered her."

"Hi, Jen, this is Zach. Come on, Calida, let's dance. This is my favorite song," yelled Jonah over the loud music.

As they were dancing, Calida asked, "How do you know Zach, Jonah? I don't remember seeing him in any of our classes."

"I just met him the other day at the hospital. I think he works there."

"Oh, okay. What does he do? He's too young to be a doctor."

"I don't know. What's the difference? I just wanted to bring someone for your friend. Let's have a good time."

"Okay, Jonah, let's relax. We've both had a stretch of long hours."

It was a fun evening and Jen seemed to be enjoying Zach. When the dance was over, the four decided to go get a bite to eat in Zach's car.

Jonah exclaimed, "Wow, this is a nice set of wheels, Zach. Must have set you back a pretty penny."

"Yeah, well, it's a long story. It's mine to use but I don't really own it."

"You mean it's leased."

"Yeah sure, that's it. Hey, where should we eat? Any suggestions ladies? It's on me."

The four decided on a local beer and burger place and it turned out very well. After eating, Zach dropped the girls off at the dorm and the two men drove off to drop Jonah at the frat house.

"Say, Jonah, thanks for introducing me to the girls," Zach said.

"That's okay, pal. Looked like you and Jen hit it off."

"Yeah, she's a nice girl, but I gotta say your Calida is some dish."

"She's a babe all right and she's got a load of talent. Some lab will be lucky to get her."

"Yeah, do you know if she's got any lab in mind?"

"It's a little early for her to commit, I think, but Dr. Casey has been working with her and has introduced her around a little."

"Are you two an item yet?"

"What do you mean, Zach?"

"No offense, Jonah. I just meant are you two going steady or engaged or anything?"

"Heck no! We've just been dating for a few months or so. But I really like her."

"Okay, well, here's where you get off. See you around the hospital."

"Okay, thanks for the ride."

***

Two days later, as Calida was riding her bike back to the dorm, a car slowed and tooted. She looked over and saw that it was Zach.

He rolled down his window and yelled, "Hey, ya got time for a coffee?"

"I'm going back to the dorm to study for finals next week."

"Come on, take your bike home and I'll pick you up in ten minutes."

Horns were blowing since he was blocking traffic. People were yelling for him to move over.

"Okay, okay," she yelled. "You better move before they really get mad."

He laughed and peeled off.

A half hour later they were sitting in Starbucks having a latte.

"I've been askin' around about you, Calida. You've really got some history."

"Yes, I have a pretty complicated past. How about you? Jonah didn't have much info to tell Jen when she asked."

"Well, I do some work for a man named Enrico Valbuena."

"I thought that you worked at the hospital."

"Well, yeah, kind of. That's where I do my recruiting."

"What kind of recruiting?"

"I look for good people that want to make good money working for *Señor* Valbuena."

"I don't understand."

"My boss has acquired an experimental laboratory. He is very interested in the development of a variety of drugs, predominantly those that promote longevity of life. He has heard of lost tribes where not only do they live to be quite old but also have few illnesses and women have fertility into their sixties and even seventies. The men are also able to procreate well into their old age."

"These are stories that I have heard also," she added.

"Are these tribes in the Amazon?"

"It is rumored to be so," she answered.

"My boss very much wants to meet you, Calida. Can I take you to him?"

"I don't know. I hardly know you. Please take me back to my dorm."

"Okay, okay, don't get upset. Just think about it, but you probably shouldn't let the cat out of the bag. My boss is still kind of doing this on the QT."

They left and he quickly drove her back to her dorm.

When she was in her room, she pondered over the conversation and an inner voice said, *BE CAREFUL.*

Chapter Thirty-Six

"That kid is outside, *patron*. He says you wanted to see him," said one of the Hispanic thugs that had been tailing Calida. "Ya mean Zach? Yeah, send him in," said a heavyset, well-dressed Hispanic man who sat behind a mammoth desk.

The thug left his office and addressed the young man standing in the outer office, who was heavily engaged in a torrid conversation with a well-endowed and pretty Hispanic girl sitting at the front desk.

"Okay, *gringo*, the *jefe* said for you to go in and keep away from Lolita. She's spoken for."

"She might be spoken for, but not by you, Pasquale."

"You got a smart mouth, *gringo*, and my name's Pedro."

"Yeah, yeah, get outta my way," said Zach as he brushed by him and entered *Señor* Valbuena's office.

"Good morning, boss," said Zach.

"*Hola*, kid, ya got any news for me? It's been over a week since I set you up in that hospital."

"I told you that you could count on me, boss. Yeah, I just had a date with our mark yesterday. I definitely think she's the one for you."

"I ALREADY KNOW THAT, *GRINGO*!" *Señor* Valbuena screamed, jumping up and standing, his face turning beet red.

"Easy, boss, easy, I got more. I approached her about coming in to meet you and she's thinking about it."

"Look, *gringo*, I've got people watching you. Ya don't take her to a hamburger joint. She's a high-class broad. Take her somewhere that she'll be impressed. Take her to a fine restaurant. Wine and dine her, and then, when she's feelin' warm and fuzzy, tell her your boss wants to meet her, but don't push it. Don't bring her to the office, bring her to my place in the country. Tell her it's a pool party for the employees or somethin'. Get creative."

"Okay, boss. It may take a little more time. I don't want to spook her. I'm runnin' short on bread. Can Lolita give me a draft?"

"Yeah." He picked up the phone and spoke Spanish to Lolita. "Okay, kid, get outta here and get to work. You're costin' me a lot of dough."

Zach left the office and stopped at Lolita's desk. She handed him a bank draft.

"Wow! Two thousand bucks, whatcha gonna do with all that money, good-lookin'?" said Lolita seductively.

"It's mine to spend, doll. You wanna help me?" Zach asked.

She whispered, "I get off in an hour, sweetie. Where can I meet up with ya?"

"I'll see you in the bar at the Hilton," he said as he was leaving.

***

"Hey, Calida, wait for me," called Jennifer as they were leaving class.

"Oh, hi, Jen," said Calida as she turned and stood waiting for her girlfriend to catch up.

"I've got something to ask you. Are you and Jonah busy this Saturday night?" asked a panting Jen.

"I don't have any plans but I can't speak for Jonah."

"Well, Zach has asked me to go out to dinner and he wants to know if you two want to double with us."

"Gee, I don't know. I'm not crazy about Zach."

"Aw come on, Calida. He wants to take me to the Breakers in Palm Beach. That's where all the movie stars go and people like the Kennedys."

"Well, you can go. Besides, I don't know what Jonah's plans are."

"Hey, did I hear my name mentioned?" said an approaching Jonah.

"Oh good," exclaimed Jennifer. "Are you free to go to dinner with Zach and me Saturday night?"

"Well, I don't have any plans. Is Calida going?"

"Sure she is. You two are going to double with us."

"Where are we going?" asked Jonah.

"Zach wants to take me to the Breakers."

"Whoa! That's too rich for me. There's no way I can afford that, even in my dreams."

"You don't need to. Zach said it's all on him."

"That's too much," exclaimed both Calida and Jonah at the same time.

"It'll be okay. Zach said his boss is giving him a bonus and putting it on the company tab. It'll be deductible or some such thing."

"What do you say, Calida?" asked Jonah.

"Oh please, please, Calida. I've always wanted to see that place."

"Okay, Jen, but I'm doing this for you. Both Jonah and I don't count Zach as one of our favorite people."

***

The dinner at the Breakers was all it was supposed to be. Zach was the perfect host and the evening was progressing nicely. They were riding in his luxury sedan on the way back to Miami, very content after a pleasant evening.

"Is anyone up for a pool party tomorrow afternoon?" Zach asked.

"What have you got in mind, honey?" asked Jen.

"I've got an invitation and can bring a few friends to this private pool where there's going to be plenty of food, drinks too, if anyone's interested."

"Where is it?" asked Jonah.

"Just up in Lauderdale, not far, and I'll drive."

"I'll go if Calida does," said Jen.

"I was planning on studying," answered Calida.

"If I was as smart as you, I'd never study," said Zach.

"I'm free," said Jonah. "Can you just go for a few hours, Calida?"

"Yeah, I can drive you back to the dorm whenever you want Calida," added Zach.

"Boy, you guys. I'd never get any studying done if it was up to you," mumbled an uneasy Calida.

"It's set then. I'll pick up everyone at the women's dorm at 1:00."

***

As planned, Zach was at the dorm at 1:00 and they all piled in the car.

As they drove up I-95, Jonah asked "Hey, you never said whose house this pool party was at, Zach."

Zach looked over at Jonah who was in the front seat with him and quietly mumbled, "It's at my boss' mansion."

Calida perked up. "What did you say, Zach?"

Zach gave Jonah a sheepish look.

Jonah turned to look at the girls and said, "I think we're going to his boss' house."

"Well, if I had known that I wouldn't have agreed to go, Zach."

"Oh come on. It'll be okay. There's gonna be a lot of people there. He might not even notice a couple more girls in their bikini."

"I may not change because we may not be there very long," said a disgusted Calida.

"Aw, don't be a party pooper," said Jennifer.

"Well, I think I was tricked, Jen. You don't know the whole story."

"What's the story, Calida?" asked Jonah.

"She's upset because I had coffee with her one day and mentioned that my boss had an interest in a pharmaceutical company and that I was recruiting her to work for him," Zach said.

"In the first place, you said it was an experimental lab and not a pill manufacturer. Other things didn't add up either," she answered.

"Well, we're almost there. Can you at least go in and make an appearance so I don't get hung out to dry?" Zach said.

"What do you say, Calida?" Jonah asked.

"Okay, but let's not stay long," she answered.

They entered a gated driveway that led to a huge estate. Cars were parked all along the front, some with drivers standing by. When they stopped in front of the mansion, a butler opened the doors for them and said, "John will park it for you, Zach."

Zach said, "Thanks, Jason." He turned to his group and announced, "Follow me around to the back. There's a gate and a sidewalk leading to the pool."

As they got closer, sounds of a reggae band along with laughter floated out of the pool area. When they entered, a waiter showed them to a cabana where they could change or just lounge if they chose to.

"Nice, huh?" said a content Zach.

The waiter asked if he could bring a refreshing drink for them. They ordered, sat back, and relaxed, listening to the sounds of merriment from a group of young people playing water polo.

After their drinks were served, the host approached them to welcome them to his home.

Chapter Thirty-Seven

The "lord of the mansion" entered in a flourish and was overpowering with his wide girth and boisterous attitude. The sweat was dripping from his brow. The Florida heat and humidity greatly affected a man of his heavy stature.

"Zach, you have brought beautiful people to my *fiesta*. You must introduce me to these lovely young *señoritas*."

"Sure, boss. This is Calida Clark and Jennifer Smith, along with their friend Jonah Davis."

"It is my pleasure to have you visit my home. Please there is food in the *solana*. Help yourselves. I will stop back to visit later."

To Calida's relief, he graciously left them.

After another drink, they relaxed and decided to eat.

Calida was sitting in a shady area with Jonah, enjoying a splendid lunch, when she felt uneasy. She turned to find *Señor* Valbuena hovering at her back. She scooted closer to Jonah.

"Ah, *señorita*, I'm sorry. Did I startle you?"

"I didn't hear you," she said uneasily.

"I'm light on my feet in spite of my size," he responded.

"Well, thank you for having us but I think we'll be leaving soon."

"If I may, *señorita*, I would like to meet with you to discuss an interesting proposition."

"I'm not ready to discuss any employment at this time. I have more schooling to complete before I can even think about it."

"But I can make that go away. I have the ability to put your knowledge to work right now."

"That doesn't sound reasonable, ethical, or possibly even legal."

"I can circumvent all those objections, *señorita*. We need someone who can give us knowledge and experience on those herbs and plants in the rain forest where you grew up. We want to develop drugs and medications hurriedly and get them to market. There is millions to be made and you can participate in this."

"That is not my interest, *señor*. Please forgive me but I must leave. Come on, Jonah, let's find Zach and Jen and get out of here."

"I think not, *señorita*," said the rotund man as he grabbed her wrist in his grubby hand. "You will come with me to my study where you will listen to my *tenedor de libros* explain the monetary benefits of working for my pharmaceutical company and what can happen if you don't."

Jonah stood up and loudly proclaimed, "Hey, you can't do that." As he stepped toward the *señor*, he was abruptly halted by a burly guard who was lurking in the background.

"Don't get foolish," said the guard as he bumped against a much leaner Jonah.

Valbuena led Calida toward the house. They were walking adjacent to the swimming pool and he was roughly leading her with a strong grip. Suddenly, Calida jerked her wrist from his grasp, flexed her knees into a fighting stance, and as Valbuena lunged at her, she quickly raised up and slammed into his fat, cushy body, propelling him backward. There was a tremendous splash as the wide body landed flush on his back in the deep end of the pool. He disappeared in the foaming water and then came up splashing and coughing.

"Help . . . Help, I can't swim," he screamed as he again disappeared under water.

The hired lifeguard leaped into action and dove in the pool. He approached the struggling man, who grabbed at him in a panic. The guard was almost overcome by this terror stricken, drowning man. He wrenched himself free of the grabbing arms of the huge man and swung a roundhouse blow that caught the *señor* flush on the jaw. He was stunned long enough for the lifesaver to turn him around and tow him to the side of the pool. Strong hands were poolside to hoist him out of the water. As he regained his senses, he lay on his back, gasping for air.

After Calida witnessed his safety, she looked for Jonah, who quickly approached her. And she said, "Let's go, Jonah. If Zach won't take us, I'll walk home."

They quickly left the house and were walking down the long driveway when Zach pulled up in his Mercedes and yelled, "Come on and get in. I want out of here. He'll probably can my ass now."

They piled into the car, and Calida was happy to see that Jen was in the front seat with Zach.

As they drove, Calida said, "I really didn't appreciate your deception, Zach. You knew that I didn't want to work for that man."

"Hey, don't blame me, Calida. I was only doing my job."

The rest of the trip back to the school was quiet. When Calida and Jonah got out of the car, she said, "Don't bother coming around anymore, Zach." And she slammed the car door shut.

Chapter Thirty-Eight

THREE YEARS LATER

Calida was now a mature twenty-eight-year-old woman with a medical degree, specializing in pharmacology. She had recently signed a contract with one of the leading research and development laboratories in the country. Her first assignment, after spending one long year in the corporate headquarters that also housed the most advanced development lab in the United States, was to report to the company office in Manaus, Brazil.

Even though she had spent all of her younger years in the Amazon basin, landing in Manaus and traveling by rickety taxi into town was a bit of a culture shock to her. She now realized that even having lived the pauperlike life of a medical student, she was now going to embark on a life devoid of many creature comforts.

The city of Manaus was hot, humid, insect-ridden, and noisy. The taxi driver rocketed through narrow streets, blared his horn at every turn, and was seemingly indifferent to the many bicyclists and other vehicles of every description if they happened to be in his way. They, thankfully, arrived unscathed at the hotel booked for her by the travel bureau used by the company.

Calida peered out of the taxi window at the seedy-looking front entrance of the Atlas Hotel, with the sign devoid of the E and L in hotel making it read HOT. She asked, "Are you sure this is the right place, driver?"

"It's the name you gave me, *senhora*. That'll be 45 reais."

"I forgot to change my dollars to reais at the airport," she said.

"Okay then, give me 15 US dollars."

She paid him. He unloaded her luggage on the sidewalk and drove off. She struggled with her two bags and dragged them into the lobby. An unkempt man peered at her from behind an ornate but equally unkempt registration desk. The lobby was large and at one time in its history was probably very well appointed. The furniture was well worn and ancient but it too looked to be expensive at some time in the past. She stood and gazed at her surroundings, wondering whether or not to remain here.

The man behind the desk said, "You might as well stay, *senhora*. Your company is paying for it, and at this late in the evening you won't find much better."

She was taken aback and said, "Oh well, I wasn't expecting—"

"I know. Others are as surprised as you. At one time during the rubber boom we were one of the top hotels, and all the companies sent their employees here. Times have changed and we still have a good reputation, but money is scarce and the new owners won't spend any more. Our rooms are not fancy but they are clean."

"Well, I'm really tired, so I guess I'd better stay."

She registered and was shown to her room by an older gentleman who also struggled with her bags. The room did seem clean, though a bit worn. After a long shower, she felt human again. She decided to turn in early and be chipper when reporting to the local office.

The next morning, she stopped by the desk and asked for a taxi to be sent to take her to the office.

The same man was at the desk, and he said, "One reason that your company uses us is that you can walk to the office. Here is a map of the area and I have marked the directions."

"Oh, thank you."

She left the hotel and followed the map. As she walked she was soon approached by street urchins begging for money. She made the mistake of giving a few coins to the first one that came begging. This brought a phalanx of additional little raggedy boys, jabbering in Portuguese and begging for more Reais. She quickly ducked into a bank to change her dollars to reais and the guard prohibited the little beggar's entrance when they tried to follow her.

Calida was now regaining her command of the Portuguese language and expressed her discomfort to the young teller.

The girl said, "They will be waiting for you when you leave. Where are you going?"

"I'm going to the office of Roget's Laboratories."

"Let me show you to a side entrance. Your office is just down that street. The boys won't be looking for you there."

"Thank you. They kind of overwhelmed me."

She went out the side entrance and was soon at her destination. It was a small office and she was shown in to the manager right away.

"*Buenos dias, senhora*, we've been expecting you. Are you rested from your long trip?"

"I'm still moving slowly, but I'm anxious to get to work. They told me that I would be going to a makeshift outpost lab and they have given me a whole raft of experiments to try and goals to reach. Are you familiar with the place?"

"Yes, I am, but don't count on me showing you where it is. Not many people can locate it."

"Well, how do I get there?"

"You get there by boat, mostly, after we fly you to Japura by way of Guajará. There, you'll find your way to Fonte Boa by boat, and someone will meet you there. Next, you'll take a trek over land into the rain forest to our most remote outpost."

"I have friends in Guajará. Will I be there long?"

"They gave me your history from corporate, Calida. Yes, I anticipated that you might want to visit with friends there. Corporate authorized a paid one-week stay."

"Oh thank you. I haven't seen them for years."

"Considering where you are going and what you'll be doing, it's the least they could do," he added.

"You don't sound very encouraging," she said.

"I've been here for ten years. That's five more than most people can take. I'm ready to go back to the States and live like a human being."

Calida hesitated and then asked, "When will I leave for Guajará?"

"Whenever you're ready. You have no duties here. If I were you, I'd pick up a few items here at the local supplier where we have a company account. I'll give you a list of suggestions. As you may know, many things are not available upriver, even in Guajará. We have a supplier there too, so more can be added if you don't want to carry too much from here."

She left and headed to the supplier. She found the warehouse after tooling around in a taxi trying to find it. It was in a down-trodden area with no real identifying sign that was readable. After scanning the buildings, she spotted a faded sign that said "Enrico's Suministra" in small Spanish letters. As with the hotel, she hesitated, but decided to go in. She asked the cabby to wait for her. She entered and was quite surprised to see a warehouse full of merchandise stacked on shelving that reached to the ceiling.

A very short, bald man bounced down the crowded aisle, peered up, and gazed at this blonde woman at least a foot taller than him.

"*Hola, señorita!* I hope you speak Spanish," he said in Spanish.

"Yes, it is better than my Portuguese," Calida said.

"How can I help you?" he offered, bowing with a flourish.

"I'm new with Roget's Labs," she said, "and I—"

"Say no more, *señorita*. I know who you are and where you are going. Put away that list. Enrico will supply you with everything that you need."

"I've got a long way to go and no one to help, so do not overload me."

"Don't worry, *señorita*, Enrico knows what you need." He started pulling merchandise down from the shelves and soon had a pile for her.

"Wow, that looks like a lot of stuff. How will I carry it all?"

"No worries, *señorita*, the last items I've got for you are these two suitcases to carry everything. I will pack them for you. Never let it be said that Enrico didn't take care of his customers."

"You've been very helpful, Enrico."

"It is my pleasure. Now can I ask a question?" Enrico asked.

"Yes, what is it?"

"Did you really come from the Amazon women in the jungle?"

She smiled. "Yes, it was so long ago though. I was born in the village of warrior women that was destroyed by an earthquake."

"How did you survive?" he asked.

"It's a very long story, Enrico, too long to tell you now, but if I ever come back I promise to tell you," Calida answered.

"I'll look forward to that day, *señorita*."

She left after loading the suitcases in the taxi, and pushed off for the hotel. Enrico was wildly waving from the doorway, smiling broadly.

The next day at the airport, the Ford Tri-Motor airplane baggage handler complained about the four heavy suitcases brought by the *gringo* woman. When the manager assured him that Roget's Labs was paying for the extra weight, he calmed down.

The ancient airplane lumbered down the runway and was airborne seemingly before it had enough speed to leave the ground. But leave the ground it did, as it had on thousands of flights before. Calida observed the rain forest as she flew over it and it brought back the pangs of past memories. She thought of the years she traveled in the jungle and of all the people she encountered along the way. She thought of the women in the Amazon village and of her mother, whom she still missed. She thought of the shaman that taught her so much about the curative properties of the herbs and plants in the jungle. She thought of the old man that she saved and how he taught her so many things and how to survive in the wild. He taught her to use a blow gun and how to make darts and coat them with poison to incapacitate game. All those friends had died.

She thought of the Indian village where she lived for three years taking care of the sick and wounded, of how they allowed her to leave unscathed when she requested it. She thought of the old priest in Guajará, and all the good people that helped her find her father. Somehow she hoped to find them again.

Time passed quickly and she soon landed in Guajará Airport. She was anxious to see old friends.

Chapter Thirty-Nine

"You have an unexpected visitor, Father. Can I show her in?" said the receptionist at the parish offices.

Father McCann answered, "If you think it's important, *senhora*, but I have a raft of paperwork to complete by the end of the day. Could one of the assistants handle it?"

"I think you will want to see this one yourself, Father," she answered.

"Then by all means send her in," said the elderly priest. He shuffled papers aside as he waited for the visitor and then looked up as he heard a familiar voice say, "Good morning, Father." A broad grin came across his face as he stood up and reached with outstretched arms. A tearful Calida skirted the desk and met the priest with a warm hug.

"Calida, it's so good to see you. How long has it been?"

"Too many years, Father. I missed you and the sisters who were so kind to me during the most confusing and vulnerable time of my life."

"That's why we're here, child, and to see you return to us as a successful medical doctor is a dream come true."

"I have you to thank for getting me on the right track. It could not have happened without your help."

"Please sit and tell me what comes next. We have followed what you have accomplished so far through reports from the school and of course letters from the Clarks, who you have been in constant contact with by mail."

"Then you probably know that I work for the Roget's Laboratory."

"Yes, we know you are doing experimental work."

She went on to explain about her assignment in the basin. The priest listened attentively and asked if she wanted to visit with Mother Superior and the others that she worked with. She agreed.

The morning passed quickly and she had lunch with the sisters, chattering about the past and inquiring about her assignment. After lunch she caught a taxi to the mission headquarters to visit with John Nash. It was another joyful reunion and lasted until midafternoon.

"Tell me, Director, is Quito still operating *chalanas* on the river?"

"Yes, we still use his boats to deliver supplies to our remote missions, but Quito is office bound now. Even Quito Jr. only makes occasional runs."

"Is Ricardo still with them as a captain?"

"I thought you might ask that. No, Ricardo left and started his own shipping business. He's done quite well and we use him when Quito is jammed up. He now has three or four boats."

"I guess he probably has an office down by the docks then."

"Yes, he does. If you want to see him, I suggest that you do so at his office."

"I may stop by this afternoon," Calida added.

"Are you going to be able to stop at the Yano-Matis village to see your parents?" he asked.

"Unfortunately I won't be able to until after I get established in my job. As you know, it's very remote and my assignment is just as bad."

"We are able to send them the new satellite telephones on the supply *chalana* that should arrive later this month. If you have one when you get to the lab, you might be able to reach them."

"That's wonderful. Yes, I already have one that the company supplied me with. I will use it to communicate with headquarters. How can I reach them?" she asked.

"I'll write their number down for you. Try in about three or four weeks. They will be calling me when they arrive and I'll tell them about our visit. If you give me your number, I'll pass it on, as well as keep it on file here."

"Thank you, Director. I will never forget what you've done for me, and it seems to continue. Thank you from the bottom of my heart."

"You're welcome, Calida. It's very fulfilling to see what you've accomplished."

She then left to visit her old flame Ricardo. She had lost contact with him over the years and was quite happy to hear that he was a successful businessman. When she reached the dock area, the first stop was at Quito's shipping company office.

"Good morning, may I see Quito please?"

"Quito is not in today. Can Quito Jr. help?"

"Yes, of course."

"Please sit. May I have your name?"

"Yes, it's Calida Clark."

The receptionist left but soon returned with Quito Jr. closely behind her. He said, "I questioned her at first but she assured me that it indeed was you. Welcome, Calida, and how are you?"

"I am fine," she responded and went on to briefly tell him why she was in town, *en route* to her new job.

"I'm very happy for you, Calida. My father will want to see you if you're going to be in town for a while."

"Yes, of course, I want to see him too. I also would like to visit Ricardo. Can you tell me where is office is?"

Quito Jr. hesitated and then said, "Yes, I can. Are you going now?"

"I'd like to. It's been years since I've seen him. If it's a problem for you, Quito, I'll find it myself."

"No, no, it's not a problem. His office is just down the street. I saw him earlier, so I know he's in today."

"Thank you, Quito. Tell your dad to contact me at the hotel." She left, anxious to get to her next stop.

It was a short walk and she entered the small, humble office of Ricardo's *Transportar Compania*. A bell tinkled as she opened the door. There was an empty desk in the tiny lobby. She heard a movement in the room behind and a male voice said, "I'll be right out."

A moment later, the young owner appeared and said, "May I help— oh my god. Is it . . . ? Calida?"

"Yes, it's me, Ricardo. It's been so long." She stepped forward and melted into his arms.

He gave her a warm hug and then stepped back. "Yes, Calida, it has been a long, long time. I have much to tell you."

"And I have much to tell you. But first I am so, so happy to see you again."

"First of all, Calida, I must tell you that I am married."

It was like a bolt of lightning hit her in the chest. Her chin dropped and her mouth remained open as she pulled her arms back from his shoulders. She was speechless for a minute. Her knees felt weak and her hands trembled. She couldn't breathe.

Ricardo said, "Calida, please sit. Are you all right? I should have prepared you. Please sit."

She sat and tried to compose herself. Ricardo handed her a glass of water. She finally said, "I'm okay. It was such a shock. I don't know what I expected. I can't say I blame you."

"I lost track of you, Calida. I hadn't heard from you for a year or more. I figured that you had your own agenda and that I was just a chapter in your life."

"I understand, Ricardo. Is she a local girl?"

"Yes, I met her shortly after you left, but we were just friends. We were at the same dance and a group of us went out for drinks later. We ended the evening together and started dating after that."

"Are you happy?" she asked.

"Very much so. I have a son. He is a year old and I love him very much."

"I'm happy for you, Ricardo. It's probably best for you anyhow. I'm not sure what my future holds. I may be in the rain forest for an undetermined time."

"Calida, I will always remember the time we spent together."

"I will too, Ricardo. I think it best if I leave now."

"Will you be okay?" he asked.

"Yes, I'm good now. I'm very clear on what I must do. Goodbye, Ricardo." She stood, and with her head held high but sad of heart, she walked out the door determined to bury herself into her next adventure. She will be back in the rain forest. There will be hurdles to climb and unknowns to discover. The past is gone and can be but a memory, a very happy memory, but nonetheless gone forever.

Chapter Forty

The next morning, Calida lay in her bed wide-eyed and fully awake. She had slept very little, if at all. She pondered her fate overnight and came to a decision. She jumped out of bed and dressed. She was famished. She skipped dinner the night before and now she felt it.

She went through the lobby and to the small restaurant down the street. She told the waitress to keep the *cafezinho* and fresh fruit coming while they were preparing her eggs, ham, and hash brown potatoes. When she finished, she hailed a taxi and directed him to the airport. She found a manager in the small terminal and introduced herself.

"Yes, *Senhora* Clark. Roget's Lab has set you up for a flight to Japura in a week or so."

"That's what I wanted to talk about. Would it be possible to catch an earlier flight, maybe tomorrow or the next day?"

He chuckled. "There are no scheduled flights, *senhora*. Yours is a charter on a small plane. Japura's airport is even smaller than ours. You are the only passenger. You will sit next to the pilot, and your luggage is loaded in the seats right behind you."

"I didn't know this. Can the charter leave earlier?"

"I need to check with the pilot for his schedule. He is out on a run now, but is returning this evening. I can call you in the morning after I talk to him."

"That will be fine. You can call the hotel or call my satellite cell phone. I'll give you the number."

"Very well, *senhora*. Expect to hear from me in the morning."

She left, caught a taxi, and directed him to the dock area. She got to Quito's shipping company late in the morning and entered the reception room. "*Buenos dias.* Is Quito in today?"

"Yes, *Senhora* Clark. He tried to call you at your hotel and they informed him that you were out. He said to show you right in if you happened to stop by. Come with me."

She entered Quito's office, and when Quito saw her he stood and in his usual boisterous manner he rushed to her and enveloped her in his arms. "Calida, Calida, it's so good to see you."

Breathlessly she answered, "I'm so happy to see you too, Quito."

"Please sit. We have a lot to talk about."

"Thank you, Quito, I visited with Quito Jr. yesterday. He brought me up to date on you and the shipping business."

Quito hesitated. "He told me that you asked about Ricardo. Did you go see him?"

"Yes, I did. I'm very happy for him. He seems to be very much in love with his wife and little boy."

"Ricardo is a special person. I encouraged him to strike out on his own, and he is doing very well. We work together on projects when one or the other is overloaded."

Calida nodded in agreement and said, "Yes, Ricardo is special. We both agreed that our time in the past was a happy chapter in both our lives, but it's just that, and we're thankful that we had it."

"I'm so glad that you feel that way, Calida, but I would not have expected anything different. It's almost noon. Can I buy you lunch?"

"I'd like that very much."

They left the office and Quito took her to his favorite restaurant. They dined and talked about old times.

Quito said, "Tell me about this new job. What exactly will you do out there in the jungle?"

She laughed and explained her duties. She told him about her aspirations on experimenting with herbs and plants, as well as with berries and fruits. "I have also been assigned a project, working with others there. They are working on a fertility drug. The local tribe has a history of older women who remain fertile." She went on in exuberance.

Quito kept asking questions, leading her to in-depth explanations. She brightened up with excited resolve on her theories of cures and treatments.

Hours passed, and when she realized what time it was, she said, "Oh, Quito, I'm so sorry that I took up so much of your day. I just got so involved and it brought back why I came here and what I want to accomplish."

"If questions from an old friend have helped you, then I too have accomplished what I wanted to do."

"You are such a good friend, Quito. This visit with you has helped me over a rough patch, and I'll be forever appreciative."

"I'm here for you, Calida, whenever you need me."

They left the restaurant and soon parted with tearful goodbyes.

***

The next morning, Calida returned to the hotel from breakfast. The desk clerk hailed her and said, "You had a call from *Señor* Garcia at the airport, *senhora*. Please call him." He handed her a note.

"Thank you, I'll call from my room."

When she reached him, he said, "*Buenos dias, senhora*. I've talked to your pilot. His plane is being serviced today. He said that he could work you into his schedule if you can leave early tomorrow morning. He would like to beat the afternoon storms. Your flight is for six hours, so he'd like to depart at 7:00 AM."

"Yes, I can do that. What time should I arrive?"

"Be here at 6:30 so we can load your luggage. How much do you have?"

"I have three suitcases and one rucksack. I also carry a pouch of herbs and medical supplies."

"We have a weight limit on this small plane. Do you know if the bags exceed 25 kilos each?"

"The suitcases are in that range. The rucksack is much less, maybe 15 kilos, and my pouch is like a large handbag, maybe 4 kilos at most."

"I pegged your weight at 60 kilos. Am I close?"

She chuckled. "You're close," she said.

"I think we're within the limit. We'll weigh everything before loading."

She hung up and felt relieved. She would soon be on her way. Before long she'll be back in the environment where she spent her first sixteen years. She spent the rest of the day writing letters to all the people that she felt close to. After this, any written correspondence may take months to arrive, if it arrived at all.

***

She pulled into the airport parking lot well before 6:30 in a loaded taxicab. Her bags were tied with rope to hold them from spilling out of the open trunk of the taxi. Her pouch with medical supplies was alongside her in the rear seat.

A baggage handler loaded the luggage on a cart. He wheeled it into the terminal to be weighed. The pilot checked the total weight and approved it for flight. Calida approached him and introduced herself.

He said, *"Buenos dias. Me llamo es Martinez. Como se llama?"*

"Me llama es Calida Clark," she answered.

He added, "I was hoping you'd understand Spanish."

"In fact, I prefer it if you don't speak English," she answered.

"Good! Then let's get loaded. Some of these afternoon storms can get nasty. We have a six-hour flight, so we should be fine."

The handler loaded the luggage on the two very compact rear seats and tied them down with the seatbelts.

The pilot explained, "I have a small luggage compartment, but it is loaded with cargo for my stop after yours. With you in the copilot seat we should be fine."

All went well and at the target time of 7:00, they were wheels up. The azure sky had a few puffy clouds, but otherwise the ceiling was unlimited and visibility was ten miles.

When Martinez reached cruising altitude, he switched to autopilot. He turned to Calida and said, "This plane will fly itself for a while. This is a new autopilot. I just had it installed yesterday. All I do is set a course and flip this switch."

"That's wonderful. It looks like we've lucked out on the weather."

"So far, so good!" he replied.

The flight continued smoothly and uneventfully for the next four hours. Calida dozed, now relaxing after a stressful several days. She awoke with a start when the plane suddenly encountered clear air turbulence and bounced with a hard, loud jolt. It was pushed up and then dropped like a rock for 500 feet or so.

Martinez flipped off the autopilot and grabbed the controls.

"Are we okay?" said the frightened passenger.

"It's all right, just some rough air. It should smooth out in a few minutes."

The plane bucked a few more times, but less than before. Martinez had throttled back a bit, so with the speed decreased it made for easier handling. Soon, they were in smooth air again.

"We've only got another hour and a half to go but I see a couple of early storm clouds ahead. Maybe that's what gave us the turbulence back there. I changed our altitude and that helped."

"Will we hit the storm?" Calida asked.

"If we do, it may not be a bad one this early in the day. The hotter it is, the worse it gets."

They flew on with the air getting more and more turbulent. They were soon in a cloud bank. Suddenly there was a single nuclear flash of lightning followed in milliseconds by a deafening clap of thunder. The plane seemed to hit a brick wall. It then seemed to be flung forward after a jolting speed decrease. The bouncing strained every rivet to its maximum holding pressure. Martinez was struggling with the controls, but the plane reacted well under his muscled command of the wheel.

Another tooth-rattling bump was too much for the restraints on the luggage. A 25-kilo suitcase flew up and forward from behind the pilot's seat. The bag hit Martinez squarely on the back of the head. Blood squirted from a 2-inch gash on the back of his skull as he slumped in his seat, losing consciousness. His seatbelt was all that kept him from falling out of the pilot's chair when he slumped forward.

Calida screamed and then quickly reacted. All the training she had in ER now came into play. *Take charge.* She grabbed Martinez's shoulders and pulled him back off of the controls. He was still unconscious, but now sitting back and slumped to the side. The plane was acting erratic with no one at the controls. She grabbed the wheel on her side of the plane, pulled back, and was happily surprised that the plane reacted by raising its nose. She tried to level off like she saw Martinez do, and was moderately successful.

It looked like they were coming out of the storm cloud and into smoother air. She looked for the auto control switch, located it, and switched it to the on position. Whatever course they were on is the course it steered. Good enough. Now she could tend to Martinez.

She had kept her medical pouch up front. She opened it and dug out supplies to tend to the bleeding gash on Martinez's head. She turned his head so she could work on him. He groaned.

"That's good," she whispered, "maybe he's coming to."

She blotted the blood, applied an ointment to stem the bleeding, and quickly sutured the gash. Not the neatest job she had ever done, but time was of the essence. She worked quickly and he seemed to be responding to her touches, but he was still under. She uncorked a vial of ammonia and waved it under his nose. He reacted by lifting his head away from that noxious smell. He opened his eyes, looked forward, and suddenly sat up straight.

"What the hell happened?" he yelled and started to grab the wheel.

Calida grabbed his arm. "It's on auto. Sit back before you pass out. You've been unconscious."

He was confused and sat for a moment before saying, "I've got one hell of a headache." He gazed at Calida with a glaze in his eyes. "Can you bring me up to date?"

She explained what happened, and with each minute he became more lucid. He reached up and touched the back of his sore head. "Wow, it feels like a pretty good gash. Did you stich it?"

"I sure did," she answered. "When we land I'll try to make it neater. You'll have a scar, but luckily you have a good head of hair. I had to cut it a little bit."

He was now back in control, corrected the course, and soon they were approaching the Japura airport. He radioed in requesting landing instructions, got them, and landed without any further excitement.

Calida breathed a sigh of relief when they stopped adjacent to a very small terminal building.

Chapter Forty-One

The baggage was unloaded and Calida waited for Martinez to check in with the authorities and report the accidental interruption in their flight. They cleared him for flight on the condition of approval from the doctor. He had a form to be filled out by Calida when he returned.

"It'll be up to you if I'm to resume my flight," he said.

"I understand that they have a dispensary here. Let's find it so I can look at your wound and make some more stitches."

They asked for directions but didn't need to go far in this tiny building. The dispensary was around the corner in a closet-sized room only big enough for one person. She found a chair and put it in the hall so he could sit while she worked on him. It wasn't long before she was done, tested his reaction time, and cleared him for duty.

"Check in with a doctor when you get back to Guajará. He will remove the stitches when the wound is healed. Also, he will make sure there are no aftereffects from the concussion."

He thanked her and they went on their separate ways.

She had been instructed to check in with a boat captain at the docks for the next leg of her journey to Fonte Boa. Finding transportation was a problem since there were no taxis. The terminal manager arranged for an ancient Plymouth station wagon driven by his brother-in-law to take her. The fare was 5 reais, in advance.

She changed into more comfortable clothes at the airport. The heat and humidity were stifling. She wore a light blouse and knee-length shorts, with sandals on her feet. Her hair was pulled back in a ponytail. She had forgotten about the horde of insects in the basin and the huge mosquitoes. She applied a liberal dose of repellant and that seemed to somewhat stem the tide, but a few had feasted on her blood before she could react. One got under her blouse and bit her back in a spot that she'd never be able reach and scratch.

She rode in front with the driver, who drove with the mental attitude of a racecar driver. The roads were not compatible with his type of driving, and she wondered whether or not she'd been safer in the airplane. Thankfully, it was not far to the docks on the river and they soon arrived intact. The smiling brother-in-law unloaded her bags, stood waiting for his tip, jumped into his car, and sped off after she pressed a bill into his hand.

She looked for someone to ask about her boat, but the dock was empty of any human habitation. Two mongrel dogs lying the shade were the only live things in sight. Then she realized the problem. It was *siesta* time. In the early afternoon in these parts, time stood still.

She pulled her bags off of the path of travel and found a shady spot to rest. It was about an hour later when she saw movement, and two young dock workers climbed up from the river where they had been sleeping on, or in, some structure or maybe a boat. They noticed her and walked over.

"*Hola, señorita*, can we help you?"

"Yes, my name is Calida Clark. Roget's Labs has hired a boat to take me and my luggage to Fonte Boa. Can you direct me?"

"*Si*, I think you want Captain Fernandez. But he is not here. I heard him say that his fare was not coming for a week or so."

"I thought I might run into this problem. I'm early."

"His boat is here, and I think maybe he is up in the mountains to get cool. Would you like me to find him?"

"Yes, would you please do that for me? I'll pay."

"How much?" he bargained.

"How much do you want?" Calida asked.

"Five reais, in advance," he said.

She laughed. "Okay," she said as she handed him the five-real bill.

196

He scooted off and she sat on a suitcase and waited.

The other dock worker approached her and said, "My brother is very slow and will be a long time finding Captain Fernandez. Do you want me to help you load the suitcases on the boat?"

"Yes, if that's okay."

"That's okay. No one else is using the boat. You pay me?"

"Yes, I'll pay you five reais. I suppose that's what you want."

"*Si, señorita*, how did you know?"

She laughed as she boarded the boat, and the boy carried her bags to the small flat-bottomed rivercraft. He stored them below decks, but there was no room below for sleeping. She saw the stanchions supporting a solid Bimini top and assumed it was going to be the same as her boat trip down the Amazon when she crewed on the *chalana* with Ricardo, hammocks on the main deck.

This boat was not as solid as the previous one and certainly not as clean. The roaches were rampant and large. This noxious insect was very common here in the tropics. They are never completely eliminated but could be kept somewhat in check with preventative measures. Those measures obviously were not met on this boat. Evidence of rodents was also noted.

She mused to herself, "Oh well, hopefully it's a short trip."

It was well into the evening when she heard talking and a presence on the dock. She saw two figures by light of the moon, walking toward the boat. An unkempt, bearded man walking with the young boy quickly approached.

As he stepped aboard he said, "*Hola, señorita*. I didn't expect you so soon."

"You must be Captain Fernandez," she said.

"Yes, this is my boat," he answered.

"I'm sorry to be early. It was unavoidable."

"No problem, *señorita*, I will prepare for the trip tomorrow and we can leave the next day."

"That's good. If you'll get me a hammock, I'll get it ready to turn in."

"José will get it for you. He will be going with us to Fonte Boa."

"How long will it take us?" she asked.

"If we went by the deep rivers, it will be many weeks, maybe six. But if we take the rivulets and shallow streams it is less comfortable but much quicker."

"Can you do this?" she asked.

"Yes, if you agree. I will need another deck hand but Jose's brother will go. Your company has paid enough to cover the cost."

"I can help too. I crewed on an Amazon *chalana* years ago."

"Very good. I'll get ready to shove off the day after tomorrow," agreed a happy skipper.

***

Early in the morning, after a day of loading stores, the small, shallow draft boat cast off for the backwater cruise to Fonte Boa. They made way downstream on the Amazon, making excellent time on a sunny day with humidity down to a comfortable level. The temperature, though, was in the nineties.

About midday, Captain Fernandez exited the big river into a much smaller tributary. They were now going upstream against the current, but speed was only slightly diminished. As the day wore on the river got narrower and the current got stronger. Darkness approached and the captain turned the helm over to José. He pulled out his pipe and joined Calida on the stern while he enjoyed a smoke.

He said, "We're going to cruise overnight while we're on this bigger rivulet, so your sleep may be disturbed. I will use one boy as lookout while the other on sleeps. I'll be on the helm most of the time, but José is a capable helmsman, so he can spell me."

She answered, "Please, Captain, I can help. Try me on the helm."

"Okay, *señorita*, why don't you try now to get the feel while there's still some daylight?"

She took the wheel and proved that she was capable, to the captain's delight.

The night cruise went well and they made good time on the rivulet. Days later the captain found a well-hidden smaller rivulet whose entrance was so difficult to spot. They passed it and had to approach from upstream.

Conditions changed on this leg of the trip. It was still hot but very humid, with trees and brush encroaching well into the flow of the stream. It now bordered on being oppressive, what with tree branches hanging over head. Any breeze was stifled, and now the danger of snakes and other varmints dropping into the boat while roosting in the branches was possible.

"We've especially got to watch for spade heads, *señorita.* That's one mean snake."

"Yes, I'm familiar with that one, Captain."

The river water now was as black as coffee. This was a very old stream with Precambrian sandstone at its source that has long ceased to erode. The water carries almost no sediment and few minerals. It is blackened by tannin and acid from leaf litter. A side benefit is that very few mosquitos can breed in this environment.

Weeks of travel through streams, lakes, and shallow water bordering on being nothing more than swampland were soon over. But not before encountering noxious, biting insects of many types, curious carnivores, while tied to a tree overnight. Also snakes that dropped out of trees, one of which landed in Calida's hammock. She was trying to sleep in the oppressive heat, and in her exuberance to vacate the swinging bed she landed hard on the deck. The snake was not a dangerous one, but it still was a frightening experience. The fall hurt, but worse was the loud, boisterous laughter coming from the rest of the crew.

They were finally back in deep water on the last leg, and will cruise on the Paraná Gajarai, a tributary of the Amazon, until it merges with Rio Solimas, the river on which the little *ciudad* of Fonte Boa was located.

They arrived late afternoon, which was after *siesta* time. There were a few workers on the city dock to assist in tie up. Captain Fernandez advised them that he was bringing a passenger for Roget's Labs. They knew nothing of the disposition, but told Calida that the lab had a small office in the town.

It was a pleasant, lazy little town and welcomed tourism. As such it had several small but efficient hotels. Calida hired a local worker to transport her and her luggage to the closest one. She bid her goodbyes to the captain, José, and his brother, but was pleased to get off of the tiny rivercraft and into a room with a shower. Tomorrow she would contact the lab for directions for the next and last step of her journey.

Chapter Forty Two

The next day was spent trying to locate her contact to arrange her transportation to the outpost laboratory. The problem was that after she was able to locate the office, she found that it was locked and none of the adjacent offices had any idea of who or even when someone would be there. Fortunately she was able to contact corporate back in the States on her satellite phone.

"Hello, Mr. Barry . . . Yes, I can hear you. I'm in Fonte Boa and no one seems to be available here to direct me to the outpost lab." She listened as static crackled in the earpiece and a distant voice said, "Go to the office."

"There's no one there, Mr. Barry."

The crackling static abated some and finally Mr. Barry said, "Stay in your hotel. I'll contact the lab and get this back on track."

"Thank you, sir," she said as the line went dead.

Hours later her phone rang and it was Mr. Barry. He said, "They were expecting you two weeks from now, but they will send someone into town to get you. They have your number and will call when they arrive. The office is only used when someone comes into town, and is just a base to work from. It will take several days or longer for them to get there."

She was getting impatient. She was anxious to get to work and this trip had really taken its toll on her.

***

It was late in the afternoon three days later when she got a call. A scratchy sounding voice said, "This is Bomar from Roget's. I'm supposed to pick up someone from the States. Is that you?"

"Yes, this is Calida Clark. I'm in the downtown hotel. Where are you?"

"I'm calling from the company office. Will you be ready to go first thing in the morning?"

"Yes, of course. Where should I meet you?"

"I'll pick you up at the hotel. Just be standing out front with your gear. I'll be driving a jeep. Don't be late."

"What time are you coming?"

"Dammit, I said first thing. That means when the sun comes up. Just make sure you're there."

She heard a click and then a dial tone. "Wow, what a reception," she muttered.

***

Calida was in front of the hotel with her bags before sunrise. She waited and soon a muddy jeep squealed up and came to an abrupt stop very close to where she stood. She was starting to burn and decided she would not give this rude man any satisfaction. She didn't budge or even blink as the filthy jeep came very close to where she stood.

A disheveled, bearded man with long hair and raggedy clothes sat in the driver's seat. He turned his head and stared at this tall blonde, neatly dressed woman and said, "Well, load up so we can get goin'."

She loaded the three bags and rucksack into the backseat of the open jeep, walked around, and climbed into the passenger's seat. She sat for a moment before she turned and with fire in her eyes and firmly said, "Dammit! Are you going to go or not?"

He popped the clutch and squealed down the street. He headed east and soon reached the outskirts of this small town. At the end of the paved city street, he picked up a dusty dirt road. A jeep or similar type vehicle was needed to negotiate this type of route. It soon turned into a muddy, rutted path that had unexpected curves and dips. It was a wild ride and he hadn't spoken a word since they left hours before.

By the end of the day, they were deep into the rain forest and he continued when the sky opened up with a pelting rain. It rained so hard,

201

Calida thought that if she looked up and opened her mouth she would surely drown. Fortunately it only lasted for about an hour, but turned the path into a quagmire, which now made for a slow go.

The jeep got caught up in a mud pit, and Bomar spoke for the first time, "Can you drive?"

"Yes, I can try," she answered.

He hopped out. She slid over, and after a half hour of him pushing and her spinning the tires they were free. He was covered with mud when he got back in. She stifled a laugh. He glared at her, then he drove on.

As they drove she said, "Back there when we were stuck, I thought I saw movement in the brush. Did you notice anything?"

"No, I didn't, I was pretty busy shoving us out of the mire, if you remember."

"I just had a feeling that we were being watched."

"It could have been an animal. There are plenty out there, if it was anything at all."

"Yeah, probably," she said.

It was close to 6:00, which is twilight anywhere close to the equator, when they arrived at a fast-flowing stream. The water was clear and Bomar came to an abrupt stop. He then hopped out and dove into the stream. He quickly washed off the mud and climbed out of the water, just before several caiman made an entrance from upstream.

Dripping wet, he returned to the jeep. He grabbed a huge, wicked-looking revolver from a holster mounted under the dash, aimed it toward the group of caiman, and squeezed off three rounds. The retort was ear shattering. The bullets splashed harmlessly in the water but the caiman scattered, causing the clear stream to become muddy and turbulent. They quickly swam underwater back upstream from where they had come.

He reloaded the revolver and said, "I'll start a fire and we'll stay here for the night. The company keeps some stores in that shack over there with some provisions, so we can get a bite to eat. There's a hammock in there. You can sleep there tonight. I'll sleep in the jeep."

"Okay, I'll check out the stores while you dry off," she said.

He grunted and started gathering firewood.

After they ate and were sitting by the fire, she said, "Tell me, Bomar, are you always this pleasant? Or did you save this attitude just for me?"

He threw a few more small branches on the fire and finally answered, "I was right in the middle of an experiment that I've worked on for weeks, and that idiot director pulled me off to make this trip."

"Oh, I'm sorry. I guess my early arrival screwed things up."

"Naw, I didn't even know someone was coming at all."

"Well, anyway, I'm sorry I ruined your experiment."

"It's not ruined. It'll wait till I get back. I just hate to be interrupted."

"Well, I do too. I think I'll turn in. Do you want to leave at first light?" she asked.

"Yep, we'll be going by boat tomorrow. I just brought the little skiff, so we probably won't get all your stuff on board. Take what you need and someone can come back and get the rest later."

She sighed, got up, and walked to the shack to get some rest. She hesitated before going in. She stopped and turned toward the thick brush alongside the campsite. "Hello, is anyone there?" Her inborn sense from living in the rain forest was telling her that she was not alone.

She stood rock still and listened with ears as sharp as a wild animal's. There was no sound, just an uneasy feeling. She waited before entering, and suddenly Bomar stole up behind her and said, "Is something wrong?"

"I don't know," she answered. "It's just a feeling I have. I guess it's a holdover from my early days."

"Hmm," he said, "maybe we should turn in. I don't see anything."

***

She was sleeping soundly when a loud series of gunshots jolted her out of her deep slumber. And the loud squeals of a whole herd of some type of wild animal shattered the thick, humid jungle air. She swung herself out of the hammock and slowly opened the door of the storage shack.

In the flickering light of the campfire, she saw Bomar standing by the jeep with a smoking gun. She could hear the thrashing of brush as something big and numerous crashed through the jungle, stampeding to get away from that terrible, loud stick belching fire.

Bomar walked to the rear of the jeep, and that's when she saw something lying in a heap at his feet.

She approached and said, "Are you okay?"

"Yeah, damn wild pigs, I hate 'em."

She took a closer look. "Oh yes," she said, "the white-lipped *queixadas*. You were lucky."

"Whatta ya mean? What do you know about these pigs?"

"Well, I know that they usually travel in bigger packs, and if so, you wouldn't have scared them off so easily. And I also know they have canines as sharp as knives that can slice flesh to ribbons. They typically go for the Achilles tendon. They'll attack horses and even a jaguar."

"Yeah, well, they don't scare me. Besides, how do you know so much? I thought you were new here," Bomar said.

"Yes, I am new, and it's been awhile since I've hunted them, but when I was younger I learned a lot about them."

He gave her a long stare. "Hey, who are you anyway?"

She laughed and said, "Since we may be working together, maybe we should get acquainted."

"Yeah, okay. It'll be light in another hour. Let's make some coffee and talk a little bit. You don't seem like the other newbies. Some of them only lasted a month or so. You seem like a veteran."

She stuck out her hand and said, "Hi, Bomar, I'm Calida and I was born in the Amazon basin."

Since he was about six inches shorter than she was, he reached up for her hand, shook it, and said, "I gotta hear the rest of the story now."

They sat around the fire, drinking coffee for the next few hours. She gave him a brief history of her life. He was wide-eyed and didn't interrupt until she was finished. "Now tell me about your life," she said.

He laughed. "I was born and raised in New York City," he said, "The only wild animals that I encountered wore pants down around their knees. My mom made me study and I found that it came easy for me. I got a scholarship to Columbia and got my master's and doctorate there under a grant provided by Roget's Laboratories. I agreed to work for them after graduation, and spent a few years in a lab in the city. I requested a transfer here so I could continue my study on the microbial diversity of our ancestors, and whether today's civilized diets and lifestyles strip us of some of the good bugs in our bodies that we might want back. There's a remote tribe near here in the Pantanal that have the most diverse colonies of bacteria ever reported living in and on the human body. I'm basing part of my study on them."

"You surprise me, Bomar," she said.

"What's the matta? Didn't you think a kid from the Bronx had any brains?" he retorted.

"No, no, I mean you gave me the impression when we first met that you were not a happy camper."

"Yeah, well, I guess I was upset about somethin' else. You'll see when you get there."

"What do you mean?" she asked.

"Ah, forget it. Let's pack up and get goin'," he said.

They put out the fire, put two of her suitcases in the shack, loaded the other one and the rucksack in the boat along with her medical pouch, and they shoved off. Bomar was in the stern steering with the outboard motor, and Calida sat in the bow on lookout for obstructions in the river. Bomar advised her to look sharp for logs and gators and that it will take most of the day to reach the outpost.

Chapter Forty-Three

This was a different kind of boat ride for Calida. It was a small open boat and she was up in the bow, bouncing along, getting splashed with the river water. Her assignment from Bomar was to look for obstructions in the water. The shallow, narrow river got wider but even shallower. Several times the boat bottomed out on a sandy shoal, but Bomar gunned it and they seemed to skip right over. Then she realized that he reveled in this. He was enjoying the wild ride, so she relaxed and thought that she might as well enjoy it too. They both were getting wet from river water and it was refreshing in this stifling jungle atmosphere.

The enjoyment soon ceased as suddenly Calida screamed, "GATOR," and Bomar abruptly turned the boat to miss this huge, 300-hundred-pound obstruction. It wasn't soon enough. He almost missed it, but that huge swinging tail caught the lightweight skiff and lifted the bow clear of the water. The boat took a violent swing to starboard and came close to a capsizing.

Calida hung on the gunwale, but as the boat tipped she lost her grip and flew from the boat and belly smacked into the shallow water. The boat continued past her, out of control, the spinning prop coming close to gashing her flailing legs. She righted herself and realized she could touch bottom. She was waist deep when she saw movement in the muddy water.

That huge gator was approaching her. She could see its head and eyes breaking the surface.

She threw her arms high over her head and screamed as loud as she could, rising up and making herself as big and aggressive as possible. The gator hesitated, but soon realized that this girl was not a threat and made his move toward his next meal. Suddenly, roaring between them was Bomar, pointing the skiff at the gator like a missile out of a howitzer. This time it was not a glancing blow but a direct hit, and he aimed right for the open jaws of the monster.

The huge predator arched back as the boat hit him under the jaws and slammed him into the water. It was not a fatal blow but enough to make him turn tail and sink into the mire to contemplate a new attack. It was a jolting blow to the skiff as well, damaging the bow.

Bomar put the motor in reverse and backed down. He located Calida and called to her, "Swim alongside and I'll help you aboard."

As she quickly swam, stirring up the water, the monster floated to the surface and even though wounded, he rose up to attack the defenseless person in the water. He opened those heavy jaws with huge yellow teeth dripping with his own blood, ready to clamp down on his prey and pull her under water, where he would hold her under until she'd drown. When she struggled no more, he could pull her into his lair, where he would mercilessly feast on her body until satisfied. He could return at will and continually ravage her body.

But wait!

Without any warning, two arrows flew out of the thick jungle. The hum of the killing projectiles was a familiar one to Calida. Each of the arrows found their marks. The one that entered an eye and buried itself into the small brain of the predator would have been enough to stop the attack, but the other one also hit in a vulnerable spot, the chest cavity, and would have caused death eventually as it bore into the heart.

As she saw the arrows hit, Calida sprinted to the boat. She awkwardly sprawled over the gunwale, sputtering from the churned up, muddy water.

"Are you okay?" Bomar yelled.

"I am now but I was a little worried awhile ago," she said.

"I think we lost one of the suitcases," he said.

"It could have been worse. If I have my rucksack and pouch, I'm happy. Is the boat damaged?" she asked.

"It looks like the bow is caved in, but if we go slowly we should be okay."

"That was one big gator. Where did the arrows come from?" she asked.

"There must have been some hunters from the village. They'll probably drag that gator out of the water and have him for dinner."

"They didn't show themselves, but whoever it was I'd like to thank them," she added.

"We'll find out when we get to the outpost."

They limped along the rest of the day, but soon arrived at the makeshift docks of the Roget's outpost laboratory.

***

Two young lab assistants met them at the outpost dock. They grabbed the bow and stern lines thrown to them and made them fast.

The husky one said, "Hey, Bomar, you did a number on this skiff. The old girl is not gonna like that."

"Mind your own business, Paul. It was a necessary collision to save a life," he growled.

Bomar and Calida climbed out and stepped ashore. She handed her gear to the same husky one called Paul.

As he offered his hand to Calida, he said, "Looks like corporate is finally sending someone that's easy on the eyes. Let me help you, miss. My name is Paul and I'm at your beck and call."

She tried to hide a smile. "Thank you, Paul. You can start by showing me where I should report."

"Right-o, miss. Can I ask your name?"

"Yes, it's Calida. I'll carry the pouch. You can take the rucksack if you want to."

"Yes, I will, and the office is this way. You can check in there."

She turned back and said, "Are you coming, Bomar?"

"No, go ahead. I want to check in with maintenance and show them the damage on the boat."

They got to the office and did the required paperwork to check in. The office clerk asked if Calida had met the director, Dr. Baruni.

"No, I haven't. Where do I do that?"

"She's not in her office and I'm not sure where she's gone, but I'll tell her that you've arrived. She may come to your room. You'll be sharing it with Dr. Beth Lawton. Paul will show you where the women's quarters are located."

They left and Paul said, "It's a short walk. This is not a big outpost, as you will see."

***

It was several hours later. Calida had settled into her quarters, met her roommate, and was resting when someone knocked on her door. She said, "Come in."

The door opened and Dr. Baruni came in. Dr. Baruni was a woman from India, small in stature, with brown skin, sharp eyes, and a piercing voice, not the typical singsong speech of a person from that country. She said, "Hello, Dr. Clark. I understand that you had an encounter with a resident of our river on the way here."

"Yes, Dr. Baruni, I did, but I'm happy to be here."

"Very well, you can put that to rest. You're here for one reason: corporate sent you. I did not ask for you. I'm assigning you to join a group working on a project studying the mosquito."

"Oh, I see. Dr. Baruni, my specialty is pharmacology. I have a strong background in medications derived from herbs and roots found in the rain forest."

"Let's get this straight. I assign the work here. You will do as I say," Baruni emphatically said.

"I understand. It's just that—"

"They told me who you are. It doesn't impress me. I know the history of Amazonian women and my belief is that it is 90 percent trash talk and 10 percent bull dung. You'll do what I say or take the next skiff back to the city," she said with venom dripping from her voice. She spun on her heel and walked out.

Calida was speechless.

***

Several weeks passed and Calida found that her fellow scientists on the mosquito project were friendly and cooperative. The study actually centered on the diseases carried by mosquitos. The group classified the different species of the insect as to which disease it was likely to carry. Among them were malaria, dengue, and yellow fever. The study was to pinpoint which and why others did not.

Calida was most interested in the daylight mosquito that carried dengue fever. This was a particularly devastating disease with no known cure or inoculation. She was studying a slide under a microscope when one of the other women in the group approached her and said, "How about a coffee break, Calida?"

"Yes, Elsa, I'm ready for one."

As they sat and drank a strong *cafezinho,* they chatted. Elsa said, "I want to tell you about a fellow worker that left here last month when Dr. Baruni severely chastised her."

"I'd rather not gossip, Elsa. Everyone knows that I'm not Dr. Baruni's favorite scientist and we can just leave it at that."

"Well, that's not what I wanted to tell you."

"What is it then?"

"Dr. Hennesy was also studying the dengue mosquito. She visited the Indian village in the Pantanal a day's travel from here. They were friendly and gave her some data that was helpful. She made several trips there. I went with her on two of them."

"Do you have something that I can use?"

"Yes, I have all her data. But the most interesting thing is that on our last trip we discovered that there may actually be a treatment for dengue, even possibly a preventative treatment."

Calida sat up attentively and said, "When can we study this data?"

"I'll bring it over now," Elsa said.

Chapter Forty-Four

The two women scientists pored over the data left by Dr. Hennesy for several days. It was very thorough.

"This is so intriguing," exclaimed Calida. "I can't imagine Dr. Baruni letting this brilliant person leave."

"That's why I decided to show this to you. Baruni would quash anything that Hennesy discovered. When she left and gave this data to me, she made me promise to pass it on to someone who would follow through on the study."

"Do you think we can visit this village?" asked Calida.

"We can make a request through channels. It probably will be approved. First we'll need two more people, preferably men. It's a day-long boat trip upriver, and we'll be gone close to a week."

"In my early days I heard of the Pantanal. It's a great ecological reserve and has the largest wetlands in the world. It's perfect for breeding mosquitos," Calida added.

"Yes, I agree, but also perfect for piranhas, anacondas, and alligators, among many other such things."

"What do you know about the tribe?" asked Calida.

"They are an ancient tribe, an offshoot of the Yanomami Indians. They speak Arawak, so that may be a problem. They love to use *curupa* powder in their ceremonies. Our main contact will be the shaman who is the custodian of botanical knowledge that we want to experiment with. He's the only one with a smattering of English and can expound on the rich mythology of the tribe."

"The language won't be a problem. I have an understanding of Arawak."

"My god, Calida, I heard that you have a broad history. Where did you learn Arawak?"

"I lived with an ancient tribe for three years when I was a teen. In fact, I acted as their shaman," Calida said.

"Well, I've got to ask," said Elsa. "The rumor is that you are an Amazon turned civilized. Is that true?"

Calida laughed. "Yes, I was born in a village of Amazon warriors. My mother was the leader of the tribe and I was being groomed to replace her. All were killed in an earthquake. At least to my knowledge, I was the only survivor. I lived in the rain forest for a good many years before I found my birth father. I don't know what you mean about becoming civilized. The Amazons have been civilized for a thousand years."

"I'm sorry, I didn't mean anything. I guess I used the wrong terminology. Do you think there may have been others that got away during the earthquake?"

"I don't know. When I got back there, everyone was dead. I suppose some may have escaped before it all collapsed. Who should we ask to accompany us to the Indian village?"

"Well, you know Bomar. He's usually willing to travel away from here," Elsa said.

"That's good. How about Paul? He seems strong and capable. Some of these scientists are a little fragile," Calida offered.

"That would be a good pair. I'll take care of asking them. Let's wait about a week. We can brush up on Hennesy's notes."

"I agree," said Calida.

The night before they were to leave for the trip to the Pantanal, Calida was studying the notes on the dengue mosquito. Her window was open when she heard a noise outside. She stood and looked out, "Hello! Is someone there?"

There was a rustling in the bushes. She ran to the door and burst outside. As she rounded the corner of the cottage, she saw two figures disappearing into the brush leading to the rain forest. "Hey, stop!" she called.

To no avail. The figures disappeared into the night.

She thought to herself, "I wonder . . . They didn't appear to be Indians. They weren't dark skinned enough. Hmmm, I guess I'll never know, they're long gone now." She went back and turned in. It would be a long day tomorrow.

It was a larger boat than the one Bomar and she took from the city. This one had a sleeping berth down below that the two women could use if they wanted. Hammocks would be used topside, and according to weather conditions, all four may sleep in the open deck. Mosquito netting was mandatory here in the Pantanal.

Bomar, being the most experienced at running the boat, was the unspoken skipper. They were underway in good time early in the morning. It was a good day to travel. A high pressure had settled over them, which cooled the temperature to the high eighties, but more important, was that the humidity had dropped to a tolerable level.

The two women were sitting on the stern deck enjoying a pleasant run on the river. Calida asked, "Elsa, has there ever been any problem with prowlers at the outpost?"

"What do you mean by prowlers?"

"I mean someone moving around the grounds during the night."

"I remember some time ago when they caught a couple of rogue Indians that were coming in at night and stealing food. But they proved to be harmless. Why do you ask?"

"There was someone outside of my cottage last night. They ran off without any harm. But I was concerned."

"It might have been some Indians again," Elsa said.

"These two looked lighter than Indians. Do you think anyone in the complex would be prowling around?"

"I doubt it, but I guess it's possible."

"Oh well, they got scared off when I yelled, so they probably weren't dangerous."

Paul ventured back with the women and the conversation turned lighthearted. It was a pleasant morning.

At about noon, when the sun was high in the sky, Bomar throttled down and eased the boat into a shady cove and dropped anchor. "Whatta ya say we have a bite of lunch?" he called to the crew.

"Sounds good to us," was the response.

Paul said, "This is a great spot, Bomar, nice and cool. Have you been here before?"

"Yeah, we used to stop here when Hennesy and her group made this run. She was a fine lady. I miss her."

"Do I detect a little sadness there, Bomar?" asked Paul.

"Just one more reason I can't respect our director," said Bomar.

Elsa changed the subject and the conversation turned lighthearted again and they enjoyed their lunch.

As they weighed anchor to get underway, Calida glanced on shore. She said "Elsa, did you see that?"

"What, Calida?

"I swear someone was watching us when we were eating."

"You are really getting paranoid. What did you see?"

"Well, it was more of a movement. My hunter's sense just kicked in and I know something was out there."

"There are plenty of animals in the jungle. You of all people should know that."

"It wasn't an animal. I would have smelled it."

"Oh come on, Calida, you can smell that well?"

"It was much better when I lived in the rain forest and I think it's coming back to me. So yes, I can smell animals."

"Well, there are Indians out there too."

They soon got underway, and by very late in the afternoon they arrived at the village. Canoes left the shore to greet them and escort the power boat into the cove adjacent to the village. The rest of the villagers lined the bank, and since it was close to evening dusk, some were waving torches.

The closer they got to the village shore, the more they could hear a chant coming from the village. It was a hum with an occasional lilting melody. In the background someone tapped on a drum or maybe a hollow log to keep time as the chant went on. In the center of the group of people there stood a tall man in ornate regalia. He stood with arms folded and a stern look on his face.

Bomar leaped ashore with a bow line and made it fast to the stump of a tree close to the river's edge. He then walked up to the shaman, who was obviously the head man here today, and said, "Hello, Quinque, I bring friends to talk to you about your fine medicine."

"What else you bring me?" the shaman answered.

"I have many fine trinkets in my boat for you."

"You bring sweets?"

"Maybe a few. Only for you. Too much, not good," Bomar said.

Quinque grunted.

"Can I bring my friends ashore to meet you?"

Quinque grunted his approval.

Bomar went back to the boat and helped them ashore.

Chapter Forty-Five

The crowd of villagers drew back as the scientists disembarked from the boat and clamored ashore. A low rumble sounded as the villagers mumbled something in the strange Arawak tongue.

"They're disturbed about something," said Calida.

Quinque stepped forward in front of the distressed crowd of villagers and said in a booming voice, "Who is this woman that you have brought to our village?"

Bomar was aghast. He looked back at Calida. There was no doubt that she stood out with her long blonde hair and golden skin, standing a head taller than the tallest Indian.

She sensed it and in the language of the villagers, she said, "Oh great shaman, why are you displeased with me?"

Now the murmur of the crowd grew louder. From the bystanders, she heard a quavering voice, "She speaks our tongue."

"WHO ARE YOU?" Quinque boomed even louder.

In their native tongue she answered, "I am Dr. Calida Clark. I came to ask you to explain how you cure the dreaded fever that is brought on by daytime mosquitos. Why are you and your people frightened of me? I have done you no harm."

"It is said in our ancient lore that the tall women with hair the color of the sun and skin with a golden hue, like the pebbles that we find in the streams, will return to fight us in a devastating battle. They will steal the men of our tribe."

"What is the basis for this legend?" asked Calida.

"Long ago, these ravaging women warriors raided our villages and captured our warriors. The captured men were never to be seen again. Our tribes banded together, and there was a great battle, causing many losses on both sides. Finally the women withdrew, but it was told that they would return someday. They were seen on a journey to the mountains where they are said to live and flourish. Are you of that tribe? Did you come to spy on us and others will follow?"

"No, of course I'm not. My medical training was in America. I work for the laboratory and was sent to study the disease carried by mosquitos."

"Where did you learn to speak in our tongue?"

She had to be cautious here. "My father is a missionary with the Yano-Matis tribe. I learned the language as a child."

The shaman gathered a group of men around and withdrew to the side. It was a heated discussion. When the conference was over, the shaman, who definitely made the final decision, walked back to the group of visitors from the lab. "Dr. Bomar, does this woman work with you?"

"Yes, she is a scientist like I am, and is studying diseases carried by mosquitos, as she has told you."

"We are wary. She can stay, but she will be watched."

"Thank you, Quinque. You have no reason to fear her."

***

The next day, the group of scientists set up the portable lab they brought with them on the boat in a hut furnished by the shaman.

"The larvae in this tray of tepid water are ready to hatch. We should transfer them into these large plastic buckets. Make sure you stretch the pantyhose over the top like those that are already infected with dengue. We don't want them to get out until we're ready to experiment with them," Dr. Bomar instructed.

"Do you think Quinque will divulge any of his secrets so we can try it out on lab rats first?" Calida asked.

"I know a little bit already," Elsa said. "Hennesy made notes about the venom from tocandira ants."

Calida added, "I've had some experience with those ants, and I can tell you they are fierce, especially if you accidently happen on a colony and they attack. They are big for an ant, about an inch long, and their bite can cause indescribable pain. I saw a man who was bitten on his feet and he was drenched in sweat, trembling all over and vomiting while writhing in pain."

"Hennesy's notes say it must be added to the bark of a tree, but she didn't know what tree or how it was done. That's why we need Quinque to give us the formula."

"He's very territorial with this kind of information. We may only get a sample to take back on this trip. It's going to take several trips and some sort of special gift before we get the whole ball of wax," Bomar said.

"I also wonder how the venom is extracted from the ant," said Calida. "That alone has to be a special procedure."

"There are many questions, none of which we will discover on this trip. So let's collect what we can, go back to the lab, inject some mice, and arrange another trip in about a month," instructed Bomar.

They did their due diligence, collecting as much data as possible and intermingling with the local tribe. A week passed quickly and they made their way back to the outpost lab.

On the return trip, Calida asked Bomar, "What's your opinion on the shaman sharing his secrets with us?"

"We'll have to catch him at the right time. He is a regular user of *curupa* powder. He takes some of the others and they go off into a special spot where they use it and hallucinate, according to Hennesy. She experimented with it, and claimed she experienced vertigo at first, then she said it kicked in and she seemed to float above ground. She said she could see beautiful scenes in the distance."

"She took a real chance taking that stuff," Calida said.

"Yeah, but that's how she got as much information as she did. The two of them got high together."

"I've heard of some terrible side effects with that hallucinogen. She's fortunate that she didn't overdose. These shamans don't always give the same dose of any medication. Most think that more is better."

"Well, she also said that after the beauty she saw savage beasts and she fell on the ground and awoke fighting and very violent for a short time before returning to a somewhat stable condition. She said she would never do it again."

"That's probably one reason for the mood swings of Quinque. His brain is probably half fried," she added.

"Anyway," said Bomar, "we might catch him in a vulnerable moment after one of his trips."

"Okay, I'm anxious to use the miniscule sample that we got on some lab animals."

"Yeah, he was very reluctant to even give us that. I doubt if there is enough to break it down. We probably will be better served to make sure it works."

***

During the next several weeks, experiments were conducted on a mouse and one very small monkey. Calida used the mosquitos that were known carriers of dengue and purposely stung the experimental lab animals. After ten days, both experienced symptoms of dengue fever and were near death. She inoculated both with the serum carried back from the Indian village.

The mouse was too far gone and died. Possibly it was too small and fragile to ward off the disease. Not so with the monkey. With more body mass, it was able to fight the initial phases of the fever and chills. It was fully involved with the disease when Calida inoculated him with the remainder of her small sample.

The first reaction was not good. He faded and was close to death during the night. Calida stayed awake, monitoring him closely. When the sun came up, the little monkey rallied. He progressed throughout the morning and by afternoon the fever had regressed to almost normal. She fed him soup through an eyedropper, and though very weak, he slept through the night. She again stayed in the lab, but was able to get some sleep.

In the morning, Bomar entered the lab. "Well, this looks promising. How did it go?" he asked.

"From what I can see so far, it worked. I still must take his vitals, but ordinarily he'd be sick for another week to ten days, if he survives at all," Calida answered.

"Well, I'll be damned. Calida, this is a major discovery."

"Let's not count our chickens yet, Bomar. This is only one case, and the mouse died," Calida advised.

"I know but I'm still excited," Bomar said.

"I guess we should tell the director what we found," she added.

"Hell no! Let's wait. If she thinks we're on to something she'll pull us off and put her sidekick on it. Then it's her discovery. I'm tired of her totalitarian attitude. She runs this place like a Nazi death camp."

"Oh come on, Bomar, she's not that bad."

"Oh yeah, wait till you get screwed over like I did."

"Okay, let's wait, but you know she's got to get involved sooner or later."

"I've put in the request for another trip for the four of us. I'm asking that we stay in the village for a month. That will give us time to run an experiment on people."

"Isn't that a little dangerous at this stage?"

"That's okay, some of them have probably already been cured a time or two anyway."

"Suppose we don't get volunteers?"

"You be surprised what some will do for a Coca-Cola."

"That's bribery, Bomar."

"Call it what you will. It works."

Several days later they were advised that the request for a one-month experimental trip for the four of them was approved. The largest boat was made ready with enough provisions for the stay. The four scientists collected all the necessary gear to proceed with the experiment offsite.

The day before they were to leave, the director called Bomar into her office. She said, "I'm expecting some results on this trip, Dr. Bomar. One month is a very long time. If you think it's just going to be one big party with hanky-panky going on, you've got another think coming. I want some results out of that loser bunch that you're taking with you. Do you understand?"

"Yes, ma'am! We're going to get some good data on this trip, I'm sure," Bomar replied.

She stood, extended her arm, pointed with one finger, and growled, "I'm making you responsible, Dr. Bomar. It'll be your ass this time if I don't get results."

Bomar walked out. When he reached the outer office and closed her door, he turned and gave her the middle finger salute.

The mosquito crew left for the village the next morning.

Chapter Forty-Six

The trip upriver to the Indian village was long and uneventful, but again when they anchored in the cove and ate a relaxing lunch Calida felt like she was being watched. The close proximity to the rain forest was, obviously, awakening her inherent skills that she learned from living in the jungle. It also awakened those inherited natural defenses that came down the line from her mother and before her for a thousand years.

The trip took longer, and with the later start, it was well after dark when they arrived at the shore of the village. They were surprised to see the shore lined solidly by the village residents, each holding a burning torch. The shoreline was ablaze with orange and red fire, and with the chant from the crowd, it almost seemed to be a holy site. The shaman was standing in the center, with arms folded in a regal pose. He was dressed in even more ornate regalia than when he greeted them on the first trip.

The boat slowly nosed up to the shore. Two husky Indians waded into the water and pulled the bow up to rest on the beach. Quinque walked the edge where the land met the water. The chanting suddenly stopped as he raised his arm and held his open hand high above his head.

He bellowed in his best English, "Welcome to our village, white doctors."

Bomar stood on the fore deck, smiled at the shaman, and said, "Thank you, great shaman. Please come aboard and enjoy a refreshing Coca-Cola."

Quinque beamed. He waved the two husky men over and they lifted him onboard the boat, keeping his feet dry. Bomar and the crew welcomed him. Quinque's eyes lit up at each gift shown to him. He stayed aboard until the wee hours of the morning, swilling Coca-Cola and admiring trinkets and candy offered by the white doctors.

***

The next several days were spent setting up equipment in the temporary lab. Petrie dishes of larvae and jars of infected mosquitos lined the tables.

"I think we'll have enough infected mosquitos to run some real tests, Bomar. What should we do about subjects?" Paul asked.

"I stayed up late last night talking to Quinque. He is reluctant to volunteer anyone and he calls the shots," Bomar answered.

"The real question is *will he give us any serum*? And more of a question is *will he divulge the ingredients and the formula*?"

"I did get a little more input from him late in the night when he was feeling tipsy from that drink that they brew here. It's pretty potent, but he seems to thrive on it. I tried it and just a sip did me in. I faked it after that," said Bomar with a chuckle.

"What did you learn?" asked Calida.

"Well, to answer your question on how do they get the ant venom, they don't. They actually use the larvae before they become ants. It seems that the ants lay eggs in the buriti palm trees, under the bark."

"How do they use them?" she asked.

"He wouldn't go into detail from there. I think he resented that he told me that much. There apparently is another ingredient besides the bark, but he clammed up at that point."

Paul interrupted with, "Hey, look, we still need a subject or two. How about if I volunteer to get a mosquito bite? And maybe someone else from our group will be the second one."

Elsa added, "Hey, if you'll do it, Paul, I'll volunteer too."

"Wait a minute. Before you guys go stinging yourselves, let's make sure he'll provide the serum to combat the fever and chills," Bomar added.

"Let's find him and get this show on the road," Paul said with excitement.

***

A week later, Paul and Elsa were lying in their bunks sweating and writhing in a semiconscious state. They both were chilled to the bone and their teeth were chattering to the point of being unable to properly converse. They were fully involved in dengue fever. Calida and Bomar were making them as comfortable as possible.

Calida asked, "Where is he, Bomar? Is he really going to bring the serum or not?"

"Here he comes now. You should know that a shaman will use as much showmanship as he can and arriving at the eleventh hour is all part of it."

Quinque came into the hut holding a gourd of the serum.

"What do you want us to do, Quinque?" asked Bomar.

"You stand back. Quinque will do," he answered.

With a flourish, chanting his unintelligible rite, he approached Elsa's bunk. He put his hand over her nose and pulled up, opening her mouth. He then poured a milky liquid into her mouth and slammed it shut while she coughed and gagged, swallowing the serum. He held her down as she struggled, retching dry heaves, her arms flailing. Quinque was much stronger than her and he held her at bay. She soon stopped fighting, laid back, and shivered even more than before. Her eyes turned back into her head and only the whites showed.

Calida grabbed a blanket and wrapped her body that was now close to convulsing. "What's wrong with her?" Calida called out.

Quinque stood back and calmly said, "It will change. Just wait."

A few anxious minutes of a violent reaction passed and slowly Elsa's seizures abated. Her body shuddered with a few spasms, and then she settled into a restful sleep. Calida wiped the sweat from Elsa's brow. The bed was soaking wet from her ordeal.

"She will sleep now," said Quinque as he moved to Paul's bunk.

Paul was conscious but his face was beet red with fever and he shivered uncontrollably. His jaw quavered so violently that his teeth clicked together in a staccato. As with Elsa, his bunk was soaked with his sweat. He moaned.

Quinque said, "I will need your help with this one, Bomar. He is much stronger than the woman and he will fight me and the drug when I pour it into his throat."

"Okay," Bomar said and stood on the opposite side of the bunk. He placed his hands on Paul's upper arms.

Calida left Elsa and moved to Paul's feet, grabbing his ankles. Quinque then proceeded as with Elsa and poured the serum down his throat. Paul fought the liquid pouring into his throat, but Quinque clamped his mouth shut and it was forced down his gullet. The reaction was the same as before, but Paul fought it harder. It took all three to subdue him.

Finally it was over and both patients were now resting peacefully.

Quinque said, "They will sleep through the night and be fully rested by morning with a huge appetite." He left the hut and the two doctors followed.

Bomar asked, "Is this the typical reaction of the people you've treated?"

"I do not wait until the fever has gained a foothold. If someone is bitten or has symptoms, I medicate as a preventative. There is very little reaction at that point."

"That's wonderful," said Calida.

Bomar asked, "Do you keep the serum on hand?"

"It must be fresh to be effective, never more than a week old. I send men out to collect the necessary grubs and other ingredients when I need more," Quinque answered.

"When is the next trip? We would like to accompany them."

"I sent them out two days ago. They have not returned. If they are not back in two more days, I will look for them myself."

"Can we go with you?" asked Calida.

"I usually take two men as escorts in case of animal attack. If you can arm yourselves, I would consider it."

"I have a rifle on the boat and Calida is an expert with bow and arrow. Is that good enough?"

"I will consider it," he murmured as he walked away.

Chapter Forty-Seven

They were getting ready for the trek into the rain forest with Quinque when Paul asked Bomar, "Are you sure that you will be okay? I mean it's just the two of you out in that jungle with Quinque."

"Sure, we'll be fine. Calida is a very capable woman. I have a feeling that she's right at home out there. It's only a half-day's hike. If we're lucky we'll be back in a couple of days."

"Well, I wonder why the three guys that he sent out haven't returned."

"He didn't seem to be concerned. Apparently they sometimes take longer because they get high on that *curupa* powder. Some of the villagers are addicted to it."

"They get on that stuff and forget about time," Paul said.

"As with all of these lost tribes, time is not crucial, nothing is urgent. Even the clocks seem to run slower when you're in their villages."

"Here comes the shaman now. It looks like he's ready to start out."

"We must leave now," said Quinque.

"We're ready," answered Bomar. "I have my shotgun and Calida found a bow and she made a quiver full of arrows."

Paul said, "I saw her practicing. You're right, she is very capable."

The village was well into the Pantanal, which covered 100,000 square miles of swampland. It is the most powerful and bioactively diverse natural phenomenon on the planet. It's now under the protection of the government of Brazil and is the home of several now known lost tribes and many other indigenous tribes that have been in existence for a thousand years.

Long regarded as hocus-pocus by science, the indigenous people's empirical plant knowledge is now thought to be the true wealth of the Amazon rain forest. The serum being sought by this small group of scientists is but one of many that has been used by these people for many centuries. It is wondered if there may be new drugs awaiting discovery that will cure AIDS, cancer, diabetes, arthritis, and Alzheimer's.

***

Travel in the Pantanal is not easy. With the rapid growth of plants, vines, brush, and trees, a trail is quickly overgrown. To traverse this rain forest takes all three people swinging machetes to cut a path. It was well past noon when Quinque called a halt.

"We will rest now," he said.

"How much farther is it?" Bomar asked.

"We will reach the palm trees soon," he said, "and then make camp for the night. I will then visit the site where ceremonies are performed to try to find my warriors."

After resting they continued until they came to a beautiful grove of trees. There was no undergrowth and the palm trunks were tall and straight. There was a feeling of tranquility in the grove, almost a sacred sensation. Even the ever presence of noxious flying insects was abated. Quinque quietly left them.

Bomar whispered, "Have you ever seen a place like this, Calida?"

"No, but in my youth, while living with the old shaman that taught me about the herbs in the forest, I remember a story that she told. It was a night with the moon round and full with a silver ring around it. In her quavering voice she told me about such a place. She said that it was a place with soil that nurtured the trees and gave them strong medicinal properties. She said that you would be safe there because all the animals shunned the grove and even the flying insects did not enter."

"Well, I wonder about the ants if that's the case."

"I don't see any ants crawling around, tocandira ants or otherwise. Let's see what Quinque has to say when he returns."

"I have a feeling we won't see him tonight. He may perform his own ceremony with *curupa* powder, especially if he finds his cohorts."

"I'll gather some kindling so we can make a campfire," said Calida.

Bomar unpacked his backpack and organized a campsite.

When Calida returned with the wood, she said, "Was that Quinque that I heard in the forest? Is he back?"

"No, he's not here. What did you hear?"

"Someone was moving about. Then when I stopped to listen, I didn't hear it anymore," Calida said.

"Well, maybe it was an animal. Did you leave the grove to find the wood?"

"Yes, I did. There are no loose branches here."

"Maybe it was Quinque or an animal. Anyway, it didn't bother us."

Calida said, "I see the red fruit on the palm trees is ripe. I'm going to try to knock some loose. I used to climb up the trunks years ago, but I think I'll try the easy way now. The fruit is very good and it's nutritious." She threw a thick stick up into the palm fronds and dislodged several delicious red fruits.

They started a fire and sat around it after dark. It was peaceful and seemed to be a safe place to camp.

"I think you were right, Bomar, Quinque won't be back tonight. I guess we'd better turn in. No telling what's in store for us tomorrow."

They rolled out their sleeping bags and got ready to call it a night. While she was busy preparing her sleeping bag, she heard a familiar humming sound. *Was that a mosquito?* She thought. It sounded like one, yet it didn't. So familiar though. Her back was to Bomar. She turned to ask, "Hey, Bomar, did you hear—BOMAR!" she yelled. She rushed to his prone body draped over his sleeping bag. "Bomar, what's wrong?" She rolled him over and then saw what she had thought was a buzzing mosquito a few moments ago. A dart from a blow gun was protruding from his neck.

She alertly stood to look around for danger as she heard another buzzing sound instantly before another dart buried itself into the side of her neck. She raised her hand to her neck as she crumpled to the ground, her legs becoming like rubber. As she lay, she was barely conscious when in her dreamlike state she heard someone approach. There were two and one spoke to the other.

What is that strange language? I know it. It is so familiar. Then it all went black as she felt herself being lifted.

Chapter Forty-Eight

The next morning, Calida awoke with a splitting headache. She was lying on a pallet with a straw-filled mattress. It was soft and comfortable. She raised her throbbing head to look around, but dropped it back when she got dizzy. The ceiling of this hut was thatched and the walls were solid looking. This was not the type of construction used by Indian tribes who moved their villages every twenty years or so. This was a more permanent structure. Something about it was familiar. Something about this hut stirred up her memory. She was now getting her senses back and able to sit up.

What happened? she thought. She then remembered the dart in Bomar's neck. She reached up and touched her neck and found a welt where another dart had hit her in the neck. *Well, I'm not a prisoner. Or if I am, I'm not restrained.* She swung her legs off the side of the bed and experienced some vertigo. She sat for a moment.

As she prepared to stand, the door opened and a very tall blonde woman walked in. She was dressed in animal skins and strapped to her waist was a wicked looking dagger. She stood in the doorway, and in that strange language that sounded familiar to Calida as she fell unconscious, she said, "Welcome, princess. Please come with me. Our leader wants to see you."

Calida was aghast. It was the language of her mother's tribe. Her memory of the words came rushing back. This was her native language. She stood. The Amazon warrior held out her hand and Calida grasped it. The warrior led her out of the hut and into a courtyard surrounded by other huts of the same type. She saw other Amazon women along with some women of smaller stature and darker hair. There were children playing in a field to the rear of the huts, all female, some blonde, some with dark hair, with bronze colored skin.

They walked to the largest hut in the complex and entered. Sitting in a chair against the far wall was a very tall blonde woman with golden skin. She was older than the one that came to her hut and awakened her. Though older, she was trim and still beautiful.

She said, "Hello, Princess Calida. It's been a long time."

Calida looked closely at this striking lady and haltingly she asked, "Nardania? Could it be you? You aren't dead?"

"It is me, my princess, it is Nardania, your mentor."

Calida rushed to her outstretched arms and they hugged one another in a firm embrace. Calida was crying. She blubbered, "What of my mother, Nardania? Did she survive as you did?"

"No, princess. I tried to save her but she was buried in the first quake. Tons of rubble cascaded down on her hut. I'm so sorry. She was not only my leader but also my best friend."

"How did you escape?" Calida asked.

"I was with my group of warriors on a training exercise in the fields. We were away from structures and hillsides. We tried to return and save the others but we were too late. All that we saw were dead bodies. We fled. The fire god was angry and we feared that he may kill again. But where were you? I thought you were dead along with Cassania."

"I was in the jungle with our shaman. She was killed by a jaguar. I was alone when I felt the earthquake and made my way back to the village. All that I saw were dead bodies and then an avalanche came and buried every one of them. You must have already been gone by then," Calida said.

"Yes, we saw the dead ones piled up by the passageway. The stench was unbearable. We panicked and ran."

"How did you get here? It's a long way to the old village from here," Calida asked.

Nardania answered, "We came on rivers mostly, if we could steal the boats to travel. We also walked many miles between rivers. We knew of a legend passed down from generations ago that told of a group of unhappy warriors that left our village and established a new village in a giant swampland to the west of our home. We captured Indians along the way to get stories and legends from them. It took us years to finally make it here. There was resentment from the old ones but we overcame them and became residents. They saw that we were strong in battle and were happy to have us for added strength. My days of battle have passed, but I still have the knowledge and experience to pass on. I have been acting as leader since the old one died."

"I'm so glad that you survived, Nardania"

"I regret that your mother was not with us. I grieved her death. Now tell me, princess, how did you get here?"

Calida told of her quest to find her birth father and all that had happened in the sixteen or seventeen years since the giant earthquake. Finally she ended with her assignment to the outpost lab and her eventual assignment to research the mosquito carrying the dengue fever virus.

"We have heard of this serum to cure the terrible fever, but we do not have it," Nardania said.

"How did you know that I was in the village of this tribe?"

"It was strictly an accident that you were seen on the river. Two of our hunters spied you and were curious. They followed your boat, and when you were attacked by a huge alligator they dispatched it."

"So that's who saved my life. I wondered. It took a pretty good shot to kill that monster."

"It was a win-win situation. We got a lot of meat from that one."

"Has someone been spying on me after that day?"

"Yes, we didn't know who you were but we knew you had to be one of us or someone who looked an awful lot like us. A few days ago we captured three Indians from the village and they told us that a woman that looked like us was coming to their village. They said that she would be coming into the bush with their shaman. We decided to bring you in if it was possible."

"What happened to the Indians?" Calida asked.

"They seemed to be very pleased when we provided them with a liberal dose of *curupa* powder. Sadly they were gluttons and continued with the powder until they overdosed. We carried their bodies back to their place of worship. One of my scouts said that another Indian came and discovered them. He looked like a shaman."

"That was Quinque. Did you capture him too?"

"No, I instructed our warriors to watch him but not to capture yet. We wanted to see who you were, and that's when my guards brought you and your friend in."

"I see," Calida said, fearing what happened to Bomar.

"I was overcome with joy when they brought you in and I saw it was you by the tattoo on your shoulder. Then I recognized you, but I had no idea that you had survived the earthquake."

"I was happy to see you too, Nardania, but I must ask what you have done with the man that was with me."

"He is here and still under sedation. I wanted to wait until you awoke before we made a decision on him."

"I'm not sure what you mean. Aren't you going to let us go? We should return to the village. We have two more of our associates from the laboratory waiting for our return. They will be worried when the shaman shows up without us."

"But, princess, don't you want to join us here? We are your people. You are destined to be our leader. Your mother, Cassania, was queen of our clan and you rightly inherit this from her."

"Nardania, I was but a young teen when I left the village to find my father. When I did, my whole life changed. I no longer lived as an Amazon warrior and my future then became more structured. I am a certified medical doctor now with a good paying job with an international laboratory. How can I give that up?"

"Tell me, princess, are you truly content living that kind of life? We have heard stories of the crime and devastating wars in the so-called civilized world. It is true that we don't have the perfect culture here, but tell me that you haven't experienced some questionable situations since you left our care."

Calida was taken aback. Yes, she remembered several situations where she would have been safer in the rain forest. "I must admit that I was very happy as a child living with my mother and with you, Nardania. It would be very easy for me to stay. I'm sure that I would be accepted into your community. I also feel that I could be an asset to all with my medical training. If I agreed to stay, will you let Bomar return to the village?"

"I'm sorry, princess, we could not possibly allow that."

Chapter Forty-Nine

"What will you do with him?" asked Calida.

Nardania hesitated. She pointedly looked at Calida and said, "You are well aware of how you were conceived, Calida. Your father was one of the few men that fathered a child in our community and continued to live thereafter. You know it is how we have survived as a *women-only* clan. It is not often that we are blessed with a man such as your friend. He is young, virile, well statured, intelligent, and Caucasian. He will make a good sire for the next generation. He can create future warriors."

"I understand how we as Amazon warriors procreate, but I cannot as a human being cast aside a colleague. I have worked with Bomar and he has befriended me. Can I at least see him and explain that I am helpless as to his fate?" Calida said.

"That is possible, Calida, but you still must make your decision on your own fate. We want you here to join us and to take our clan to the great force that it was in the past. Will you stay and become our leader?"

"I've got mixed emotions, Nardania. I loved the life of the Amazons and I miss it. But after the quake, I had lost all hope of living that life with my mother and all that I knew. I saw it all destroyed, but I found hope with others. An old derelict Indian helped me and taught me how to survive. An Indian chief took me into his tribe, where I lived for years. A

Christian priest took me in and helped me survive in a city. I was sent to America, where I was educated in the best schools. I was hired by a large company and sent to study drugs in the Amazon basin. I owe all this to my father and stepmother, who embraced me with no hesitation. Do I abandon them?" Calida implored

"I understand, Calida, and only you can decide. I, as leader, must protect my clan. We have suffered a devastating blow with most of our people destroyed in the volcano eruption and earthquake years ago. We have started to rebuild our clan, but we have a long way to go. We need leaders like you to get started to be what we were."

"Let me talk to Bomar."

"Yes. They tell me that he is conscious now. We have given him some nourishment. He is in a hut nearby," Nardania said.

A young warrior took Calida to an adjoining hut. When she entered, she observed Bomar ensconced on a pallet, leaning on pillows behind him. Plates of sliced meat, fruit, and nuts were being fed to him by two young maidens. He, very obviously, was enjoying the attention.

He saw Calida and joyously said, "Hey, Calida, I don't know where we are or who these wonderful people are, but I love it."

Calida couldn't help but chuckle. She said, "Enjoy it, Bomar, and that's not all you'll enjoy."

"How could it get better?" Bomar asked.

"Those two young maidens are feeding you to build up your stamina. They'll be taking you to their bedchamber later, and you'll be expected to perform. You may even enjoy several nights of this, but there is a price to pay."

"What can I possibly pay them for this kind of treatment?"

"How about giving up your life?"

Bomar sat quietly for a minute and then he said, "Oh my god, these must be the storied Amazons the Indian legends tell about. So they are real. Is it true that the men are killed after they sire children?"

"That's what happens," she answered.

"What's going to happen to you?" he asked.

"I was born an Amazon, Bomar. They want me to join their clan and become their leader."

"Yeah, I kind of figured. Can you put in a good word for me?"

"I'm really not sure what will happen if I don't join them. We've got a little time, so you might as well enjoy yourself."

"Do what you must to save yourself, Calida. Don't worry about me. I'll make do with what's given to me."

She left. The warrior took her back to her hut, where she rested.

***

Quinque found the three dead Indians and the remains of the hallucinogen that they overdosed on. He noted that it was a much stronger mixture than he provided. That is why they overdosed.

He returned to the campsite in the grove of palm trees to find it abandoned. There was enough evidence to determine that the two scientists had been attacked and abducted or killed. He searched the area and could not find them or their remains. Rather than risk another attack, he made tracks for the village. When he got back the next day, he reported that the three scouts he had sent to harvest grubs were given a lethal dose of *curupa* powder by unknown assailants. These same assailants either abducted or killed the two scientists that he had in his care.

Paul was upset that he would leave them for such a long period of time. He asked for a man to help him take the boat back to the outpost so he could report this to the director. They left immediately and the trip back was uneventful.

Paul immediately went to the director's office. He quickly entered the lobby and burst through into her office. She was livid that someone had the audacity to burst into her office like that. Her jaw dropped as she looked up from the paperwork on her desk and loudly exclaimed, "What the hell is this?"

"Director, I've got terrible news."

"It better be terrible, you nitwit. I don't like *anyone* bursting into my office."

"Bomar and Calida are missing."

"Missing? Where? I suppose they're playing games. I told Bomar that I wouldn't put up with that hanky-panky. I'll take care of them. Now, how did the experiment go?"

"Please listen to me. They're gone. Someone abducted them or maybe killed them."

"Hmm. Well, I'll notify the authorities and let them handle it."

"Thank you. I've got to rest," Paul said as he got up to leave.

"JUST ONE MINUTE," she bellowed. "What about the mosquito experiment?"

Paul turned and calmly said, "The serum works," and he walked out.

***

Calida confidently walked into Nardania's hut.

"Come in, princess," said Nardania, "are you rested?"

"Yes, I am. Nardania, I've been giving thought to my future." She sat. "I am not naive enough to think that my beginnings and my history in general would not have an effect on my future in the civilized world. I'm probably limited to experimenting or ministering in the rain forest. If I accept your offer to come back and live with the Amazon clan, I possibly could make a difference. Even though there are many remedies and cures found in the rain forest, all discovered in their natural state, modern science has made great strides in preventative medicine and hospital care. I'm giving very serious consideration to staying and practicing some of what I have learned."

"That's wonderful, though you sound tentative. Do I hear a 'but'? Nardania asked.

"Yes, I'm still concerned about the fate of my friend Bomar."

"I understand, but you surely must see why we cannot allow him to return to the village and divulge what he has seen here. We would be overrun with attacking Indians from an assemblage of tribes."

"May I talk to him?" asked Calida.

"Certainly, but I'd advise you not to plan an escape. It would only hasten his demise," Nardania said.

"No, I promise that I will not do that. I have another thought." She left and entered the prisoners' hut where Bomar was shackled.

He was alone, with a guard posted at the door. Calida asked that she step outside while she was there.

"Hello, Bomar, are you still being treated well?"

"Hello, Calida, yes they still feed me well and one has tried to teach me some words in her language. I think I get the gist of what happens tonight. But I must admit that my good treatment is somewhat less enjoyable since you told me my ultimate fate."

"That's what I want to talk about. What is your feeling about returning to the outpost lab?"

235

"What do you mean?"

"I couldn't help but notice your dissatisfaction with the director and her management of the lab."

"I hate her and she hates me. Given the choice, I would never go back. If I did, I think I would resign just like Hennesy did."

"Those are my sentiments exactly," Calida said.

"Well, at this stage of the game I guess it's a moot point. What about you, Calida? Will they let you go?"

"They want me to stay, Bomar. That's the only choice they've given me so far. I haven't given them a firm answer as yet."

"Good luck," he said.

Calida left the hut.

Chapter Fifty

The meeting was between Calida and Nardania. The mentor and the pupil were face to face.

"This is what I respectfully propose, Nardania," Calida droned in a monotone, her eyes cast down.

"I understand, princess. I know that you have given much thought to this and it's difficult. Please speak."

"I want to live the rest of my life as an Amazon warrior, as well as use my skills in medicine to further the health and wellbeing of my sisters," Calida said with deep emotion in her voice.

"That is good," interjected Nardania.

"But I also want the life of my friend Bomar spared," Calida stated emphatically.

"Go on," stated Nardania, now with a disapproving squint.

"You have made the observation that he is a prime candidate to sire children here in our village. He is willing to do so for as long as you would require it. He has also made known to me that he no longer wants to work for the outpost lab. He wants to resign and never return to the site," she stated.

"Does he have a plan of how to do this? And what happens after his resignation?" Nardania asked.

Calida laid out her resolution. "First, he and I will leave together. Before leaving, I give to you my solemn promise to return and live my life as an Amazon. Bomar, in turn, promises to bypass the Indian village and also the outpost lab. We as a couple will travel by foot and by boat to the closest large city, Corumba, the capital of the Pantanal. Here we will post letters of resignation to corporate headquarters. At that point we part company. Eventually I will make my way back here and report to you, to live as I was born to live. Bomar will book passage back to America. He will return to his home in the Bronx in New York City, where he'll practice medicine in his old neighborhood. Neither of us will divulge to the Indian village or to the outpost lab or anyone else what happened here or where this village is located."

"What's to keep them from finding out anyhow? What protection do we have other than your word?" Nardania asked.

"Please, you have to trust me. I give you my word on my mother's grave, Nardania. I have one more important part of this plan that will give us as Amazons the protection that you want."

"Go on," she said with skepticism.

"Before making my way back here I will travel to Brazilia, the capital, using the funds from my lab earnings. I will visit FUNIA, the Bureau of Indian Affairs. This bureau has set aside vast protected areas so that indigenous tribes can live as they have lived for the past thousand years or longer. These tribes are now protected from infringement by land speculators, ranchers, miners, and other raiding jungle tribes. I'll lobby that our village be included and fall under their protection."

"But, Calida, we are not Indians," Nardania advised.

"No, but we are an indigenous tribe. We have been here as long as any Indian tribe, longer than some. We live in the Pantanal. And those are the requisites needed, as far as I know. Our numbers have been decimated by invading foreign soldiers, as well as marauding tribes and notorious land speculators."

"How long would you be gone?"

"It may take as long as six months. We must travel far and without creating attention. After that, my time in Brazilia is unknown. I will stay until I get the answer that I want."

"You will make a great leader, Calida. Your mother would have been proud. Tell your friend to sire strong girls. He is a lucky man to have a friend like you. Carry out your plan and come back to lead your people."

They embraced.

***

Months later, many changes had taken place. The director of the outpost laboratory, Dr. Baruni, was fired and replaced by a progressive young man. His name was Paul.

Quinque, the shaman for an Indian tribe in the Pantanal, no longer welcomed scientists from the laboratory. His serum for dengue fever remained a secret.

Years later, Bomar was practicing medicine in the Bronx. His patients were many that he grew up with. He was married and had four children, all girls.

Calida was now the leader of the clan of Amazon warriors living in a village deep in the Pantanal. She was instrumental in moving the village even deeper than before. She was successful in gaining protection under the guidance of FUNIA. The village is growing.

Dr. André Clark and his wife Caroline had received a long letter from Calida expressing her gratitude and explaining her decision to live with the Amazons. They understood, and felt confident that their daughter had chosen the correct path for her life.

Printed in the United States
By Bookmasters